Frankie's Confections

Amy Denson

Vineyard Seeds Book 3

Frankie's Confections is a work of fiction. The characters, names, offices, ideas, incidents, and events (historical and future) are products of the author's wild imagination and are used to tell a story fictionally. This book is inspired by the story of Dinah in the book of Genesis.

Published by ADB Bridgeport, WV

ISBN-13: 978-1-7341579-3-2
978-1-7341579-4-9

Library of Congress Control Number: 2021924126

Marchio Family

- **Salvatore** — **Mary**
  - **Esther Marchio (m. John Robinson)**
    - **Ruth Marchio (m. Malik Lavalier)**
      - **Maryssa Lavalier (m. Beau Baker)**
        - **Chloe Elizabeth Baker (stepdaughter)**
        - **John Boaz Baker**
    - **Haddie Robinson (m. Jackson Cashe)**
      - **Elizabeth Robinson (m. Beau Baker)**
        - **Chloe Elizabeth Baker**
  - **Samuel Marchio (m. Hanna Meade)**
    - **Samuel Joseph Marchio II**
    - **Francesca Josephine Marchio**
  - **Dominick Marchio (m. Tamra Kelley)**
    - **Dominick John Marchio II**
    - **Alexis Marchio**
  - **Josephine Marchio (m. Matthew Slater)**
    - **Matthew Slater II**
    - **Olivia Slater**
    - **Trey Slater**

God never uses a person greatly until He has wounded him deeply. The privilege He offers you is greater than the price you have to pay. The privilege is greater than the price.
—Dr. Helen Roseveare

Prologue

Thwack!

Bam!

Thud!

The punching bag spins as the next hit connects with the synthetic leather. *Smack!* The rattling from a metal chain connecting the heavy load to the rafters can barely be heard over her tempered breathing. *Thump!* Frankie Jo reaches out to steady it before turning, bending, and delivering a roundhouse kick. A direct hit to its logo. *Kathunk!* The bag swings back to her and is met with a series of blows on each side. Sweat pours down her face. Sweet satisfaction fills her entire being.

Half Italian and half Irish, Frankie Jo Marchio sticks out among her family. She has secretly wondered for years whether or not she was adopted. Her skin is fair and freckled, while her eyes could not be greener. Every other Marchio cousin has the olive skin of their Italian grandmother, even her own brother Sammy. *Traitor.* Frankie looks just like her petite Irish grandmama on her mother's side. People often underestimate her fierceness based on her fragile appearance. Frankie may look like a tiny porcelain doll, but she fights like a machine now.

Her hands, expertly wrapped, will still bleed when the workout is finished. The pain only pushes her harder. Deena, her trainer and closest friend, will yell at Frankie later for not using gloves, but some days she needs to feel the bag's impact. Deena has a lot to say about the psychological reasons Frankie resists gloves, but she'll save those thoughts for later too. The dark green hand wraps are a stark contrast against her pale skin.

Frankie began boxing a few years ago. During her senior year of college, she took a self-defense class after unexpectedly meeting the instructor, Deena Finnegan, at the police station. Deena's family owns a gym and are well known in the professional boxing circuit as the Fighting Finnegans. Deena saw something in Frankie on the first day of class. They have been close friends ever since. She spends more time with Deena at the gym than she does at home. The Finnegans are loud and intrusive, much like the Marchios, so Frankie feels at home in their gym.

Creaking floorboards above pull her mind from the workout. She grabs the towel from the workbench and checks her phone, six in the morning. She's been downstairs in the basement since four. The nightmares have started again, so her middle-of-the-night-workouts have intensified too. Frankie's counselor warned her that massive life changes might ignite her anxiety, and she has had her fair share of those lately. They have worked on coping exercises, but nothing makes her feel as strong as whacking a shock-absorbent punching bag.

The basement door squeaks open. "Francesca Josephine, I see you were up before the chickens again. Do you want some coffee?" Nunnie calls down the rickety wooden stairs.

Her new roommate knows very well that Frankie wants coffee, but that is her grandmother's way of checking on her without checking *in* on her. Other than spending more time with the family's spunky matriarch, moving into the family farmhouse has two added benefits. One, she is saving money to start her own business. Two, her commute to work is literally just over the next hill.

"Yes, Nunnie. I would love coffee. Thank you. I'm finishing now so I'll be up in a minute." Frankie smiles before tossing her towel back onto the bench.

"Mmm, hmm. Lord, help that girl get some sleep. She is so stubborn." Nunnie mumbles loud enough to ensure Frankie hears.

"I heard that," Frankie laughs.

"You were meant to." Nunnie grumbles as the door closes.

Frankie turns her attention back to the punching bag. Focusing on a quick barrage of punches directly to the bag's center, Frankie ends with a knee targeted at pain level for any male attacker. Satisfied, she backs away and steps off the mat where her feet have been dancing with the heavy bag.

Frankie wipes down her face and begins removing the layers of hand wraps. Her hands are tiny, giving her more padding around the knuckles and wrist. Dropping her hand wraps on the workout bench, she winces as she flexes all of her fingers. Both hands, now naked, plunge into a bucket of ice and water. She learned quickly to perform this act downstairs, away from the keen eyes of Nunnie. That woman is very perceptive. No matter how much energy Frankie puts into faking calmness, nothing keeps Nunnie from commenting on the pain that laces Frankie's face when her hands hit the frigid water. Nothing gets by that woman.

Icy tingles overtake her body as she shivers with a satisfying determination. Her ringing phone breaks the silence. Annoyed, she glances at the screen before rolling her eyes. Frankie's cousin Maryssa knows she wakes up early for workouts, but calling at six in the morning is not like Maryssa. She must be worried about something going on at the restaurant today. Frankie glances between her phone and her ice bath and decides to call Maryssa after some coffee. Maryssa is much easier to handle after coffee.

Frankie thoroughly dries her hands, then begins the ritual of rubbing in liniment Deena gets for her. The smell is potent. The first time Deena applied it on her hands, Frankie

3

almost passed out from the odor. Once it started working, Frankie didn't care what it smelled like. The obnoxious scent isn't as bad as the manure from Nunnie's chicken coop in the backyard, but it is pretty close.

Frankie's phone begins ringing again as she peers down at the screen. Maryssa. About two years ago, Frankie quit her office job at the family vineyard to manage Poppy's, Maryssa's restaurant. Frankie's plan was to learn about the food industry while pursuing her passion. The end goal is to open her own bakery. Since starting, orders for baked goods have taken on a life of their own, but Frankie still hasn't left her gig working at the restaurant. Poppy's is Frankie's safety blanket.

Frankie works out of Poppy's kitchen all morning, baking and crafting her sweet confections. She then puts on her manager's hat at lunch to help run the restaurant. As bakery orders continue to pile in, she has added some evening baking sessions with Nunnie at the family farmhouse. Italian cookie trays, cupcakes, pies, cheesecake, you name it, she bakes it. But her very favorite is to design wedding cakes.

She finds this ironically satisfying. Something perfect to begin the imperfect farce of a marriage. Frankie doesn't hate the idea of marriage. She just doesn't buy into the fairytale of happily ever after. She has seen good marriages, terrible marriages, some that are more partnerships than romance, and marriages that are shams. The only happy marriages Frankie has witnessed ended in death long before the rocking chairs. No, Frankie Jo Marchio is not waiting on prince charming to sweep her off of her feet. If she needs rescuing, she'll ride her own horse and do her own sweeping.

Frankie reaches down to answer her phone. The top right corner has a crack from bouncing off of her mixer onto the floor. She doesn't have time to get a new phone, but it's on her never-ending to-do list. She slides the green phone icon across the screen and lifts it to her ear.

"What's up? Is the restaurant on fire?" Frankie smirks, knowing Maryssa is overreacting about something.

"Bite your tongue. No, I actually have something exciting to tell you, smarty pants. Do you remember Lisa Fox, my producer?"

"She's the one who worked on *Future FLOTUS?* with Haddie, right? I like her."

"Yes, the very same. Anyway, Lisa wants to meet with you today at Poppy's. She's flying into the North Central Regional Airport and will be here this afternoon. Isn't that exciting?" Maryssa's voice reaches a high-pitched level that only she can hit.

"Why on earth does your producer want to meet with me? Don't even think of signing me up for some reality TV dating show like you did to poor Haddie." Frankie's voice is laced with conviction.

"For the love of all that's good. This family needs to stop giving me grief about submitting Haddie for *Future FLOTUS?* against her will. I WAS RIGHT! She is currently married to the man from the show and is, in fact, the First Lady of the United States." Maryssa's voice is faint for a second before Frankie realizes she is talking to someone else in the room. "All right, Babe, I know I need to let it go, but they need to let it go first. Seriously, it's getting on my last nerve."

"Tell Beau, I'm on his side." Frankie laughs before continuing, "Back to my original question, why does your producer want to meet with me?"

"Good grief Frankie, do you ever watch TV or look at your phone? I know you are one busy lady, but you really need to pay more attention to the world around you."

"Maryssa, what are you talking about?" Frankie is already exhausted from this conversation. The only things on her mind right now are coffee and a shower.

Exasperated, Maryssa responds, "Bring your portfolio to work today, and after we hang up, search your name in that cracked phone of yours so you can see for yourself. I'll see you soon. Love you, bye." Maryssa talks away from her phone again as she hangs up, "It's sad when I'm the sane one in this crazy family. Beau, stop laughing...."

"Bye." Frankie drops her phone on the towel mid-eye roll as she shakes her head. Rolling her neck back and forth, she loosens her stiffening muscles. A few more stretches help to release the tension. She collects her used hand wraps and the bucket of ice water before heading upstairs for coffee and a protein shake. With her free hand, Frankie taps her name into the search bar of her phone as she begins to trek up the basement stairs.

Freezing on the second step, Frankie's mouth drops open as she furiously scrolls down to reveal more and more headlines. "Haddie!" Her cousin's name escapes like daggers from her lips.

The American Post
Scene & Heard

By: Tabitha Telall

What do they put in that West Virginia water? Three celebrities from the same family? Watch out, Kardashians, the Marchio girls are taking the world by storm! Walk with me as I make my case.

Exhibit A: Haddie Robinson is a contestant on *Future FLOTUS?* where she woos President Jackson Cashe. After a whirlwind romance, the two marry and form a super couple. Haddie wins the hearts of both the United States of America and the Allied States of America. She is SEN-SA-TION-AL!

Exhibit B: Haddie's cousin, Maryssa Lavalier, scores a coveted internship with renowned chef Jacques Boucher (ooh-la-la) and wins the prestigious Geoffrey Barton Rising Star Award. She opens a restaurant on their family vineyard in West Virginia, where she pumps out cookbooks and cooking show specials as fast as the artisan pizzas from her brick oven.

Exhibit C: The newest member of the Marchio family to stake her claim at fame is Frankie Jo (is that not the cutest, down-home name ever?). Frankie's sugary confections have graced tables from local birthday parties to the West Virginia Governor's Mansion to the White House. Frankie's latest creation for President Cashe's second Inauguration made waves across both countries. Rumor has it, she will be the third family member to sign a TV contract!

Who to watch next: Chloe Baker. She is Haddie's niece AND Maryssa's step-daughter (that's a tell-all book in itself!) Though technically a citizen of the Allied States, her frequent visits to Washington, D.C. make her the cutest White House visitor ever recorded in history. She puts the sass in sassy!

I, for one, cannot wait to get more and more of this family. The grapes at Rafaluzza Vineyard must grow from some magic beans. Gimme more! We are following this family like bees follow a glass of sweet tea. Check back for more family deets in our print issue out next week.

Frankie

The hot shower does little to calm Frankie's nerves. Her mind has been racing since Maryssa's phone call. Maybe she *has* been in her own little bubble. She had no idea that her name has been trending all week. She even has a hashtag, #frankiesconfections.

Frankie may have a big personality, but she is not comfortable with attention directed at her. Attention leads to panic, which leads to more talking, which leads to Frankie wishing she had shut up ten minutes earlier and crawled into a hole. Contrary to popular belief, she is not a fan of the spotlight. The Internet doesn't seem to understand this and is blinding her with it.

As if she's not stressed out enough with work, baking, sessions with Deena, finding a location for the bakery, now she gets to add a cooking show to the list. Her counselor is going to have a field day at her next appointment. It's no wonder the nightmares have returned. Frankie feels bile rising in her throat just thinking about her regular nighttime visitor.

She finishes drying her hair. Her fingers deftly braid long brown locks at an angle across her head and down to her shoulder. Chloe calls it her "Elsa" hair. Frankie laughs, thinking about the sassy eight-year-old who loves to watch Frankie bake. She throws on her oversized WVU t-shirt and yoga pants and grabs a change of clothes for her meeting later. Thanks to Maryssa's change of plans, Frankie needs to make a pit stop at the grocery store. She hates the grocery store. No, that's not right. She loves the grocery store, it's people she's not crazy about.

As Frankie descends the stairs of the family farmhouse, she hears the strains of worship music floating out of the kitchen. The memories of this house wrap around her like a warm hug. She loves the smells and the sounds of Nunnie's house. From dark wood accents to the photos that line the walls, this house elicits all the feels. Her heart is full before entering the kitchen, which is the heart of the Marchio family.

"Ah, there's my famous roommate." Nunnie lays down the newspaper in her hands and lifts the warm coffee mug to her lips.

"Not you too," Frankie quips. "You can't get famous for baking one cake."

"Ah, but the news begs to differ, sweet girl." Nunnie offers a sly grin along with her hearty laugh.

Frankie rolls her eyes and heads for the coffee pot. After filling her green travel mug with liquid gold and creamer, she tilts her head in the direction of the counter. Her question is quickly answered.

"Yes, the bacon and eggs are yours. Maryssa texted that you have an important meeting today. I wanted you to have something on your stomach instead of watching you grab a granola bar and running out the door. You burn off more calories in the basement than you actually eat all day. Even with all of those goodies you bake and taste, you're losing weight. It's not fair to the rest of us."

Frankie takes the plate from the counter and sits next to Nunnie. She leans over and kisses her grandmother. "For the record, I was going to make a protein shake today, but this is way better. Thank you."

"You are very welcome." Nunnie picks up the paper and begins reading again. The bacon is thick, crispy, and savory. Frankie enjoys every bite as Nunnie fills her in on the information she is gathering from the local newspaper. Frankie now knows everyone who has died this week, who has given birth, transferred property, and how renovations at the public library are coming.

As she listens to the local news being read by Nunnie, Frankie thinks back to Haddie's phone call the day after the Presidential election. The whole my-cousin-is-married-to-the-President-of-the-United-States aspect is still surreal for her. What happened next was otherworldly. Jackson requested that Frankie design a cake for one of the Inaugural Balls.

Frankie drove to D.C. the following week to meet with Haddie and the Presidential Inaugural Committee. Her head was spinning during the visit. After her trip, Frankie was inspired to design a cake that showcased Jackson's love of history and patriotism. The goal was to emphasize his top priority of reuniting the two countries back into one great nation. The final design was nothing short of inspirational. The buttercream base was a shimmery silver. She hand-painted the words from one of Jackson's reunification speeches around the layers of the round cake. Each tier displayed American symbols throughout history embedded in between the words.

The cake topper was a risk. Frankie and Jackson talked extensively about it before making the final decision. Frankie always had a rebellious streak, but the topper would be pushing Jackson's limits, not hers. He loved it. Together they designed a hologram with waving, overlapping flags of the United States of America and the Allied States of America.

The whole family traveled to Washington, D.C., for Jackson's Inauguration. They are Italian, they travel in packs. After a crazy few days celebrating with Jackson and Haddie, they all returned home and went back to normal. Well, normal for their family. Frankie has been too busy to sit down and watch TV, much less do anything else. Now, she is trending.

11

The design was a massive hit at the ball. The balance between detail and simplicity was ethereal. She loved the end result but had no idea the impact it made nationally and internationally. After Maryssa's call, Frankie was blown away by the results of her search. The comments and reviews about her artwork were overwhelming to read. She had to put down her phone and shower so she could get to work. Surely there must be something more exciting to hashtag about than a cake.

"Then Chicken Little saved the day and the dish ran away with the spoon."

Frankie glances over at Nunnie like the woman has lost her mind.

"Oh, you *were* listening. I thought you were in outer space with Chicken Little."

"I was listening," Frankie defends herself, but Nunnie's smirk tells her it's not working. "All right, I was only half listening. This trending thing is a little overwhelming. I just want it all to go away."

Nunnie closes the paper and folds it in half to reveal the front-page headline. She places it beside Frankie who takes one last bite of breakfast. Frankie reads the headline, *"Local Baker Shines at United States Inaugural Ball."*

Frankie's head collapses into her hands as a groan slowly escapes. "I don't understand why this is newsworthy. Isn't there a war or a natural disaster or some political scandal to cover? This is crazy. It was just a cake."

Nunnie pats Frankie's back. "You're just upset because no one has commented on your right hook."

Nunnie has a way of making people smile when they don't want to. "That's it, Nunnie. You got me. Ha-ha."

"Frankie, I know you don't like attention. I think you're actually allergic to it, but it's okay to accept a compliment. You don't have to fight the system at every turn. Sometimes it's okay to shine." Nunnie kisses the top of Frankie's head as she rises from the table. "Anyway, Maryssa is very excited about the meeting today. She thinks this may give you the startup money for your own bakery."

"Why? Is Maryssa tired of me managing the restaurant?" Frankie hears the brattiness in her own voice.

"You know that's not true. Poppy's was only supposed to be temporary until you learned the business and got your name out. It's time. You're ready. You love taking risks in all things, but you. Jump!" Nunnie's smile can inspire anyone.

Frankie allows her grandmother's words to sink in as she rinses her plate. Warm water stings the minor cuts on her knuckles, reminding her to wear gloves tomorrow morning. Deena nags her frequently about it.

Nunnie waves a yellowed index card in the air, "That reminds me, I found the old gingerbread cake recipe my Nona used to make. We can give it a try this weekend if you want. I know you were looking for a new recipe for fall."

"Gingerbread and cake? Umm, yes, please." Nunnie taught Frankie to bake. When Frankie's parents would argue, Frankie would retreat to the farmhouse. The two would bake anything and everything they had a hankering for that day. When the creations became more elaborate, the assistant became the master, and the master became the admirer. Frankie still feels like a little girl adding ingredients to Nunnie's bowl. Her reputation has grown organically as people ate at Poppy's and raved about the desserts. Now, her business is exploding.

"Do you really think I'm ready? Somedays, I feel like a fraud." She leans back against the counter. "I have no formal training, no credentials. Maryssa graduated from a top culinary school and then interned with Jacques. What makes me think I can run a bakery, let alone host a cooking show?"

Nunnie turns and stands beside Frankie at the counter.
"I love baking. I always have since I was a little girl, and I
have definitely eaten my fair share of desserts." She chuckles
to herself. "But you, you have a gift. You are not a fraud or
inexperienced. When God gives you a gift, you must use it."
Nunnie leans against Frankie's shoulder and nudges her.

Frankie shifts uncomfortably at the mention of God
and gifts. She hasn't been to church in years, despite
Nunnie's guilt and persuasive daily arguments. "I'll make you
a deal. I'll ride this out as long as you agree to be my sassy
assistant."

"I don't think the world can handle my sass." A quick
hip-bump to Frankie and the spunky octogenarian floats
around the kitchen to the oven.

Realization dawns on Frankie, "Do I smell your
heavenly cinnamon rolls? The eggs and bacon were filling,
but I can always eat one of your cinnamon rolls."

"These, my dear, are not for you. I invited Tony over
this morning. I have a project for him. You can stay and
have one with us, if you like." Mary glances over her
shoulder as she places the pan on the stovetop.

"Tony," it's more of a grunt that a word. "I'd rather go
grocery shopping, and you know how I feel about that."

"Suit yourself. That just leaves more goodies for us.
Enjoy your grocery shopping." Nunnie glides out of the
room without another glance at Frankie.

That woman is up to something.

Already feeling anxious, Frankie grabs her grocery list,
keys, and purse. She squares her stance and breathes deeply
to steady herself, just like Deena taught her. On the exhale,
she pictures her worries floating off her shoulders and out
through her breath. She repeats the process. At some point,
this exercise for anxiety is bound to start working. Frankie
sighs, gives up, then heads out the back door for work.

Frankie's Confections

Tony

Squeak.
Crunch.
Creeaak.

The screw twists smoothly into the stud. The wire shelving unit protests loudly, but it has a few more years in it. At least Tony hopes it does. Rebuilding the outdated shelving system in the hardware store is not the best use of his resources right now. He keeps trying to talk his dad into reorganizing the layout, but Big Tony won't hear of it.

Anthony's Hardware hasn't changed in Tony's lifetime. Based on the pictures, it hasn't changed since Tony's dad bought it decades ago. This place was Big Tony's baby before he had babies, and he has no intentions of updating it now. His dad is famous for the cliché of "If it ain't broke, don't fix it," which is ironic for the owner of an independent hardware store on its last leg.

Tony stands and stretches out his back before dropping a screwdriver into the toolbox. Big Tony called his son at six this morning about an electrical question. After rewiring a light switch, unloading a delivery truck, and making a few adjustments to a broken shelf he found, Tony is almost finished and ready to start his own workday. He lifts the rack into its place then checks the stability of it. Once Tony secures it, he rearranges the inventory on the shelves making sure the bigger boxes end up on the bottom, not the loose shelf.

"Pop, I fixed the shelf. I'm leaving for work. Do you need anything else?" Tony yells from the front of the store to the back storeroom.

"Why are you yelling?" His mother yells in response. "You can't walk back fifty feet to tell your father goodbye? What? Were you raised in a barn?"

16

Tony learned early in life not to mess with an Italian woman. "Ma, you know good and well I wasn't raised in a barn. A zoo would be a better description of our house." He walks behind the counter and plants a big kiss right on his mother's cheek. She leans into his kiss before turning around and smacking him in the back of the skull.

"A zoo. I'll give you a zoo. Sapientone." Rosemary Devono mumbles under her breath as she organizes paperwork beside the cash register.

"Language, Ma!" Tony laughs and ducks before her hand connects to his head again. "Tell Pop the shelf is fixed and not to put heavy boxes that high up anymore."

"What? You think he listens to me? I told him not to put that box there in the first place. He didn't listen. Now you have to clean up his mess. Maybe he'll listen to you." She grunts before adding, "Testardo come un mulo. I blame his mother, you know. Your Nona Anna, God rest her soul, she made him un mulo."

"Well, he's your stubborn mule now, so I'll let you nag him about the shelf." Tony laughs, his mother glares. "I have to go, I have a meeting, but I'll stop over for dinner this week. Love you, Ma." Tony tightly squeezes his sturdy mother and heads for the door.

"I don't run a restaurant." She calls out as he opens the front door to leave. "But if you come, bring Sammy. I doubt you two have anything to eat in that apartment of yours. I'll make tiella, or whatever you boys want to eat. Maybe a lasagna."

"I thought you didn't run a restaurant?" Tony ducks as his mother throws a tennis ball at him from the display bucket. A wide grin covers his face, exposing his deep dimples. Tony retrieves the bouncing ball and lobs it perfectly into the bucket, "Love you too, Ma."

17

Tony Devono is the only son of Anthony Senior, aka Big Tony, and Rosemary, Rosie, for short. His older sister works part-time at the store when her daughter, Harmony, is in school. According to Big Tony, as the only son, Tony is the sole heir to the hardware store. He is also the only person in the family who doesn't want it. Tony held tools in his hands before learning to walk. In fact, he learned to walk in Anthony's Hardware. He loves the store, but he doesn't want to be tied to it.

A contractor by trade, Tony loves working with his hands. He worked at the store from the time he could reach the counter. He knows every contractor with an account and their specialty. Tony learned all the trade tricks from the store's loyal customers before starting his own company. Now, Tony runs the most successful commercial contracting business in the area. His parents don't understand why he can't give it up and take over the family business. The arguments have only intensified as his parents near retirement. The guilt weighs heavily on Tony every day.

Conversations swirl through Tony's head as he drives out of town toward the Marchio family farm. This drive is second nature to him. He practically grew up on this land with his best friend, Sammy Marchio. The stone sign for Rafaluzza Vineyard beckons his truck to turn onto the paved road that will take him to the Vineyard Tasting Rooms and Poppy's.

Pulling into the parking lot that he paved two years ago, his truck takes up three spots right in front. The restaurant won't open for a few hours, but it will be packed from open to close. He saunters through the front doors, which he helped to design, and admires his handiwork.

"Thor, your chariot awaits," Tony bellows as he peeks around corners to find his favorite carpenter.

Beau Baker enters the dining room from the swinging kitchen door. He's holding a travel coffee mug in one hand, the other is extended with a delicious looking muffin. "Maryssa says to give you this." He tosses it to Tony. The muffin soars in a perfect arc.

Tony catches it mid-air and inspects the delicious and still warm muffin. "Did she lace it with laxatives?" He asks Beau, half-serious.

"Nope, rat poison," Maryssa answers as she strolls out behind her husband. A baby, wrapped around her front in a swaddle, practically knocks over the lumberjack-sized man in her way. "I know this may shock you, Tony, but sometimes, I can be nice. Its chocolate chip, by the way. I know you love those."

"Mm-hmm. Sure you can be nice. Like the time you, Frankie, and Haddie dropped Sammy and me off at the cemetery and made us walk home?" Tony peels the wrapper from the muffin but takes an exaggerated sniff first to test it.

"First of all, you two deserved it. Second of all, well, that was actually Frankie's idea, and I forget why we did it." Maryssa becomes lost in the memory. Her brows arch together before she laughs to herself.

"Every day, I wake up thinking, there can't be more crazy family stories to tell. Sure enough, you lunatics have one to top the last." Beau shakes his head at both his wife and boss. "Rubber snakes at the lake, stealing toilet paper to TP houses, then returning the toilet paper. Oh, and let's not forget pulling the fire alarm at the bank. That was a quite a story."

Tony laughs so hard he chokes on his muffin. "That was a good one. They evacuated the entire building."

"Oh, stop, Beau. You knew what you were marrying into, and you love us. In fact, you married into this family twice, so what does that say about you?" Maryssa blows him a kiss. "Besides, Tony and Sammy had their fair share of pranks as well. Haddie and I only had to endure them over the summers. Poor Frankie had to deal with you two knuckleheads year-round."

Tony glances in the direction of the kitchen at the mention of Frankie's name. The lingering look does not go unnoticed by Maryssa.

"Frankie ran into town for supplies. My producer wants to talk with her about a baking show, so we're all meeting later today. I asked Frankie to make her famous tiramisu inspired cake. You can stop by later for lunch if you want to see her." Maryssa smiles at Tony warmly.

He shakes the cobwebs from his head and pulls himself together. "Why would I come by to see Frankie? She wouldn't think twice about giving me arsenic."

"I highly doubt that. I've seen the way she...ouch!" Beau's attention is drawn to his arm, which was just tightly pinched by his wife. Beau hasn't seen her move that fast in months.

Tony's confused expression is met with an innocent smile from Maryssa and an even more confused expression from Beau back to Maryssa.

"The way she what, Beau?" Tony is watching them closely, scrutinizing the awaited answer.

"The way she loves to bake good food and not kill people, Tony." Maryssa rubs Beau's arm, where she had just vise gripped him. "Don't you two have errands to run? And it would be nice if you could finish the cabinetry in our laundry room. Chop chop, get moving." Maryssa pulls Beau close to her and tugs on his chin before kissing him sweetly, then swatting his behind. "Get to work."

"She's bossy." Tony pops the last of the muffin in his mouth before lobbing the crumbled wrapper at Maryssa, which she catches.

"She is the boss. Love you, Babe. Love you, J.B.." Beau kisses the top of the baby's head then follows Tony to the front of the restaurant.

"Thanks for the muffin, Mary Mary Quite Contrary." Tony offers a bow before ducking behind the wall built between the hostess stand and bar area.

"Tony, one of these days, you're going to have to grow up and stop calling everyone by these crazy nicknames you inflict on innocent people," Maryssa shouts.

"Never, Shrimp-ryssa!" His fake, evil laugh reverberates through Poppy's. Maryssa's grunt can be heard from the front door.

The two men climb into Tony's silver truck with the Mountaineer Construction logo displayed on both sides. As usual, Tony has country music blaring as soon as the engine starts. The pickup makes its way out of the parking lot. They drive onto a service road between the vineyard side of the property and the family farm on the other. They are surrounded by varying shades of green along the hillside. The sun is still to the east but rising steadily. White puffy clouds float along the vibrant blue sky. A flock of geese flies in a V shape overhead. Tony loves this place.

Legend has it, Salvatore Marchio won the run-down farm in a poker game. The farmer died, and his son was a drunk who gambled away the deed. Sammy's dad told the boys stories about the Klan burning crosses on their front lawn when they first moved onto the property. Once Salvatore and Mary got the vineyard got up and running, those visits slowed. The family built their brand by selling wine at fairs and festivals around the state. One of the hooded men was a regular at their tents. Salvatore recognized him by his limp and fancy shoes. The Klan didn't like "Tallies," but they sure liked alcohol.

Salvatore was a man with a vision who laid out the property flawlessly. Tony admired the land and the man. The tasting rooms and Poppy's were situated on the western side where the sunsets could take your breath away at night. The vineyard warehouse was a football field away from the front showpieces. This may be Marchio land, but Tony feels tied to it as well.

Salvatore had a large barn built for family gatherings. They all thought he had bigger aspirations for it. Sadly, he died before seeing what his grandchildren would build on this land. When Maryssa finished culinary school and her internship, she began designing her dream restaurant. Tony took her dreams and expanded them to fit inside that same barn. With the help of his newly hired carpenter, Beau, and the rest of his team, Poppy's became a landmark. The building has been featured in regional and national magazines for both its culinary and architectural integrity.

The vineyard takes up most of the acreage. Still, the family farm was large enough to host a pond, a pavilion, a farmhouse, and land for children and grandchildren who want to build their homes. Beau and Maryssa picked a spot across from the pond where her parents married and where she and Beau married as well. Tony's crew finished their house right before the baby was born, but Maryssa quickly requested a larger laundry room be added.

"We can run by your house in a minute to check on the crew. Mary called me this morning and asked me to stop over for a project." Tony explains to Beau.

"As long as the laundry room at my house is finished before school starts next month, I don't care where we stop. If that room isn't finished on time, I might have to move in with you and Sammy. Don't laugh, I'm serious."

They drive around the pond and end up on the main road leading to the white farmhouse. The house is a simple three-story, with lots of windows and character. With her wrap-around porches and swings, she welcomes every visitor to come and sit for a while. Tony loves this house.

"What project does Nunnie have? We just had dinner with her last night, and she didn't say anything."

"I have no idea, but I wasn't about to tell her no. The last time she called, Sammy and I spent an entire weekend building her a pen and coop for her chickens. Knowing her, it could be anything. A castle for goats. A treehouse for her rooster. She never ceases to shock me." Tony pulls up and around the circular front drive before cutting off his engine. "That's why I brought you. You will either be my witness or my protection."

Both men laugh as they climb out of the truck and up the front stairs.

The screen door opens before they reach it. "Right on time. Good morning, boys. I made coffee and cinnamon rolls."

Mary Marchio amazes Tony. She is always two steps ahead of everyone and lighter on her feet, too. She is a force to be reckoned with, just like her granddaughters. The burly men follow her through the house until they reach her iconic kitchen. Mary motions for Tony and Beau to sit while she pours coffee in mugs.

"You have three cups ready. How did you know I was bringing Beau?" Tony questions the spritely woman.

"I didn't. I figured you would either bring Beau or Sammy. I knew you would want some backup in case my idea was too crazy for you." She winks at Beau then pats Tony on the shoulder. "Let's get down to business, shall we?" She pushes the cinnamon rolls toward the men.

"After eating your cinnamon rolls, I'll agree to anything." Tony takes a piece of gooey goodness from the pan.

"Well, eat up because it's a doozy." She smiles sweetly in her ornery way.

Warily, the men exchange glances.

Mary begins with a bang, "Anthony, I would like for you to redo my kitchen."

Tony stops his fork in mid-air while Beau chokes a little on his coffee.

"I'm sorry, what?"

"You heard me, Anthony. My kitchen. It needs to be opened up and updated. I want that open concept everyone talks about on TV. We can knock out a wall and get some new cabinets. I want my farmhouse kitchen to look like, well, a farmhouse kitchen." Mary chuckles at her own joke.

Tony stares at Beau, begging for help. Beau glares in response to Tony before turning back to Nunnie.

"Nunnie, are you sure? Have you talked with E, or Jo, or the boys about this? I don't know if the family is ready for you to change your kitchen. This is the epicenter of the Marchio family. I'm not sure how such a drastic change to their family home will go over with everyone." Beau tries to reason with his grandmother-in-law, knowing his wife will have his hide when she hears about Nunnie's plan.

"It's my kitchen and my house. They'll get over it." Mary watches their worried faces. "I'll tell you what, you boys do the work, and I'll worry about the family."

"Kitchen renovations are a big deal. It will take weeks or months. Not to mention that you won't be able to cook or use it while it's being renovated. What about Frankie and Esther?" Beau shifts in his chair.

Mary touches her hand to Beau's cheek. His devotion to his first mother-in-law can't be described in words. Esther and Beau have been to hell and back together, twice. "I know you're concerned for Esther, but she'll be fine. She's been spending a lot of time at Wes's home. I have a feeling they will make some permanent decisions soon. She needed her mama after John passed, but she ran her own household for decades. Permantly moving back in with her mother isn't healthy for either of us anymore. She needs her own space. That just leaves Frankie and me, and I want to do this for Frankie. God has given her a gift. She needs the space to grow into it. She needs a kitchen that is up to the task. This one is retired, like me. We need a facelift." Mary pulls back at her temples and hairline.

"Whoa, whoa, whoa. A kitchen update we can handle. Don't go crazy with anything else. Maryssa will definitely lose it." Beau rubs his forehead with his hand.

Mary rolls her eyes. Tony has seen that particular family trait many times. "Mary, are you sure about this? Have you thought about the nuisance it will cause? The dust, the noise?"

"What do you boys take me for? A sissy? I know what I'm doing and what it means. For goodness sake. Tony, do you want the job or not? I can find someone else, but then I'll have to call your mother and tell her you turned down my business."

"No, Ma'am. There is no need to call my mother. How could I ever say no to you? When do you want my crew to start? Have you worked with a designer on the plans?" Tony pulls out his phone to check his calendar for an opening.

"I don't need a designer. I have you and Frankie. You two will work together to design the kitchen and pick out what we need."

The pieces are falling into place. Mary Marchio is one sneaky lady. Beau has witnessed firsthand this woman's meddling power, and he can't hold back the laughter.

Tony stares at Mary, his phone hanging in his hand. "Does Frankie know about any of this? Is she okay working with me? We don't exactly get along."

Mary pats Tony's hand. "You're not the only one who can't say no to me." With a wink, the woman sits back in her chair and takes a long sip of coffee. Beau chuckles before taking a big bite of his cinnamon roll, a giant smirk covering his face.

Frankie

Group Chat: My insane family (22 contacts)

Nunnie (Mary Marchio): Family dinner tomorrow night. Be here by 6. No excuses.

Annoying Brother (Sammy Marchio): I have a date I'm not coming.

Nunnie (Mary Marchio): Yes, you are coming. Bring her.

Annoying Brother (Sammy Marchio): UR Kidding, right? Bring a date to a family dinner. No way.

Daddy (Samuel Marchio): Son, why would you argue with your grandmother? You won't win.

Aunt E (Esther Robinson): Says the man who spent our childhood arguing with her.

Uncle Dom (Dominick Marchio): I'm her favorite. I never argued with you, right, Ma?

Nunnie (Mary Marchio): All five of my darling children are equally as guilty when it comes to arguing. I have an announcement. Everyone comes.

Haddie (Haddie Robinson Cashe): You know I'm living in another country, right?

Annoying Brother (Sammy Marchio): If I have to come, Haddie needs to fly in on Air Force One.

Haddie (Haddie Robinson Cashe): Smart@$&

Annoying Brother (Sammy Marchio): Language! Nunnie, Haddie needs her mouth washed out with soap.

Maryssa (Maryssa Lavalier Baker): Nunnie, your favorite granddaughter, who has a young baby and doesn't get any sleep, is craving menasha. Will you make me some? I have potatoes, spinach, and sausage at the restaurant. (Please hear my underlying whine)

Annoying Cousin (Dominick Marchio, Jr.): If shrimpy-ryssa gets to whine, then Sammy and I want our menasha with just potatoes and green beans.

Maryssa (Maryssa Lavalier Baker): Grow up boys.

Aunt Jo (Josephine Slater): What announcement? Is it bad? I can't handle bad. I have back to back meetings at the middle school. I can't do bad tomorrow.

Nunnie (Mary Marchio): Enough. Maryssa, you come early with ingredients. Everyone else, be here before 6pm.

Jackson (Jackson Cashe): Malik, can we have menasha tonight in the Residence?

Annoying Brother (Sammy Marchio): How does every text string end with Jackson asking for food?

Uncle Malik (Malik Lavalier): Sorry, Jackson. I'm off tonight. Victoria and I have a date night. If you want menasha, you need to listen to Sammy and take Air Force One.

Haddie (Haddie Robinson Cashe): Uncle Malik, don't encourage him.

Frankie: Got it, tomorrow, 6. I'm turning off my phone.

Annoying Brother (Sammy Marchio): Someone's in a bad mood.

Nunnie (Mary Marchio): Tomorrow. Farmhouse. 6pm. No excuses.

The phone continues to beep, but Frankie silences it then tosses it into her purse. The inside of her car is silent and calm. She inhales deeply, exhales, then repeats. Going out in public is stressful. The bulk store wasn't as crowded early this morning, but it was enough to give her the heebie geebies. She's tired from her restless night and an early

28

morning workout. The last thing she needs is more family drama.

Lately, sleep ends with the same nightmare she used to have years ago. The one that wraps her tighter than the weighted blanket she sleeps under and suffocates the air right out of her lungs. She sees a horned creature coming at her with outstretched arms. It is shrouded in shadows and fire. Waking her at the same point each time, right before the face comes into view. Frankie shakes the image from her head to try and clear the memory, again.

As if that wasn't enough, her day has been hijacked by Maryssa's producer and a surprise family dinner tomorrow. Frankie hoped to hit the gym tonight, but sparring with Deena is now out of reach. With a heavy sigh, Frankie collects the grocery bags from the passenger seat and heads into the restaurant's back door.

Poppy's has become Frankie's home away from home. Working out of Maryssa's commercial kitchen allows Frankie to increase output and try new things. Maryssa used to spend the mornings in her office planning, but since the baby, she's been working from home. Maryssa's new schedule gives Frankie free reign in the mornings. The best part is the quiet. No one to distract her. No static, only focus.

Frankie moved into the farmhouse with Nunnie and Aunt E last year to save money. She wasn't about to move back in with her parents. Nunnie's kitchen is too small to do the scale of work Frankie needs if she wants to launch her own specialty bakery. The arrangement with Maryssa is perfect.

Today's schedule will be different now that Lisa Fox is coming to meet them. Frankie's anxiety has been heightened since the call this morning. Thankfully, the hefty list of bakery orders will keep her mind focused on recipes and measuring. She finds comfort in the consistency of a recipe and the control over the ingredients. Goodness knows she has no consistency or control over the rest of her life.

Poppy's is so quiet. The calm before the storm. Frankie steels herself before pushing open the kitchen door, not knowing what she'll find on the other side today. Maryssa came in early to organize and take stock of her calendar and to brainstorm show ideas for the meeting with Lisa.

Empty. Nice. Placing bags on the counter, Frankie turns to store her purse and clothes bag.

"Frankie?" Maryssa calls from her office. "Is that you?"

"Yeppers, it's me. Do I still have time to bake? Staff won't trickle in for a couple of hours, do you need me for anything?" Frankie walks to the office door with the hope of an answer already in her heart.

Knowing Frankie and food, Maryssa understands the profound cathartic benefits of cooking. "Go crazy. Just make sure you have time to change before we open, so you're ready for Lisa."

Frankie sighs in relief. "You got it, boss." The smile lights up her face.

A few minutes later, Frankie's tendrils are secured by an elastic headband. Her braid is wrapped into a nice bun on the back of her head. She pulls on her gloves and gets to work. Music fills the space as she hits her stride. Securing a crate of eggs on the counter as the butter melts, she cracks some for the cake and separates the others for another recipe.

The whirring of the mixer sounds blissful as it whisks mascarpone with sugar, vanilla, and heavy cream. The sweet aroma envelops Frankie. *Awn, sweet, sweet sugar.*

Growing up, her family called her Fearless Frankie. She's still fearless but in a more guarded manner. That makes

30

her sad to think about, so she doesn't. Life has a way of knocking the courage right out of a person. She spends every day fighting to make herself fearless again. Baking helps.

Time flies as Frankie flits and floats around the kitchen. Sugary confections line the counters of the kitchen. Some already boxed, some cooling, and some waiting to be placed in the display case out front. Frankie works on the tiramisu cake. She finishes the last few dollops of mascarpone whipped icing then sprinkles chocolate shavings along the top. Standing back to look at the finished product, an inner smile overflows to her face.

Perfection.

After cleaning her tools and the counters, Frankie races to the bathroom to change and freshen up before staff arrives. She tightens the belt on her shirt dress before rolling up the sleeve cuffs. She slides on her nude, open-toed, scalloped booties. A few spritzes of perfume, a dab of lip balm, and a swipe of mascara are applied. One last look in the mirror, then she's back to the kitchen to finish icing some cupcakes.

Maryssa emerges from her office at the same time. Frankie marvels at her older cousin, "You look absolutely adorable." Frankie smiles at Maryssa in the doorway, wearing her chef's whites. Hot pink Crocs peeking out from her casual linen pants. "I can't believe you just had a baby."

Maryssa examines herself then smiles in genuine gratitude. "Thanks, I feel like a hot air balloon."

Maryssa and Haddie are retired ballerinas. They danced professionally for years before age and injury beat down their doors. Frankie doubts there is one inch of fat on either one of them. Both have tiny frames like Nunnie. Small and fierce, not fragile. They were powerful and fluid. Frankie imagines that Maryssa feels out of place in her body after having a baby.

"Well, you look like a gazelle."

"A gazelle? I think you've been spending too much time breathing in sugar, but I'll take gazelle over a hot air balloon any day." Maryssa snorts then begins her prep for service. Frankie loves watching Maryssa and her staff. The fluidity and high level of communication are astounding. Sounds of cars pulling into the staff parking lot draw her attention back to the job at hand.

"Staff is here. I'll head to the front of the house to check menus."

The afternoon rushes by Frankie in a blur. Thanks to the state tourism commission's new West Virginia vineyard tour, the tasting rooms and Poppy's have been bustling all summer. The restaurant is packed with patrons every day except Sunday. Frankie loves watching Maryssa pop out to visit with her diners throughout service. Maryssa's love for the culinary arts and people is inspiring.

In between the late lunch and early dinner crowd, Maryssa pulls Frankie from the floor. Frankie saw Lisa and her assistant arrive and head into the bar area a few minutes ago. She was secretly hoping they'd changed their minds about meeting her or the plane was delayed. No such luck. The four of them grab a high-top table near the brick pizza oven that opens to the kitchen.

After a quick round of hellos, Maryssa chuckles to herself as Lisa and Frankie look at her questioningly. "Sorry, the last time I had a propositional business meeting in this room, it didn't end so well for me."

Frankie shivers and makes a creeped-out face, which makes Maryssa chuckle more.

Lisa appraises the sanity of both women, confused by their private joke. "Your family is highly entertaining."

"That's an understatement. You have no idea," Maryssa snorts.

Lisa Fox is precisely how you would picture a television producer, serious. She dresses smartly. Navy pantsuit topped off with an enviable silk scarf. A perfect balance of comfortable professionalism. Her red lob framing an oval face. She lifts her glasses and rests them on her head. "Should I be worried about this previous meeting?"

Maryssa half explains, "Unless you are secretly a sixty-year-old womanizer with character issues, a crazy daughter, and the stipulation that one of us dates you, I think we're okay."

"Well, I definitely don't fit into any of those categories, but I would love to hear that story." Lisa laughs suspiciously as she pulls out her tablet and a file folder from her designer briefcase. "This family never ceases to surprise me."

Frankie and Maryssa exchange a glance before Frankie offers a "we can't argue that" shrug.

"All right, ladies, let's get down to business. I know you are busy, and I would like to fly back tonight and process these contracts." Lisa starts whipping her finger across and over the tablet, clearly looking for something. "Ah, here is my file." Lisa tilts the tablet in Frankie's direction.

In a past life that Frankie wants desperately to forget, she earned a business degree. Her role in the family business was to help Aunt Jo with the financials at the vineyard office. She understands every chart and graph whipping in front of her eyes. No matter how hard she tries, she cannot avoid facts and statistics.

"Frankie, I will forward these charts to you for closer examination. You can probably read these faster than I can say 'statistics' based on your business background." Lisa looks directly into Frankie's muddled eyes. "The bottom line is that you are off the charts right now. Your name was searched for more times last week than the name of Haddie's dress designer. That never happens. Your cake. The personal touches, the intricate details. Your cake is on fire. We want to strike while the iron is hot. Our parent company would like to offer you an eight-episode season with the option to add holiday specials based on the ratings."

Lisa and Maryssa expectantly stare at Frankie, gauging her reaction.

"All this because of one cake? Aren't you taking a gamble on me?" Frankie is floored by the offer.

"Seriously? Let's review. Your cousin Haddie made television history falling in love with the President of the United States on a reality dating show. The attempted assassination episode is still the most streamed show of all time. Then, Maryssa blew up network ratings after her pilot holiday special. We can't get enough air time with her. Your family is television ratings gold. Your Inauguration Day cake may have launched you, but the shuttle has been prepped for a year now. You, Frankie, are a no brainer. We have advertisers begging for a place at the table since a rumor leaked that we are courting you. Eight episodes are just the beginning."

Frankie begins earnestly studying a chart then scrolls to the next and the next and the next. She takes a deep breath. Six years ago, Frankie would be popping champagne corks and bouncing from the ceiling at this offer. Fearless Frankie is hiding behind her fear. She sits back in her chair and searches their faces. "Are you sure about this? Because I'm not. That is a lot of pressure riding on someone who just started a baking business a few years ago in her grandmother's kitchen. They only training I've had is from an old Italian woman."

"Ooohh, you better never let Nunnie hear you call her old." Maryssa shakes her head in shock and concern.

Frankie rolls her eyes. "You know what I mean. Lisa, you are not propositioning a professional. I'm flying by the seat of my pants half the time. You want to hire an amateur who knows enough to be dangerous. Everything new is a risk that I'm brave enough to try while I'm hiding in the back of Poppy's." Frankie takes pause at the revelation that she is still taking risks, but pushes it aside for her boxing session tomorrow morning. "It might take me a hundred takes to get one cake perfect."

Lisa leans in to close the gap Frankie created. "That is exactly what I want, authenticity. Not all people want to see a professionally trained chef or pastry chef." Lisa turns to Maryssa briefly before returning to persuade Frankie. "No offense, but it's true. Viewers want to see real people in the kitchen. They want to see a dreamer following a dream so they can keep following theirs. Your story gives hope."

A sardonic chuckle escapes Frankie's usually stone resolve. She draws in a breath through her nose, holds it, then exhales through open lips. "My gut is telling me yes, but I'd like a week to think about it. Maybe the hype will die down, and the network won't want me."

"That's not going to happen, but I can give you some time. Just remember, the longer you wait, the harder we work at PR. Right now, we have a wave of free publicity. We don't want to look a gift horse in the mouth." Lisa smiles then hands Frankie a manilla envelope. "Here is the contract. Look it over and let me know if you have any questions or changes."

Lisa reaches over to touch Frankie's hands, but they recoil before the connection. "Frankie, this is a great opportunity. You can try it out for eight episodes and get enough money to open your own bakery. If you don't like it, let the contract run its course and move onto something else.

Don't miss an opportunity jumping up and down right in front of you."

Maryssa senses the heaviness in Frankie's eyes. "Well, let's move on to me and let Frankie have some time to think." Maryssa winks at Frankie, who returns the kindness with a smile.

Tony

The soles of his boots stick to the floor with every step. The air is heavy with stale beer and perspiration. Lingering cigarette odors are embedded in the walls from years of smoking in public. The added humidity makes Tony feel five pounds heavier. The bar is packed wall to wall with people waiting to see the band.

Tony and Sammy are here for the wings and to support their high school buddies who play in the band. The drummer crashes at their apartment sometimes when he's not on tour. They are playing one of Tony's favorite songs, so he knows they just started the set.

Sammy sits at the bar with a direct view of the stage. Tony nudges his way through the college crowd. He catches a tipsy blond girl as she stumbles into him. "Thanks," she says breathily as she smiles and appraises him. Tony returns her response with a polite nod and continues to walk through the mass of people. By the time he makes it to the stool saved for him by his best friend since first grade, he feels dirty and exhausted.

"What took you so long?" Sammy continues without waiting for an answer. "I had to fight off ten girls to save this seat."

Tony shakes his head, "If even one girl asked for this seat, I would be standing right now." The stool has a slight wobble as he climbs on to it. Tony thinks of ten different ways to fix it.

Sammy shrugs in agreement. "You're right. Here, eat." Sammy pushes red plastic baskets, lined with waxed paper and bar food. "Working late on a job?" Sammy asks while he looks beyond Tony and scans the bar.

"Sorry I'm late honey." Tony jokes as he shoves hand-cut fries in his mouth. He realizes he hasn't eaten anything since the cinnamon rolls at Mary's, unless you count the coffee grounds from the pot in the construction office. He knew better than to drink coffee made by one of his crew members, but he was desperate. Tony is starving.

"Actually, it's your grandmother's fault I'm running late today."

Sammy stops scanning and looks questioningly at Tony, "Nunnie?"

"Sweet tea and another basket of wings, please." Tony orders then eats another handful of fries. "Yeah. I felt like I was being summoned to the Corleone house on baptism day." Tony laughs at his own joke. "She called me this morning and said she had a job for me. I brought Beau over as backup. That woman scares me. I never know what I'll be talked into doing with her. I love your Nunnie, but she can be a real boss lady."

"Tell me about it. I can't leave the farmhouse without at least five chores under my belt. What does Nunnie want you to do this time? Build a new chicken coop with a spa?" Sammy laughs.

The wait staff, wearing referee inspired shirts, knows Tony and Sammy well. They always seem to get the same bartender, "Here you go, Tony." She lingers a few seconds longer as Tony grabs napkins from the dispenser. "Did you watch the Pirates game last night?"

"It was close, but they pulled it out in the seventh." Tony nods his thanks to the blond with straight hair before taking a long drink of the sweet, cold tea. Sammy shakes his head at Beau before offering a shrug to the bartender.

"What? Why are you laughing?" Tony looks down to make sure he didn't spill anything on his shirt.

"We come here every Tuesday night for wings. Every. Tuesday. And every Tuesday, Aubrey flirts with you. I don't get it. I'm starting to worry about you." Sammy chomps on a celery stick drenched in house-made ranch dressing.

"She's not my type."

"Hot? Funny? Knows sports? Hot? Hot isn't your type?" Sammy stares astonishingly at his roommate. "You're crazy."

Tony turns in the barstool and looks at his best friend. Trying out the words his mind has been kicking around for months. "Don't you want more? More than another fling with a bartender or waitress or whatever girl happens to hit on you? We both have jobs, trucks, money. Don't you want more than our apartment with a broken stove we've never fixed?"

"Neither of us cook," Sammy deadpans.

Tony turns back and sighs. "I'm not interested in *her*. Can we just leave it at that?"

Sammy, finally reading the situation, "Sorry, man. I didn't mean to push. You just haven't dated anyone in a while. No offense, but you've been kind of a downer lately. I think a nice girl might help."

"Now, you just sound like my mom. A nice girl might help? Seriously? I didn't realize my lack of a dating life was bothering you." Tony drinks his tea and grabs one of Sammy's fried pickles and dips it in the mystery sauce inside the basket.

Awareness dawns on Sammy, "Wait, did you say you're not interested in *her*? Is there someone you *are* interested in? Are you holding out on me?" Sammy reaches over and squeezes right where Tony's neck and shoulder meet. "Do you need some advice on how to get a lady?" Sammy's laughing now.

Tony closes his eyes and drops his head. "From you, no thanks. Let's move on. I liked talking about your grandmother more than this conversation."

"All right, all right. What does Nunnie want you to do anyway? Do you need help or can you just have one of the guys work on it?" Sammy returns to normal, checking out the prospects in the room and eating.

"Right, because Mary Marchio would let me put someone else on one of her jobs. Beau and I can handle it, but she wants me to work with your sister. I'm not sure how well that will work out since Frankie seems to hate me more each time I see her."

"Frankie hates everyone since she came home from college. Just ignore her." Sammy rubs his chin in frustration.

"Why is that? Did anyone bother to ask why she changed from fun-loving and fearless Frankie to tough-man contender overnight?" Tony stares directly at Sammy, hoping for a different answer than he knows he's going to get.

"Who knows. She won't talk about anything with me. Frankie is still the same pain in my rear she's always been. I'm just glad she's not working at the warehouse anymore. Working with Maryssa seems to calm her down more than handling the books for the vineyard. She was miserable before she started at working Poppy's. At least now she smiles." Sammy shrugs and waves Aubrey over, "If you're not interested, I'm asking for her number."

"Go for it." Tony settles in and thinks about Frankie as he eats his first wing of the night. Sammy has Aubrey laughing in no time. They are both ignoring him now so Tony focuses on Frankie. She's never far from his thoughts, but even more so lately.

He remembers the exact moment when Frankie Jo Marchio became more than Sammy's annoying little sister. It was the middle of summer and very hot. The whole Marchio family spent the day boating at Tygart Lake with friends. Frankie, Haddie, and Maryssa were laying out on the sandy shoreline, working on their tans. Everyone was resting from their morning spent skiing and tubing on the water.

Sammy and Tony had walked the steep dirt trail from the lodge down to the beach. Once they made it to the sand, the boys were bragging about some girls they had been flirting with in the parking lot. Sammy's cousins called the boys out for their lack of skills as they protested. The teasing was intense, but par for the course with that family. Without a word, Frankie walked right up to Tony and planted a kiss square on the lips. In that second, an electric current zapped his entire body. Butterflies floated up from his stomach into his throat. His lips were still puckered when she abruptly pulled away from him.

"That's what I thought. You two idiots have no idea what you're doing." She walked away like she had just given him a high five and plopped back down on her tie-dyed beach towel. Sammy and the girls were laughing hysterically. Tony felt like a deer caught in headlights. He shrugged it off, but it made a mark on him. The two boys proceeded to dump a bucket of water on all three of the sun soakers.

From that point on, Frankie looked differently to him. He listened to her stories around the kitchen table and asked questions to prolong conversations. Tony tried to walk with her in between classes without Sammy, or Frankie for that matter, thinking it was more than just a coincidence he always seemed to be outside her classroom. He helped Sammy intimidate would-be-suiters. He almost got away with asking her to prom until he realized the state baseball playoffs were the same weekend. Sammy and Tony played baseball in college, and Frankie attended every home game. Tony remembered that initial spark every day and wondered how the flame would feel.

He always thought there was a connection, but never knew for sure. Frankie didn't say anything to him, and he didn't say anything to her. Tony respected his relationship with Sammy too much to make a move, but he pushed any limit he could to get closer to Frankie. He took a baby step the night before she left for her junior year of college. There was an end of summer cookout at the farmhouse. Frankie was climbing into her car to leave when Tony ran out to say goodbye. He told her not to forget him, then leaned in through the car window to kiss her cheek. It was a brief moment, but it felt intimate and sacred. Her smile filled his heart.

"Never." Frankie touched his cheek as kids ran around the house and broke the silence, and the moment.

She started her car and drove off into the summer night. That was the last time she looked at him with stars in her eyes. Her emerald eyes lost their luster that year, and no one knew why.

Nunnie Mary

The sizzle of garlic frying in olive oil hisses while Mary gathers the spinach. She has been cooking for her brood in this kitchen for decades. It is only fitting that the final meal is menasha.

Mary has already diced the potatoes, now she needs to get the greens in the pots. One batch of traditional menasha with potatoes, spinach, and sausage cooks on the stovetop. The second pot holds only green beans and potatoes. The second, makeshift, version she made for the kids when money was tight, and food came from the garden only. When the vineyard started breaking even, and Mary began making the traditional version again, the kids only wanted green beans and potatoes.

She picked up some fresh Italian bread from the bakery. The soft bread with its hard crust is perfect for dunking into the menasha and cleaning plates. Breadbaskets, butter, salt, and pepper already line the table in the dining room. She has a platter filled with meats and cheeses ready to go out with the food. A pan of Italian sausage links warms in the oven.

Mary loves cooking, but it's more about filling the bellies of those she loves. It's not the food, it's the experience. The breaking of bread together is healing. Passing plates back and forth. Laughter and stories passed out with the food. This is where Mary Marchio holds court. Family dinner is her legacy.

The spinach cooks down as Mary plops in the cubes of potatoey goodness. Everything begins melding together. The aroma is rich and savory, and garlicky. Her memories go back to another time in her life. When her husband Salvatore came home one night after a poker game, she thought he was teasing her when he said he won a patch of land outside of town. The deed was warm from his hands holding it so tightly all the way home.

The next morning was a warm summer day as they drove out to see the acreage. They were surrounded by lush green hills and trees. The white farmhouse sat far back on the property making it invisible from the road. It was old and covered in overgrown landscaping. The fields hadn't been tended to in some time. Salvo saw potential, Mary saw work. Work she didn't have time to do while working full time and raising four young kids, with a baby on the way. The shutters were hanging off the windows, and paint was peeling. She looked at her husband and saw a spark she hadn't seen since his baseball days.

She watched him as he explained what he saw. Their visions were different, but she saw the hope in his words. "Mary, I know it doesn't look like much, but the bones are great. It just needs some paint and a good cleaning. And, look over here, there's a pond behind all that brush. We just need to clear it out with a tractor."

Mary scoffed, "A tractor we don't have."

Salvo just kept talking, "I can fish there with the boys." He paused while Mary looked at him, knowing he was picturing two little girls with fishing poles. "And the girls."

"Salvatore," Mary began to protest.

"Mary, I think we can do it. We can buy a few vines and plant them this summer. The only thing we have to pay for is taxes. I can cover that after we plow the fields and sell the hay. If it doesn't work, we're only out the first two hands I lost last night." He stared longingly at her, waiting for an answer.

"Salvatore, I don't understand. How on God's Earth could someone gamble this much land away? Aren't they going to want it back? Can we handle all this ourselves?" Mary paces. Salvatore Marchio has always been a dreamer.

His parents sailed from Italy with a suitcase full of them and passed each one down to their kids. Most Italian immigrants came to West Virginia to work in the coal mines. Salvatore spent one day a mile underground and never went back. He worked at the glass plant and did odd jobs to stay above ground. Mary had to grow up pragmatically. She had her own dreams, but they were emotionally expensive.

"Mary, we can do it. I know we can do it. The land is old man Simpson's farm. It's been closed for years since he died. His only family left is a son who lives an hour down the highway and wants nothing to do with farming. The neighbors don't want him to sell it because they're afraid some big warehouse or factory will take it. He can't get it sold before the next tax payment. I think he was actually relieved he lost."

Salvatore snuggled up close to her from behind. He wrapped his arms tight around her and leaned down to kiss the top of her head. "I promised you a lifetime of dancing. Do you trust me, Mary?"

She sighed. Salvo was the only man in her life who had never let her down. "You know I do, Salvo." She shook her head, laughing, "I guess we're farmers."

Salvo had kept his promise. They danced every night in that kitchen before bed. The first ten years were hard, but they had each other, and they made it work. They couldn't have done it without their families. Brothers painted and repaired the house to make it livable. The fields were cleared as the hay was baled and prepared for sale. The neighbors weren't happy about the *I-tal-ee-uns* owning land next to them, but after a few cases of homemade wine, they seemed less outraged. A couple of them even offered to help during the third harvest.

Not only was the pond spruced up, but after the vineyard took off, Salvo built her a pavilion next to it for the family to gather. They planted large oak trees in the backyard for each child born, five in total. The farmhouse still stands today. They were able to purchase the adjacent farm and added more acres. Maryssa and Beau built their own home on the land, and there is room for other houses. The vineyard boasts an office, a warehouse, a tasting center, and Poppy's Restaurant. The farm grew into much more than even Salvatore Marchio could have dreamed that day. Not too bad for three hands of poker.

One of the pot lids begins rattling as steam interrupts Mary's walk down memory lane. A stray tear escapes her eye. She wipes it quickly before coming back to reality. Mary stirs the pots and does a quick check of the contents. She breathes in the familiar aroma and smiles intensely as she blows a kiss to her dear Salvo.

"Nunnie, can I do anything to help?" Maryssa crosses the room with baby John wrapped up tight across her chest. "Mmm, it smells so good. Do you want me to taste test it? Make sure it isn't poisoned?" She kisses her Nunnie's cheek.

"Give it a few more minutes, so the potatoes soak up the liquids. You can grab plates from the cabinet and set the table." Mary looks around for potholders. Maryssa gets them out before she is asked. The two women were roommates before Maryssa married Beau. They learned to dance perfectly together in a kitchen.

Voices begin trailing in from the front door. Mary smiles in anticipation of seeing her entire brood gather around the table in the dining room. She stirs the pots then peaks at the sausage.

"Hey, Ma. Smells delicious." Sam makes a beeline for his mother and presents a kiss to her cheek. His brother Dom follows in turn. Their wives Hannah and Tamra are next in line.

The family trickles in and settles into a routine. The glasses are filled with ice. Pitchers of sweet tea and water are placed on the counter. Pots and baskets are carried to the long dining room table like an assembly line. When the food is ready, they are all ushered to their seats.

Mary Marchio sits at the end of the table while everyone bows their heads and joins hands. A blessing is spoken over their family and the food. "Amen" resounds around the room. Stories and laughter fill every second of the meal. Mary's heart warms as she takes in the table set before her.

Sam notices his mother's face and kicks off the conversation they have been assembled to hear. "All right, Ma, what has us all gathered together tonight? What's the big announcement?"

Silverware and glasses still. A rare moment of silence fills the typically boisterous space.

Mary sits up in her chair, ready for dissent. No one likes change, and this is a big one. "Well, it's time for a change. I'm making some updates to the farmhouse to make it more, well, open concept if you will."

"Open concept? I see Frankie has you watching her house renovation shows with her," Sam chuckles while smiling at his daughter.

Esther asks, concerned by what this means for her, "Mom, what exactly are you saying? Are you gutting the house or just making updates?"

"A complete overhaul."

A chorus of "Mom" and "Nunnie" ring out from around the table. Mary holds up her hands to silence everyone and explain.

"Well, I want to knock down the wall between the family room and the kitchen and make the two doors for the dining room wider so you can see into it better from the other rooms. Mainly, I want a new kitchen. I want to open it up and add more storage and a big island that we can all fit around instead of a little table. Salvo promised me a new kitchen, but other projects kept moving up the list. Now, I'm ready. The kitchen has always been the heart of this house. It deserves some TLC. Some pizazz."

"Pizazz? Nunnie that scares me." Frankie chokes on her water. "What exactly does your definition of pizazz look like?"

Mary leans down to pat Frankie's hand. "I'm glad you asked, dear, because you and Tony are in charge of the project. I've already signed a contract with him. He'll do the work himself, with Beau, of course helping. Together, you two will work on the design. He is coming for dinner tomorrow to plan."

Sammy starts laughing at Frankie. "Oh, that will be fun, Tony and Frankie working together. Now, that would make great TV. They hate each other." He is stopped short with a kick to the ankle under the table from his mother, Hannah. He looks up at her with a questioning look.

Trying to change the subject, Beau uncharacteristically jumps into the conversation as everyone sits confused and unsettled. "Mary has some great ideas. Tony and I took the measurements and will be able to start next week. It should only take a month to six weeks to finish.'

Beau nervously continues as Maryssa glares at him. Mary is sure there will be words tonight at the Baker house about Beau keeping her secret. "Frankie, you'll have a blank slate. Tony can work on sketches with you as you plan. I can help if you want."

Mary observes Frankie's frozen face as Beau rambles on and on about demolition and materials. The rest of the family starts to squirm. Mary decides to end this before everyone panics and starts questioning their entire existence.

"Thank you, Beau." Mary takes control of the conversation.

Mary appreciates Beau's gift of observation. He looks at her with genuine gratitude for putting him out of his misery. Beau is a good judge of character. He has carried a lot on those broad shoulders of his. She is grateful he and Maryssa balance one another out so beautifully.

"I have given this a lot of thought. I know you all are attached to this house and this kitchen, but the truth is, it's long overdue. Instead of making this a sad thing, focus on the fact that our family is bursting at the seams, and we need more room to bake and cook and celebrate. This is a blessing, and we will treat it as such. Now, tonight we'll enjoy our last evening together in the past, and then we'll only focus on the future. Your father promised me a new kitchen, you can send all complaints to him."

All eyes focus on Mary. Squirming bodies and shock are the only sounds. Everyone at the table knew that was the end of the conversation. "Sam, pass the bread please." Nunnie has spoken, the matter is settled.

Jackson

Jackson: Did you find out more information from your mom about the kitchen? Is everyone still upset?

Haddie: Nothing from Mama, but according to Maryssa, the siblings were having lunch today to talk about it. Maryssa was mad, but honestly, I think she's more upset that Nunnie is remodeling after Maryssa moved out of the farmhouse. Although she would never admit it.

Jackson: I'm still confused by the whole Frankie and Tony angle. They hate each other.

Haddie: Oh honey, you're so cute. Did you forget that I hated you when we met?

Before Jackson can enter his witty response, Haddie quickly texts that her mom is calling. He can't wait to hear the latest update and get back to Marchio family drama. Last night, the kitchen saga kept his mind off of presidenting, as Haddie calls it, for over an hour. That is hard to do in his line of work.

Jackson is struggling in Washington. Everything has changed. Politics is no longer about people debating positions. Politics is controlled by big money and the media. The art of debate had been lost. The kingdom now belongs to the best sound bite. The noble field of journalism has replaced the cornerstone of their profession from seeking and providing information, to performing and crafting reality for the highest bidder.

After an assassination attempt that almost killed Haddie too, Jackson's entire political platform shifted from party loyalty to common sense decisions. His first act of power declared that any bill containing hidden agendas or funding brought to his desk would be automatically vetoed. Bills and amendments were to be straight forward without quid pro quo stuck in between the lines by special interest groups, from either party. He reads each bill line by line now. That means no more three-thousand-page bills that no one actually reads.

With help from West Virginia's Governor, John Marchio, Jackson's reunification summit between the Allied States of America and the United States of America was a success. The final division of the transportation and military systems are paused. At the same time, both countries remain in negotiations for a possible reunification. It has not been easy, but Jackson is steadfastly focused on making one great nation from two.

The media hailed Jackson as the brave unifier leading up to the summit. A modern-day Honest Abe, he was attempting the impossible. During the summit, he was a poised and wise leader. A rare breed who could cross long instilled party lines for progress. The summit was a huge success. The media began drooling and churning out clickbait. A reunification effort would give them years of debate and unrest to cover. However, the media attention spooked the Allied States. Now, they're dragging their feet about the second summit in Washington, D.C. that Jackson is proposing.

As the first elected president after The Separation of States, Jackson has always felt the burden to reunite. He faced an uphill battle during his first term, but he is feeling confident this time around. Today's meeting with his team is crucial in planning the initial stages of the next summit.

Knocking from the side door signals to Jackson, the meeting is at hand. He stands and stretches his spine tall to work out the stress that envelops him each day. Jackson readies himself for the task as the paneled door opens.

Madison Lyn and Jackson have been friends since college. She looks exactly the same, whereas Jackson is greying and gathering deep lines around his eyes. Madison is followed by Rich Miller, the third member of their collegiate trio. Jackson can tell by the pinching on the bridge of Madsi's nose and the pained look on her face, that Rich is obviously trying to talk her into something.

"Rich, please stop. I know you think you're invincible, but not even you could spin that idea." Madison sounds exasperated.

Rich stops dead in his tracks and grabs his heart in a mock stabbing, "Ouch Madsi, that hurts. I'm the master of spin."

With an incredulous gaze and shake of her head, Madison makes her way to the champagne colored silk settees. "Jackson, are you interested in speaking to the UFO Society of Fiji?"

Jackson chuckles, knowing this will be a good one. "No, but I am intrigued about the request."

"A resort contacted Rich about a conference they're holding. They offered Rich a free suite for life if he can get you to speak to a group of their very eccentric and wealthy clients." Madison sits and spreads out the contents of her folder.

"Rich, we have talked about the balance between political favors and illegal activities before, do you need a refresher?" Jackson laughs, relatively sure his best friend is only joking.

"A guy can dream, right? I mean, we traveled to a Colorado ski resort so you could wine and dine beautiful women for a reality dating show. When do I get a vacation like that?"

"Here we go," Madison drops her head into her hands, waiting for Jackson to blast Rich. Jackson fought them tooth and nail against that dating show. Regardless of the fact he met and married Haddie because of *Future FLOTUS?*, it is still a sore subject.

Jackson counts silently in his head. *Eight. Nine. Ten.* "Rich, while I'm grateful for the outcome, you know full well I was opposed to that entire adventure. It was a waste of resources, money, and time that I could have been working. We are not using the national budget for you to conga your way through Fiji. Now, can we get some real work accomplished today before we host party leaders from both the House and the Senate?"

"You two are killing me. Just wait until my tell-all book comes out in three years." Rich pokes Madison as he walks by her with a smirk.

"You would never. I know where all of your skeletons are buried, Miller." Madison replies with a sweet smile in Rich's direction.

The three long time friends converge around the American Victorian walnut table. Jackson chose a table inspired by the décor used by President Ulysses S. Grant. Jackson studied both Grant and Lincoln extensively in college. At the time, he had no idea he would be emulating their reconstruction policies as his own. Looking back, Jackson can see the providential leadings in his course studies.

The presidential heroes Jackson admires bravely looked across party lines and aimed at doing what was right instead of what was expected. Grant took on the KKK and created the Department of Justice. Lincoln strengthened the federal government and updated the economic structure. Jackson Cashe spent his first term tackling immigration and education reforms. His second term is set to reunify two broken countries. His lofty ambitions can be unbearable at times.

Rich pulls Jackson from his thoughts. "Earth to Jackson. Did you read the latest numbers my team sent about your approval rating?"

Jackson shakes the thoughts from his mind and reconnects to the task at hand. "Approval ratings, yes, still in the low fifties. Something about the Federalist Party purchasing post-election ads. That is unusual, right? I know media and PR are your areas of expertise, but historically, after an election cycle there is some reprieve. A regrouping of sorts. Why would they be spending money on attack ads right now?"

Rich pointedly looks at Madsi, "How does he do that? He looks like he's in another world, but repeats everything I said."

"It's a gift. How do you manage to never directly answer a question?" Jackson pins Rich with a stare as Rich bows his head to receive the comment as an accolade. Jackson searches their faces inquiringly when Madison responds to the original question about political ads instead of Rich.

Madison speaks calmly, which has Jackson paying close attention. "We are wondering that ourselves. I have made a few targeted calls, and we're working some angles. It could just be the new norm, no relent. Or, there could be an undercurrent developing. This could also be a direct attack based on the campaign finance reform we are pushing. Neither party wants us peeking at their pocket books. Not to mention, any proposed bill would expose their revenue streams. Regardless, Rich's team is monitoring and reporting directly to me."

Jackson glances back and forth between the two, "Should I be worried?"

Rich leans back and stretches out his arm across the couch. "I'm leaning toward the no relent theory. With twenty-four-hour news cycles, everyone has a target. No news is no ratings. Either way, we're following it closely. I don't like the post-election personal attack ads. They are irritating me. I'm going to walk the floor today and ask some questions. I'll let you know what I hear."

"What about the negotiation points for the reunification? Any follow up questions or recommendations from either party?" Jackson is personally invested in this movement. He has built his entire presidency on reunification.

"Not yet, but we're hopeful they'll come with something in writing to the meeting today. Rich will give a press briefing afterward, and we would like to give some type of update, if possible."

"Speaking of the meeting, is everything set?" Jackson rubs his temples.

Madison hands Jackson a folder with talking points, "Yes, they are meeting us in the Roosevelt Room within the hour. My team organized the packets and are arranging place cards as we speak. Usually, the Speaker's office calls to confirm before she leaves the Capitol. Either they forgot today, or the delegation is running late."

Madison looks down at her phone as it begins beeping and pinging repeatedly. Rich's phone jumps in unison. Everything seems to happen at once.

Madison grabs the television remote from Jackson's side table. The door to the Oval Office swings open as Haddie enters breathlessly. As the TV comes to life, the four leaders of the House and Senate stand side by side. The Speaker emerges to walk in front of the podium. Jackson reads the ticker across the bottom of the screen, "Joint, bi-partisan task force formed to open an investigation on President Jackson Cashe in regards to collusion with the Allied States of America."

Haddie walks over and stands behind Jackson. She places a hand on his shoulder. A volume of words passes between them in silence as he reaches back and grasps her hand. Madison Lyn crosses her arms in annoyance.

Rich lowers his head in defeat. "Well, at least we got both parties to agree on something."

Frankie

The television has a loop of Jackson and Haddie stock photos. Frankie sits stunned with Nunnie and Aunt E as they huddle around the family room TV. The news anchor reports the same information repeatedly as they show clips from the press conference that just ended.

"Every time someone goes after Jackson, they always show pictures of Haddie from that darn show. It's as if they're subliminally blaming her for all of Jackson's political hurdles." Esther wrings her hands together in worry. "Not to mention, they always seem to pick the most unflattering pictures of her."

Frankie thinks back to Uncle John's funeral. The media called Haddie a terrorist for wearing a dress sold in South Carolina to her own father's funeral, as if Haddie cared what she was wearing that day. Camera crews shut down the roads surrounding the funeral home and graveyard. They could barely hear the sermon on account of the helicopters flying over the cemetery. It was so awful. Haddie couldn't even escape the vultures to mourn her own father, and the media supposedly loved her. Frankie shivers thinking about that kind of attention. She can barely handle the coverage she's getting now for a cake. Haddie must be a mess of emotions right now.

Nunnie stands up and turns off the television. "Haddie Marie is strong, she'll be fine. Same with Jackson. We will pray and trust God to direct their paths. Let's not sit here and give those people more ratings. Come on, we need to get dinner ready. Tony will be here soon."

Frankie rolls her eyes at the mention of the unwelcomed dinner guest. She jumps on the opportunity with a fake sweetness, "Nunnie, I'm sure Aunt E would rather call Haddie than entertain Tony for dinner. Tony will understand if we cancel."

"Nice try, Frankie. I'm actually taking Chloe and baby John to Chick-fil-A with Wes's grandkids tonight. Maryssa and Beau need a night alone. I'll call Haddie on my way to the restaurant. Knowing her, she'll stay by Jackson's side all night and won't pick up the phone."

"She's so protective of him." Nunnie pats Aunt E's shoulder.

"I might get a text with a string of symbols and mad face emojis, but that's about it. I'm going to get ready." Esther stands to leave the family room and strides down the hallway for her shoes and purse.

Nunnie calls after her daughter, "Tell Wes we said hello. You two try and contain yourselves in front of the little ones," Nunnie winks conspiratorially at Frankie.

"Mother!" Aunt E returns to the kitchen, ready to head out on her play date. "Wes and I are just friends. Old friends."

"Mm-hmm. I think the term is 'old flames,' not friends. I'm sure he's getting tired of all your *play-dates* with grandchildren in tow. Doesn't he keep asking you for a real date? If he wants to take someone to the Wonderbar Steakhouse, I'll volunteer." The ornery laugh can't be contained in the tiny woman.

"Wes and I are just fine, thank you very much." Esther glares at her mother, daring another observation to be shared. Nunnie laughs.

"Man, Nunnie, I'm glad you don't meddle in my love life. You're relentless." Frankie walks to the oven and peaks in at the bubbling baked ziti before placing the garlic bread under the broiler.

Now it's Esther's turn to laugh. "Oh, Frankie dear, she's an Italian grandmother, she's always meddling. She's remodeling an entire kitchen to meddle in your love life, and you didn't even see it coming." Esther kisses her mama's cheek, then the cheek of her niece's shocked face before floating out the back door. She leaves a trail of laughter in her wake.

"Nunnie!" Frankie grunts in frustration, "What is Aunt E talking about?"

"She's just trying to change the subject from Wes. That poor man has been pining for her since he was sixteen years old. Who said God doesn't give second chances? The roads of life might be curvy, twisted, and sometimes seem like dead ends, but He always has some lovely destinations built into the journey. We just need to look at Him instead of the road."

"Who is changing the subject now?" Frankie is annoyed.

"Frankie, dear, check the garlic bread, it smells ready." Nunnie tosses the salad in front of her before placing it on the table as Frankie peeks into the top oven.

"How do you do that?"

"What, honey? Change the subject so well or smell when food is ready?" Nunnie chuckles out loud.

"Both," Frankie grumbles.

A knock at the front door alerts the women their guest has arrived. Tony knows to just walk into the house without a formal greeting, he's family. Everyone who comes to this house is family.

Frankie pulls out the pan of baked ziti and places it on the stovetop to cool. She listens to Tony's footsteps coming down the hallway as she retrieves the tray of garlic bread from the broiler. She knows where she is and that she is safe, but the sound of male footsteps makes the hair stand up on the back of her neck.

"I wish all of my design meetings included a cougar and delicious food." Tony walks over for a famous Nunnie Mary hug.

"That's my Tony. Always the charmer. It's no wonder you and Sammy are still single."

"Hey!" Tony grabs his chest in mock hurt.

"Grab the bread basket and hand it to Frankie Jo, then have a seat. We'll be ready to eat any minute." Mary busies herself and attempts to seem disinterested as Tony saunters in the direction of the stove.

Their eyes lock, along with their smirks.

"Francesca."

"Anthony."

"Are you two going to pull out your dueling banjos next? Come on, let's eat before the food gets cold. After dinner, we can talk about kitchen design. I'm so excited to hear your ideas." Nunnie keeps talking as they all work together to bring the food to the table and sit.

Nunnie offers a prayer of thanksgiving and blessing over the food they are about to eat. She is acting more squirrelly than usual. She scoops food onto Tony's plate then Frankie's, but not her own. She checks her phone twice and busies herself at the kitchen sink filling a pitcher with water.

"Nunnie, what are you doing? Sit down and eat your dinner." Frankie watches the woman closely, trying to figure out what her meddlesome grandmother is up to. It doesn't take long to figure out something is amiss.

Nunnie's cell phone begins ringing. She quickly answers it and utters a string of, "I see, mm-hmm, I can, yes." Nunnie finishes her mysterious call. In one swoop, she clears her place setting, grabs her purse, and rushes to the back door. "I need to go help Jo at her house. You two eat then work on the kitchen. Don't wait up for me." She's out the door before either of them takes their first bite.

A broad, Cheshire cat grin crosses Tony's face as he realizes that the two of them were just played by a spry grandmother. Frankie bows her head in defeat.

Wounded by Frankie's reaction, Tony tries to lighten the mood. "Oh, come on Francesca Josephine, is being left alone with me that bad? There was a time when we used to have fun together." He lifts his glass of sweet iced tea and takes a long, slow drink.

Frankie looks up and studies Tony for a minute. She has known him forever. He was a fixture at her house, or her brother was at his. His parents were invited to significant family events and holidays. Tony has always been a part of her life. She used to dream of him becoming *her* family. That was before, before she changed. Frankie has a decision to make. Finish dinner like a normal human being who has known him her entire life, or make him leave. The debate is a tough one.

"Do you remember the time we spent the night outside of Sweet Creamery? I think I still have a concrete imprint on my left leg."

Her own unexpected chuckle catches her off guard. "How can I forget? You and Sammy whined all night about the cold. But, come on, that was totally worth it. We won ten free waffle cones for being the first in line the next morning."

"As I recall, we decided to split the reward three ways, but you stashed the coupon card. The way I see it, you own me three and a third ice cream cones." Tony's grin brightens his whole face.

"No way! I was going to camp out on the sidewalk alone, but Daddy made you two come with me. If anyone owes you an ice cream cone, it's him." Their laughter is seamless.

"There was not a chance Sam Marchio would let his baby girl spend the night on a sidewalk trying to win a promotion. Sammy and I were planning on sleeping in his car and babysitting you from afar until that guy from your class ended up being next in line. We both jumped out of his truck and lugged over our chairs and sleeping bags." He takes another drink to stifle the laughter.

"Babysit? I'm barely two years younger than you two. I didn't need a babysitter." Her voice is laced with defiance and sarcasm.

Tony's voice deepens, "No, no, you didn't, Francesca. You've always been good at taking care of yourself." A moment of awkward silence sits between them for the first time that Frankie can ever remember.

She picks up her fork for another bite of cheesy, tomatoey pasta. "Why do you call me Francesca?"

"That's your name." Tony recognizes the chess move and counters.

"Yes, but you are the king of nicknames. You make up nicknames for everyone you meet. Maryssa has three. Poor Beau has your entire crew calling him Thor. You never call people by their birth names. Why me?" She moves food around on her plate before lifting another forkful to her mouth.

"Does it bother you? Do you want a nickname? I can call you Rocky. Or maybe Miss Tyson. How about snickerdoodles? Do any of those work for you?" Tony chomps into a crunchy piece of garlic bread.

"No. Please no," she softly laughs at the thought of those options. "I'm just curious. I think you do it to irritate me." She scrutinizes his reaction. The small curl of his mouth shows she has made some type of impact. She just can't figure out what that means.

"Irritate?" Tony plays with the word as he repeats it. "Definitely not that one. Flirt? Maybe. Or, maybe I just like the look you give me when I say it." He shrugs and eats a bite of salad. *Checkmate.*

Frankie locks eyes and glares at him while taking a drink.

"That look is almost as cute as your wide range of eye rolls," Tony grins.

Frankie chokes a little on her sip of tea. She sits back and crosses her arms, sizing up her competition. She knows it's her move, but she isn't sure how to counter. This banter between them is second nature, but he's never called it flirting. The confession adds to her caution. Tony is her brother's best friend. He is a player, just like her brother.

"You flirt with everyone," She counters.

"That's not true. Your brother is the flirt. I'm charming. There is a difference."

More ziti is pushed around the plate. They sit in silence for a few minutes. The only sound is the symphony of crickets and birds floating in through the open windows and screen door, and the scraping of their silverware.

"Can I ask you a question?" Tony knows he's taking a chance, but he doesn't get many opportunities to talk with Frankie when she can't bolt, or they won't be interrupted.

She nods.

"Why did you start hanging out with the Finnegans? Why boxing?" This has always been a question he couldn't answer about her. Frankie was naturally athletic and tough, but he didn't know why she became obsessed with boxing and how she got mixed up with up such a rough boxing family.

Frankie weighs his question and her answer before opening her mouth. She can't, she won't, tell him the truth of why, but she's not sure she can articulate how it makes her feel now. "Boxing makes me stronger. I can control my punches, my body, and my reaction to punches that land on me." She pauses, "It gives me strength. I like being in control."

"You've always been strong," now he pauses, "I love that about you." His warm chocolate eyes pin her in her seat. "Well, one of the many things I love about you."

"Tony, I, I, just stop." Frankie has no idea where this is going, but she needs to get out of this room. The walls are closing in on her. She takes a deep breath, trying to pull together her thoughts.

Tony reaches across the table and places his large, calloused hand on hers. "Frankie, I need to tell you something. It's more than just flirting."

"Stop!" Frankie pulls back her hand and draws it to her stomach. She quickly stands and heads directly to the counter. She turns her back to him. She needs to pull herself together and stop this. "Tony, I can't. Not now."

"Why? Because of your brother? Because you think I'm a player?"

Her head is spinning. She's breathing deeply like Deena taught her. Tony walks over toward her.

"I've always felt like there is more between us. I kind of thought maybe you felt the same way. Am I wrong? Did I do something to blow it?" He reaches out and gently places his hand on her shoulder.

The reaction is feral and fast. Tony doesn't see it coming, and neither does she. Her training takes over, and her body does what it is supposed to do. Reacts. Protects.

Tony's moan is guttural. One hand holds tight to his face while the other grasps the edge of the counter to steady himself. Blood drips down his hand onto the floor and off of her stinging knuckles. She quickly grabs paper towels from the counter and hands him the wad.

"Tony, I'm so sorry." Frankie opens the freezer to find a bag of veggies. Wrapping them in a towel, she pulls out a chair for him and helps him to sit. He stumbles back into it and takes the makeshift ice pack from her hand. She quickly wipes the blood with paper towels as he attempts to stop the bleeding.

They sit in silence until the situation is under control. Frankie offers him a warm washcloth for his face and hands. He looks at her over the bag of peas. Her eyes are filled with regret and something he hasn't seen before, eyes that he has studied for almost two decades. "Francesca, you could have just told me you didn't feel the same way." His sly grin is unmistakable, even hidden behind the bag of frozen peas.

A relieved chuckle slides out of her throat as she drops her head.

"I didn't mean to catch you off guard, Frankie. I just thought you should know how I feel. If you don't feel the same, I understand, but if we could keep this between us, I'd appreciate it. No need for your dad and brother to get a shot at the other side."

For a brief moment, she softens. "Tony, I've wanted to hear those words for a long time, but, but I just can't hear them right now. I'm not myself. I've changed. I don't know if you would like this new person. I don't know what I want anymore, and I don't know how to get back to who I was." She briskly wipes the stray tear that betrays her resolve.

"Frankie, what happened to you? What changed? Talk to me." His concerned voice crushes her.

She shakes her head and looks away from him. She can't see herself in his eyes, not anymore.

Tony watches as the walls build back up between them. "Can I decide for myself if I like the new Frankie?"

She stands up and walks to the sink, her back to him once more. "I think it's time for you to leave, Tony."

He sits at the table a moment longer, staring at her. Studying her. He quietly stands and slowly walks to the front door. She hears the screen door squeak open and the bounce back when it closes.

"I'm so sorry," she whispers to herself before the tears stream down her cheeks.

Frankie

Frankie heads to work early. Even her pre-dawn workout couldn't take her mind off of Tony. She has orders piling up and she's donating a dozen pies for a church raffle. Hopefully work will help clear her mind. She spent the entire night replaying his words. Even worse, her reaction to them. All these years, Frankie thought Tony liked her. She just assumed he didn't like her enough to jeopardize his friendship with Sammy. She finally knows his true feelings, but can't do anything with them.

The nightmares were worse last night. It's as if the past caught a glimpse of hope and put a stranglehold before they could plant a seed. She awoke in sweat more than once. They are becoming more and more vivid. The demon's face is the only thing blurry. Each time he gets closer to her.

On the nights when fear grips her like a vise, she battles it out on the bag. This morning was an exceptionally intense session. So rough, Frankie had to text Deena about ordering a new heavy bag after she cracked the leather on her current one. Deena suggested they meet for coffee this week. Frankie doesn't have time for Deena's psychoanalyzing.

After nailing Tony last night and punishing her bag this morning, Frankie's right hand is swollen and bruised. It will be challenging to cover up at work. To add to Frankie's misery, Maryssa scheduled a virtual meeting with Lisa Fox before the lunch service starts today. Frankie wants off of this merry-go-round.

Poppy's kitchen has been quiet all morning. Frankie snuck out of the house before Nunnie could corner her and ask about the kitchen plans. She was in bed last night when Nunnie came home and pretended to be sleeping. Frankie knows there will be questions today, but she bought herself some time before she has to talk.

Tony texted her when he got home and apologized for catching her off guard. He also told her to work on some sketches and design ideas so he can get quotes from his suppliers. She knows that Nunnie has something up her sleeve, but she has no idea what it is and why she must participate. One thing is for sure, she and Tony can not work together on this project.

Noise coming from the front door of Poppy's draws her back to the task at hand. She boxes the last two pies and places them into a delivery bag. She begins cleaning her station as voices come closer. Maryssa and Beau walk into the kitchen, laughing and smiling at each other. Beau is carrying a box that Maryssa asks him to put in her office.

"Hey, cugina. What are you working on today? It smells like fall in here." Maryssa investigates Frankie's space. She swipes a finger across Frankie's spatula and tastes the sweet cream cheese icing. "Good grief, Frankie, this is amazing. Did you crush pecans for the filling?" She stares at her younger cousin in awe.

Frankie wryly smiles, "I did. It's good, right?" It's more of a statement than a question. "I made a few extra pumpkin rolls for the dessert tray this week to kick start fall."

"I might eat one loaf all by myself." Maryssa takes the spatula from Frankie and starts licking it. "I'll clean this for you." They both chuckle as Beau comes back into the kitchen.

Frankie turns around to take off her gloves and roll down her sleeves. She isn't quick enough. "Ouch, Frankie, what happened?" Beau instinctively walks over and picks up her hand in his. He turns it over to inspect the damage.

She yanks the evidence out of his grip and pulls down her sleeve to cover her knuckles. "I had a rough boxing session this morning. I didn't secure the end of the wrap good enough and it slipped off of my knuckles. No biggie." She is relieved that no one in her family knows a thing about boxing.

Beau quizzically stares at Frankie as Maryssa attempts to dig deeper into the hand situation. "You box every morning. I've never seen your hands like that. What made today so intense?"

"I was picturing my brother's face." Frankie tries to laugh it off and move onto a new subject. "What time is our call with Lisa?"

"Here's an interesting coincidence for you." Beau leans against the counter and crosses his arms as he launches into a work story. "Tony came to the warehouse today with a busted-up nose and a shiner. Apparently, he was carrying a box and 'walked into a display case' at the hardware store last night. The funny thing is that I thought he was supposed to be meeting you and Nunnie last night to talk about the kitchen. How crazy that you both have complimentary injuries today." He watches for Frankie's reaction as he shares his story, complete with air quotes.

"Well, the meeting was cut short. Nunnie got called out to help Aunt Jo. I guess Tony needs to pay more attention to where he's walking. That seems like a no brainer for a contractor. Maybe Nunnie needs to cancel the remodel." Frankie shrugs off Beau's passive accusation.

"Mm, hmm, that sure is a coincidence. Well, I guess I better go. The crew is putting the final touches on our house today." Beau leans down and kisses Maryssa. "Love you, Babe. I'll call you later." He nods suspiciously, "Frankie."

"Bye, Beau." Frankie leans against the counter and watches him leave, knowing that he knows.

Maryssa turns to study Frankie, who holds up her good hand. "I don't want to talk about it, Maryssa."

"Oh, you're talking about it all right, but I'll wait if you're not ready." Maryssa heads in the direction of her office, but she keeps talking loudly. "This is definitely something we're talking about, for sure. My days consist of talking to food, two small children, and a carpenter. I need some excitement. You better believe we're talking about this." Maryssa is muttering now, "Not talking about it, does she even know me?"

Frankie lowers her head into her hands as they rest on the counter. She hopes beyond hope this will at least stay between the three of them. It will be harder to keep it from Nunnie, but she has to try. It was Nunnie's fault in the first place for leaving them alone. As far as Frankie is concerned, Nunnie should have known better.

She spends the rest of the morning making sure Poppy's is ready to open by lunch. Menus are straightened. Reservations are checked. Staff straggles in and prepares for a full lunch and dinner service. The end of summer and beginning of fall is a busy time for both the vineyard and the restaurant. The changing leaves bring visitors from all over to admire the mountains.

With thirty minutes to spare before they are set to open, Maryssa calls Frankie into her office for their virtual meeting with Lisa. She answers on the first ring. The screen on the laptop comes to life as Lisa's face appears. "Good morning to my favorite chefs! How are things in West by God Virginia? Did I get the saying right?"

"You sure did," Maryssa laughs. "Things are great! How are things in sunny Atlanta?"

"I wouldn't know. I've been locked in meetings since seven o'clock this morning. You two were the main topics, so I blame you," Lisa chuckles at her own comment.

"Well, I hope they were good meetings then." Maryssa curiously smiles.

"That depends on the answer to my first question. How is your studio coming along?"

Last year, the network had to rent space and create a makeshift kitchen for Maryssa to film her specials. It became more costly than if she had just flown to Atlanta. The agreement to film a new show in West Virginia was contingent on Maryssa acquiring a permanent space for filming.

Beau and Maryssa were living in an apartment above Poppy's. Once their house was built, they decided to turn the full-sized space into a studio.

"According to Beau and Tony, my contractor," Maryssa begins but is interrupted by Lisa.

"Tony? Is that the hunky guy we met with last spring? The tall, dark, and handsome one?"

Maryssa laughs, Frankie inwardly cringes. "Well, I only have eyes for Beau, but yes, we met with Tony."

"Yummy." Lisa winks into the screen.

"Anyway, Tony's crew completed the demo last week. They will be completely finished with the plumbing and electrical prep this week. The design portion will begin shortly, but we have all of the appliances and materials on-site, so it should be seamless. The space will be completely open with two kitchen sets on opposite sides. One set for my show, the other kitchen set will be used for my specials, and for Frankie's series. Tony's estimate is three weeks. That should give us plenty of time before filming begins to work out the kinks."

"Great, great! That is wonderful news. Can he still build the lift system to hoist the heavier equipment up, so the crew doesn't have to navigate the stairs?"

"Oh, I almost forgot. Yes, Tony actually has a great idea for that."

"I'm loving this guy! Tell me the plan." Lisa grabs a pen to take notes.

Frankie listens as the two women plan and strategize the space and the timeline. Her heart is as battered as the hand resting in her lap. Her bruised and swollen hand mirrors her thoughts as she realizes that for the next six weeks, she will see Tony at the studio during the day and all evening at the farmhouse.

Sam

The oven-fired pizza smells heavenly after a long day in the sun. A thin, crispy, just blackened crust supports the perfect amount of tomato sauce, fresh mozzarella, Italian sausage, and spinach. A vibrant bowl of red tomato insalata sits in the middle of the table. The deep red tomatoes are drizzled with olive oil, oregano, garlic salt, pepper, and just a dash of white wine vinegar. Hard crusted bread sits next to the bowl, perfect for dipping into the juices from the salad. Sam enjoys his lunch while listening to his son talk about work.

"I'm worried about nitrogen deficiency in some of the young vines in the south block. I took additional samples today. A few of the leaves are small and pale, so I think we caught it in time. I'll know more tomorrow, and we'll make some soil adjustments. Other than that, we're pruning and monitoring rain levels as normal." Sammy briefs his father about the vineyard happenings.

Sam Marchio retired from the family business last year. He had run the vineyard since his father's death with his younger brother Dom. Both of their sons are continuing in their footsteps. Dom's son, Dominick, runs the warehouse and oversees the barrel system. Sammy has the gift of growing like his great-grandfather. It's a natural sixth sense for Sammy. Sam's baby sister Jo runs the business and financial aspects with the occasional help from their older sister, Esther. Frankie went to West Virginia University for a business and economics degree. She was supposed to work with her Aunt Jo until she admitted that her true love was baking, not crunching numbers. They miss her at the warehouse, but her desserts are heavenly. Sam is so proud of Frankie for following her dream.

Once a week, Sam tries to meet with Sammy to talk shop. He never wants his son to feel as if he doubts the running of the vineyard. Sam missed out on the value of having his own father as a sounding board. Now, he works hard to mentor without intruding. Sammy appears to value his input as Sam mostly just listens and enjoys the meal. The bonus is getting to see Frankie, even for just a few minutes. He worries that she is burning the candle at both ends so he takes any chance he can to check in on his baby girl.

Their conversation is interrupted when Tony walks into the restaurant. Sammy waves as Tony struts to the table, shakes Sam's hand, and pulls out a chair. "I'm glad you made it. Sammy said he invited you." Sam points to the yellowish-black-and-blue coloring represented on Tony's face. "I heard about your run-in with a shelf. It looks like the shelf won that round."

Tony reflexively touches his eye, tenderly, before shaking his head. "I won't be asking for a rematch, that's for sure." Tony's sad laugh is uncharacteristic for him. "I didn't think I would make it in time for lunch. I promised Maryssa we'd officially be out of her house this morning and I didn't dare show up here with even a hammer left behind."

"Between her house and the studio, Maryssa is keeping you busy." Sam pops a forkful of tangy tomatoes in his mouth.

"Frankie and Maryssa will be sick of me soon enough. I almost didn't come for lunch to give them a break from me. Frankie will have to deal with me upstairs in the studio all day and at the farmhouse at night for the next few weeks." Tony's laugh sounds heavier than Sam is used to hearing it.

"How are the projects going so far?" Sam has always been genuinely interested in Tony's business. He watched Tony grow it into something bigger than anyone saw coming, certainly not Tony's parents. They thought construction work was a side job he could do until it was time to run the store. They had no idea how passionate Tony was about it, but Sam did.

"I'm heading to the farmhouse after dinner to drop off tools, and start some of the light demo work. I could nail the project out quicker if Mary would let me bring in my crew, but she only wants us there in the evenings. I'll have to bring a few guys tomorrow to help me demo the big items and to deliver the dumpster, but most of the work will be handled with the help of Beau and Frankie, per Mary's instructions."

"I just hope Frankie doesn't kill you." Sammy laughs, with food in his mouth.

Sam shakes his head. Sammy needs a good woman in his life. "Son, I don't need to see your food."

Sammy smiles broadly, enjoying harassing his dad and friend.

"Sam, I hear you and Hannah are heading off on an Appalachian vineyard tour. Retirement must be working for you. You know, the guys and I had bets on whether you would actually let him run everything." Tony's thumb points to Sammy. "I thought you wouldn't leave that office until you were a hundred and on your way to your final resting place." Tony laughs as he scoops a spoonful of tomato salad into his waiting bowl, careful to make sure he doesn't lose any of the juice for dipping bread.

Sam slaps Tony on the back and smiles. He coached Sammy and Tony all the way through Little League, making Tony a second son. Not to mention that Tony was a fixture at their house with Sammy on a daily basis. "You two keep giving me a hard time about retirement, but you are the ones with the commitment issues. I made a decision, I've stuck to it, and now I'm enjoying retirement with my beautiful wife. You two should be so lucky as to find someone to spend your lives with. You aren't getting any younger." It was Sam's turn to chuckle.

Sammy practically spits out his drink, laughing so hard. "Dad, that's not happening. I'm not getting tied down. We'll spend our retirement traveling and meeting new women in every town. Right, Tony?"

Tony shakes his head at Sammy but doesn't rebuff him. Sam notices Tony scanning the restaurant, followed by a look of disappointment. Sam files that look away for another conversation.

"Sammy, before I forget, how is the new distributor handling the Wine and Jazz Festival? Do they know how many cases we'll need? I know last year there were growing pains, but we need it right this year." They severed ties with their longtime distributor after Ben Stanley hit on Maryssa, and his daughter keyed Beau's truck. They found out the hard way that the Stanley family did not align with the values of their family business.

"We had a meeting last week about festival season. Not only are we ready for the regional events, but we're branching out this year to the Savannah Wine and Food Festival. That should take us to the next level. The Stanleys could never have handled the larger scale events. Savannah is the perfect festival to launch our brand to a vast audience. Severing ties with the Stanleys was the best thing we ever did." Sammy grabs another slice of pizza and takes a big bite, proud of his accomplishments.

"I'm sure Beau and Maryssa are happy too," Tony adds with a chortle.

"I think we all learned a lesson with the Stanleys. I actually have something to talk to Maryssa about involving them." Sam waves over his daughter, who is walking out of the kitchen, carrying a tray of glasses for the bar.

Frankie stops by her dad's table and places an arm around his shoulder and a kiss on his temple. "How is the pizza? Do you guys need anything?"

Sam could be wrong, but he senses that Frankie is doing everything in her power to ignore Tony. Typically, they begin firing jabs at first sight. Today, they both are oddly silent.

Sammy lifts his empty glass, "I could use a refill of sweet tea."

"Get it yourself. I'm not your waitress." Frankie offers a snarky smile at her older brother. They both knew she wasn't waiting on him. This makes Tony smile.

"Daddy, do you need anything? More tea?"

Sam laughs, "No, sweetheart, I'm fine. The pizza was delicious, but I'm ready for some of your desserts. A little bird told me you made a double chocolate German cake. Did I hear that right?"

"You did. I altered the menu this morning when I found out you were coming today. That's what makes me your favorite child."

Frankie was definitely Sam's baby girl. They always had a special bond until she graduated from college. They are still close, but something happened between them during her last two years of school. Something happened to her. She was already fearless, but she became guarded, and that built walls. Sam ached to find out why and fix it, but she shuts down anytime the subject is broached.

"Favorite? Hardly. We both know the firstborn is the favorite, and that's me. I'll take some cake too, in case you were wondering."

Frankie slaps her brother in the back of the head. "I have to drop these off at the bar, then I'll cut your pieces myself. Extra-large for Dad, extra small for Sammy. Tony, would you like some dessert?" She surprises them all by asking. Again, Sam could be reading into something that isn't there, but he thought her face softened slightly.

"I could never turn down your cheesecake. Unlike your brother, I will offer my help carrying plates if you're busy." Sam's suspicions are officially raised. Their silence and lack of teasing are out of character for both of them. He's wondered for years, but now he will keep his keen eye on this situation. Something is happening or not happening. Sam is not sure which bothers him more.

"I'll be fine." She turns to go, but Sam calls her attention.

"Sweetheart, will you ask Maryssa to come out when she gets a minute? I need to ask her something about the Stanleys. Wait, what happened to your hand?"

Frankie freezes. "It's nothing. My bag broke yesterday. No big deal." She tucks her hand under the tray. "I thought the Stanleys were dead to us. Why would you need to talk about them?"

"Ben called me today. He wants to make sure there are no hard feelings between us. He may need some catering and knows that using our name would help. I want to be careful, but I also don't want them to sabotage us either. He wants the connection with Haddie and Jackson, so I know they will walk a fine line. It seems his nephew is running for the House of Delegates. Tying his name to Jackson might help him."

"Nephew?" Frankie's voice has an edge. The Stanley family is a sore subject.

"Chase? I think that's his name. Chase Stanley."

Frankie's bruised knuckles scrape the bottom of the tray as she shifts the weight of it. Sam sees the tray slip seconds before the sound of shattering glass draws the attention of everyone in the restaurant. Clinking, screeching, crunching draws everyone's attention. Frankie mumbles words of frustration as she quickly bends to pick up the fragments of glass. Sam and Sammy both jump up to rescue and help her. Tony retrieves the small vacuum hidden behind the bar for emergencies like this.

"We've got this. Go ahead back to the kitchen, we'll finish cleaning." Tony looks at her directly in the eyes. Sam sees something he's never seen there before, concern or fear, he can't be sure which one.

Frankie quickly composes herself. The walls are back. "Thanks. I need to tell Maryssa before she worries. I'm sure she heard the crash. I'll get your cake while I'm back there." She heads toward the kitchen doors. That is the last time Sam will see his daughter today. After they finish cleaning the shattered glass and sit back down, Maryssa comes to their table, carrying a tray filled with their dessert orders.

Frankie

Frankie's car pulls around the driveway of the farmhouse. She grabs her purse before climbing out and trudging up the back stairs to the screened-in porch. When she enters the kitchen, she sees two mugs with tea bags, a jar of fresh honey, and a tea kettle on the stove.

"Who called? Maryssa or my dad?"

"Both."

"Well, it was nothing. I knew everyone would freak out about it. I dropped a tray. It's a restaurant. It happens."

"And what about Tony's face? Did that just happen too?" Nunnie turns off the gas burner and grabs her favorite potholder with a frog on it.

Frankie pulls out a chair and plops down at the table. "How did you know about Tony's face? Did he tell anyone?" Frankie lowers her head onto the tabletop. This day keeps getting worse.

"Beau figured it out and told Maryssa. Tony is still blaming an innocent shelf at his parent's hardware store," Nunnie chuckles at herself. "When I left you two alone, I didn't realize designing a kitchen could become so heated. I underestimated your passion for appliances and countertops."

"It had nothing to do with the kitchen. In fact, we didn't even talk about the kitchen. Tony just started talking. He's always running his mouth." Frankie sits back in the chair as Nunnie fills the mugs with hot water. Mary places the pot back on the stove and sits down next to her granddaughter. This table has been privy to thousands of conversations over the years. It's a member of the family in its own right. Nunnie reaches over to pat Frankie's good hand but says nothing. Nunnie is excellent at the waiting game. She always says that enough silence brings forth the words that don't want to be found.

"I didn't mean to hit him, you know." Frankie rubs the handle of the mug with her finger and thumb. "Tony just knows how to push my buttons. He started talking about ridiculous things instead of the kitchen. I was at the counter when he came up from behind. It was pure instinct. I didn't even realize I was doing it until I saw the blood. It wasn't his fault, either. It's my training. I move on instinct. I didn't mean to hit him. Why does Tony insist on driving me crazy?

Nunnie bobs her tea bag in her favorite mug as Frankie rambles. She listens. She's always listening. She adds honey to her tea and then to Frankie's. "Tell me when to stop." Frankie holds out her hand after a generous pour of honey.

"This honey is from Wes Anderson. Apparently, his grandfather was a beekeeper, and Wes always wanted to learn. He needed a hobby after he retired and thought he would try his hand at raising honey bees. It's nice having Wes around again, for the honey, and for Esther."

"How nice for Wes." Frankie wonders where this conversation is heading. Nunnie never says anything unless it means something.

Frankie sits, staring through the mug and the table. Nunnie removes both of their tea bags then stirs the honey and tea in her mug. She hands the spoon to Frankie, breaking her granddaughter's stare. "You know, Wes and Esther have a similar story to you and Tony."

Frankie hasn't heard this one before. She looks perplexed. "How so? I thought they were high school sweethearts."

"Well, Wes and your dad played baseball together all the way from T-ball on up to high school. Wes was a year older than Sam, but they were good friends. Poppy and I started noticing that Wes would sit near Esther on the bleachers talking between doubleheaders or after games. Sam was so clueless it was happening, but we saw. Wes teased Esther mercilessly. They were constantly bickering and flirting, but neither of them realized that the other had feelings. It was entertaining for us to watch until Sam figured it out. I'm not sure if he was madder at Wes or Esther, or at himself for bringing the fox into the hen house." Nunnie takes a small, careful sip of her tea. A smile spreading across her face.

Frankie sits, listening. Not wanting to have this conversation. Not wanting to think about Tony and his flirting.

"Next thing you know, Wes Anderson shows up on our front porch with a black eye and asks Poppy if he can start dating Esther." Nunnie laughs at the memory. She shakes her head, thinking about Salvo making Wes sweat a little. "Your grandpa said he didn't want his daughter dating a boy who went around fighting. Wes explained that he earned the shiner honestly because he broke a code and wanted to date his best friend's sister. I remember your dad sulking up the steps behind Wes with a huff, holding his hand tight. He nodded at Poppy before heading into the house to talk with Esther and ice his hand." Nunnie drinks a little more tea as she settles into her story.

Intrigued now, Frankie asks, "What happened then?"

"Poppy told Wes that his daughter had her own mind and if she deemed him worthy to date that he trusted her judgment, but he warned Wes that if he hurt his little girl, he should expect Sam to get the other eye."

"But they broke up, right? Aunt E moved to South Carolina with Aunt Ruthie. That's where she met and married Uncle John. Why did they break up?"

"That's where the story gets good. Wes and Esther planned on getting married after graduation. They were to attend the same college. He had a baseball scholarship when a minor league team called him up to play. There was a miscommunication, then an even bigger miscommunication, followed by a rash decision. Next thing you know, Wes is engaged to marry Peggy Anderson, who was supposedly pregnant. It all happened so fast. Esther was devastated."

"Figures. All men cheat. They do whatever they want to whomever they want. Good for Aunt E for running. She looked out for herself first. And I'm still not sure how this story relates to Tony and me." Frankie is back to sulking in the chair and holding the mug handle.

"We'll come back to the cheating comment, but for your information, Esther was just as guilty as Wes. She was stubborn and reactive. Esther didn't communicate with Wes. She jumped to the wrong conclusion and made a rash decision which was made worse by his own stubbornness and retaliation. Two stubborn people who refuse to admit their true feelings usually cause more hurt feelings, or black eyes in your case. By the time the dust settled, Esther was packing her bags for South Carolina. Wes was marrying a woman who faked her pregnancy, and your father fractured his pinky on Wes's other eye and had to sit out the summer baseball season."

Frankie's face is filled with disgust and resignation. "My dad isn't the picture of perfection either. Talk about a hypocrite. Punching Wes for cheating then cheating on his own wife. Nice." Saying it out loud didn't make her feel better or relieved. Frankie's Daddy sat on the highest pedestal in her mind until he came crashing down. Her world went right down with him. This confession to Nunnie opens the gaping wound all over again. A tear trickles down her cheek. She quickly and forcefully rubs it away.

Mary's cup is suspended in midair. She places it down on the table gently. She sits up in her chair and stares directly at her granddaughter. "Frankie Jo, I don't know what happened to you. I do have a pretty good guess, but it's your story to tell and I'll wait for you to tell it. With that said, you need to face your demons, or they'll haunt you forever. The Bible tells us not to let the sun go down on our anger. You, my dear, have let seasons pass, and it's leaving new scars each day. You need to shine the light on your feelings and your past. Tony deserves the truth, so do you. I will not comment on your father, that is his story, but I can tell you one thing for certain, things are not always as they seem. On that note, I am going to bed."

Nunnie steadfastly marches away from the table, leaving her cup in place. Frankie has never seen that look on Nunnie's face. She hears the bedroom door close upstairs, which is also unlike Nunnie. Frankie drops her head back on the tabletop in surrender and cries.

Haddie

Walking the halls of the White House still feels surreal to Haddie. Her life has been entirely flipped upside down in the past few years. It wasn't smooth sailing before that, but at least there was order. As a ballerina, Haddie thrived on structure and consistency. Practices and performances were scripted and methodical. She had marks to hit and routines to master. After a fluke landing went terribly wrong, her days of professional ballet ended so she began act two of her life.

This made Haddie the oldest person in her pre-med program. She was chugging along just fine until senior year and *Future FLOTUS?*. She started physical therapy school right after marrying a man she just met thanks to a whirlwind romance on the world's stage, literally. Now her life is anything but ordinary. Due to death threats and safety concerns, she had to take a sabbatical from her doctorate program, thrusting her into full-time work as the First Lady of the United States.

An unforeseen blessing has been her work with online bullying. As a daily victim herself, she relates to the people she meets along the way. While the press is still a painful part of her new life, she has learned to use her platform for change.

Lately, her main priority is bolstering Jackson. He is having a personal struggle between the noble work of servant leadership as a politician, and politics. Ever since Jackson was gifted with the personal Bible of Governor John Marchio, he can't stop reading it. At first, it was in search of the knowledge John spoke about, then it turned into finding the peace Nunnie Mary exudes, and now it's a quest for discernment. Jackson was baptized while on a diplomatic tour of Israel a few months ago. He reads the Bible at night, long after Haddie falls asleep, and in the morning when he rises. Her faith is growing, watching his.

Maryssa's dad, Haddie's Uncle Malik, and his new wife Victoria offered to host a Bible Study on Monday evenings for Jackson. They are studying the life and ministry of Paul. It started with the four of them, but Jackson invites anyone he passes in the hallways. Haddie stopped him from inviting the press corp. She is working on forgiveness, but turning the other cheek while still being hit is a little harder for her. Haddie told Jackson he could host a separate study for them in the press wing if he felt that strongly about it.

Tonight, there will be six attendees. Marcus, Jackson's aide, has joined them, and Madison is intrigued by the changes she has witnessed in Jackson's life. Haddie is straightening up the residence for their guests. Victoria is bringing baklava from her Greek restaurant in downtown D.C. Uncle Malik, the head White House chef, is bringing Haddie's favorite spinach dip in a homemade bread bowl.

Haddie prays this will pull Jackson from his funk. Jackson dedicates himself fully to reunification and the country. This latest political stunt has the Allied States rethinking the entire reunification process. Their president was quoted on air saying, "These are the same shenanigans that separated our nations. Why would we want to subject ourselves to their continued drama. Reunification is off the table for now." That interview was the final blow this week for Jackson.

The cracks in the nation began after the previous president was elected by the electorate, but lost the popular vote. After only one month in office, a shadow government formed. The House and Senate voted to overrule the electoral college. States outraged that the federal government ignored their right for equal representation came together during a secession convention stating that California and

New York dictated the rights of the other forty-eight states. They drafted a plan of secession unless the United States took steps to ensure their rights and pass legislation dealing with voting irregularities. Neither group wanted war, nor could they find a middle ground. Little did they know at the time, a Color Revolution had been in the works for years. A lot of money was made on the downfall of America, and they didn't even see it coming.

After marrying a Republican from South Carolina, an assassination attempt, and ending up on the wrong side of the media, Jackson's eyes have been opened to corruption on every side of the aisle. As he fights for reunification, he is attacked by extremists from both countries who caused the Separation in the first place.

In trying to distance themselves from the other, both nations are struggling without a balance. This weighs on Jackson. Haddie sees it. With an open investigation about his relations with the Allied States of America, the question remains how does he move forward with reunification? How does he do his job if he's not allowed to speak with other governments? Politics interferes with governance. While making decisions based on the good of the nation, Jackson must play a media chess game and the weight is heavy.

Haddie walks into the kitchen to grab the brownies she made today. She bakes when she's stressed. There has been a lot of baking in the residence lately. She places the plate on the baroque table and rubs the smooth mahogany. Her mind drifts back to her first time sitting at this very table. The night she and Jackson almost died. She inhales deeply to steady herself. Back then, Haddie was worried about Jackson being assassinated. She worries now that his job will kill him with a broken heart or a stroke.

She hears voices from the back stairs that lead up from the central kitchen. Jackson, Malik, and Victoria emerge.

Haddie is so grateful to have her uncle still in D.C. He helps keep her grounded. He preserves her South Carolina and West Virginia roots in the swamps of Washington that envelop her husband.

"I'm glad you guys are finally here. I was about ready to eat the entire plate of brownies myself." She leans in for a sweet kiss with Jackson.

"Mmm, did you make your famous butterscotch brownies?" Jackson looks at her in anticipation.

"Sorry, no. I ran out of butterscotch chips when I made the oatmeal scotchies last week."

"The First Lady can't get access to butterscotch chips when she needs them? You should complain to the head chef." Victoria laughs as she adds some baklava to the antique table before turning to hug Haddie.

"I heard the head chef is a butterscotch hoarder. At least he was when I was growing up."

"One time. One time I wouldn't let you and Maryssa raid the pantry for an ice cream binge, and I'll never live it down." Uncle Malik tightly wraps his arms around his niece, who is more like a daughter. He feels her relax before placing a kiss on her forehead. "Hello, my sweet girl." She leans into the warm security of his embrace.

Jackson excuses himself to change and grab his Bible. "He seems in better spirits today." Uncle Malik unwraps the plate with his bread bowl. "I know he's taking the impeachment inquiry personally."

Victoria, always the voice of common sense, "How could he not? The man dedicates his life to government service. He tries to bring unity and honesty into politics, then gets his hands slapped. They're attacking his character. They made this personal."

The truth of Victoria's words settles over the room. Jackson reemerges from his bedroom with his Bible and a notebook in his hands. "Well, this sounds ominous. I have never seen anyone in this family quiet. Is something wrong? I'm not sure I can handle more bad news."

Haddie tries to lighten the mood. "Haha, nothing bad. Just debating whether it's polite to break into the food before the others arrive."

"Well, I know you're lying because you twisted your hands, but I'll let it pass." Jackson kisses her on the cheek. "I'm glad we're the only ones here. I have something I want to run by you all. You already know I'm not backing down from the investigation. I'm going full steam ahead to fight this. It is a waste of time, money, and resources. This is why people hate politics. We're so busy throwing sticks at each other that we're not getting any actual work accomplished." Jackson shakes his head to refocus. This group of supporters has heard his argument for weeks. "I would like to call Sandra and ask her to produce a documentary about families who landed in different countries after the Separation, and I'd like our family to be interviewed. Do think the West Virginia clan will do it?"

"Sandra? As in the fire breathing dragon producer from *Future FLOTUS*? That Sandra?" Haddie stands open-mouthed, staring at her husband.

Again, Victoria speaks words of wisdom, "Haddie, dear, I didn't know any of you when that show was produced, but even I know that you need to get over it. You married the man, move on." She pats Haddie's shoulder before turning to Jackson. "I think that is a wonderful idea. You can touch on other areas too, business, education, medicine. I'm sure people will be willing to share the good and the bad. You could use the information during Reunification negotiations. You're always talking about how politicians need to listen to the people they represent. A documentary could help show them."

"Exactly. I just want honest stories. I think having our family speak would bring authenticity. If I'm being accused of collusion, I want to show who with and why." Jackson looks at Haddie for her opinion.

"I think we need to pray about it, but I trust you. Sandra, not so much, but you? You, I would follow into battle." Haddie squeezes Jackson's hand.

"That's good, because the battle was already waged against us, and I'm claiming victory."

Malik places a hand on Jackson's shoulder. "Nunnie always says that the greatest battles are won from one's knees."

Jackson beams with excitement. "I'm not arguing with Nunnie. Let's pray!"

Frankie

Her head is throbbing. Her mouth is dry and her lips are cracked. Her eyes fight as she attempts to open them. A faint light is in the corner, her vision is blurry. The room spins around her like a funhouse mirror. Her body feels like concrete and her bones ache. She hears heavy footsteps on the other side of a closed door, then a man's laughter. She tries to scream, but nothing comes out of her mouth. She grabs her throat. It feels like she has swallowed a bag of glass. She's suffocating. A dark angel with horns and red scarred hands leaps at her from the direction of the door. He is faceless.

Frankie jolts up in bed. She grabs at her neck and gulps in as much air as she can take. Her heart beats out of her chest. She is drenched in sweat. She looks around the room, trying to get her bearings. *I am safe. I am in my own bed. I am in control of my situation.* She steadies her breathing. She closes her eyes to reset her mind.

One hour later, she is driving twenty minutes to Pounders. The gym doesn't open to the public until seven, but she knows Deena gets there at six. Frankie pulls into the parking lot on the backside of the strip mall. The sun is rising and trying to peek out from behind the thick clouds. She parks the car in front of the glass windows and grabs her bag. Deena is already walking to the door as Frankie raises her fist to knock. The keys jiggle on the other side, and the door opens. Inside stands a petite redhead with marbled muscles and a six-pack that makes men cry.

Frankie met Deena Finnegan in the waiting area of a police station. Deena was dropping off pamphlets for a self-defense class. A detective introduced them and suggested Frankie take a flyer and get to know Deena. Frankie learned that Pounders offers self-defense clinics every Sunday evening. Frankie went the first week and has been there every week since. Frankie's big Italian family has nothing on Deena's crazy Irish family. Frankie and Deena hit it off immediately. Deena is the youngest, and only sister, of seven children. Her mother died during childbirth. Together they run Pounders Gym. They all, including Deena, are professional boxers. Deena picked out Frankie that first night of class. She saw a hunger and fire in Frankie that she recognized, intimately. It took weeks for Deena to break down some of Frankie's walls. Eventually, after an hour-long session left Frankie spent and broken, Frankie let down her guard. Deena called out Frankie on her new obsession with boxing and invited her to a group meeting. Deena is the only person in Frankie's circle who knows the truth.

"Another nightmare?"

Frankie nods and drops her bag on the nearest chair, by the door. She drops ten pounds of anxiety as her dear friend wraps her in a tight hug.

"I thought they were getting better."

"I guess that depends on your definition of better. If you mean not as frequent, but still suffocating and terrorizing, then yes, the dreams *were* getting better. Can we talk about something else?" Frankie sighs as she pulls away from Deena.

"Someone's in a chipper mood today. Do you want me to hold the bag while you sulk?" Deena can read Frankie a mile away and knows it will take a while for her to talk. Deena isn't good at waiting. She likes results. "I'll tell you what, I'll hold if you spit out one thought with each punch. They don't have to be lucid, just honest."

Frankie nods as she pulls out hand wraps and gloves. Her hands are tiny, allowing an extra layer around her bruised knuckles. She adjusts the wrist strap around her hand wrap and pushes on her gloves while Deena heads back to her office to turn on the music, loud. Frankie stretches and swings her arms to warm up. Deena turns on the lights and straightens the equipment and chairs. It can get messy in this gym.

"Ready?" Frankie nods, Deena secures the bag. "Remember, one truth with each connection."

Thwack. "My family is crazy."

"Mine too, next."

Crackle. "Everyone's up in my business."

"Oooh, shocking. Come on, that's not what has you here at six in the morning, punching like a sissy boy."

Whack. "The nightmares are every night."

"Now we're getting somewhere." Deena holds tighter as the punches come faster and with greater intensity.

Thump. "I can't sleep."

Whack! Crack! "I signed the contract for the TV show."

"Congratulations." Now Deena is holding the bag with the ferocity equal to Frankie's hits.

Whack! Thump! Crack! "Tony likes me." *Thud!* "I punched him."

That's what Deena was waiting to hear, the root of the attitude. "Now we're talking."

Frankie stops, hands falling to her sides. She walks in circles trying to catch her breath.
She lowers her head between her knees. Her right arm wraps around her stomach. Deena waits.

"He tried to tell me how he feels about me, and I walked away from him."

"Shocker." Frankie's glare has Deena holding up one hand and zipping her lips with the other.

"He came up behind me, and I freaked. I turned and connected a right hook to his eye."

"Yikes! Did you break his nose?"

"No, but I definitely popped it. There was blood everywhere. What's wrong with me, Deena?"

Deena walks over to her friend and rubs her back. "Nothing is wrong with you. You just have a lot going on in your mind. You really need to process it all up here and not with your fists." Deena taps Frankie's temple.

"Says the boxing champ." Frankie makes a rueful laugh.

"Hey! I don't use the bag to beat out my feelings. I deal with them. You need to deal with your crap, Frankie."

"Nice. Thanks for the pep talk." Frankie plops down in the chair behind her.

"I've never advertised myself as a coddler. I'm serious, Frankie, and I care about you. I don't even think the nightmares are your problem. That night wasn't the problem. That night was the brick wall at the end of a road you were speeding down headfirst. You can't deal with the crash without dealing with the reason you were on the road in the first place. You keep trying to fix your car so that no one knows you crashed, but the problem is that you're going to keep crashing until you fix the engine."

"Geez, Deena. How many metaphors can you fit into one sentence?"

"Laugh all you want, but you know I'm right. You need to talk to your dad. You also need to tighten your left jab. It's fading right on impact. You're lacking follow through."

Frankie throws her towel at her friend. She's right, about everything. "Wanna spar?"

"I thought you'd never ask. Let me grab my gear."

Frankie

Sunday dinners at the family farmhouse are not optional. After church, the entire family gathers to break bread. Since the kitchen is under construction, Nunnie reluctantly agreed to allow Sam to host it at his house this week. Frankie drove over early so Nunnie could help roll the meatballs and make sauce with her eldest son. Uncle Dom even came over early to help them. Nunnie is proud she raised sons who know their way around a kitchen.

This Sunday, Sam's house is alive with movement as everyone does their part. Hannah mixes the salad and has fresh sweet tea ready. Frankie finishes icing a new cupcake recipe she's trying for her television show. Dom and Sam set the table while Nunnie stirs the sauce and watches the spaghetti. Aunt Jo is picking up fresh bread and pepperoni rolls from the Italian bakery.

The Marchio clan begins arriving one group at a time. Aunt E arrives with Wes Anderson. Maryssa, Beau, Chloe, and baby John arrive on their heels. Haddie is coming in this week for a visit, so Aunt E is on cloud nine. Dom carries a bag of ice as Aunt Tamra holds the door for him. Aunt Jo's family comes in like a hurricane. She looks disheveled and tired.

The volume increases as everyone pitches in to get the feast on the table. This is Nunnie's happy place and everyone knows it. Truth be told, no one would miss it, even if they had a good reason. And according to Nunnie, there weren't any good reasons. Frankie watches as Nunnie orchestrates the prep work. This family works well together.

Just in time for dinner, Sammy and Tony walk in through the front door and up the stairs of the split-level house. Frankie freezes.

"Nice of you to join us." Uncle Dom starts teasing as soon as he hears Sammy's voice.

"They always arrive just in time to eat," Sam adds on to the roast.

"Hush, boys, you both did the same thing when you were his age." Nunnie ends the conversation. "Anthony, I'm so glad you came. Where are your parents? You should have brought them with you. We have plenty." Nunnie hugs him tightly.

"They're babysitting at my sister's. I'm heading over to their house later today. I'll tell them you asked about them."

Frankie sees Tony from across the room. Their eyes meet before she ducks back into the kitchen and looks for a job to do. She tries to stay busy while nonchalantly watching Tony make his way around the dining room. He stops to hug and kiss every one of her aunts, uncles, and cousins. Frankie keeps her head down as he rounds home plate to one person, her. Frankie busies herself with the task of filling cups with ice and getting drinks ready. She feels his presence next to her.

The wide-open space makes it impossible for a private moment. Frankie just hopes for a non-violent one. Tony picks up the extra marker and helps Frankie write names on the red plastic cups. The way people get bumped around a table, their cups need nametags. He observes which names she has already written, then starts writing.

"Francesca."

"Anthony." Frankie is relieved at the appearance of a truce.

"My crew finished up the demo at the farmhouse on Friday. I can't get too much farther without your plans. I also need to start the layout for the network set. Is there a time we can meet tomorrow to go over your ideas and wish list? My face promises to keep a safe distance from your fist.

96

Or, maybe I can buy some headgear from the sporting goods store at the mall, if that works better for you."

He gets the exaggerated eye roll he is looking for from her. A tiny grin peeks out from his lips.

"I'll check my calendar," Frankie coolly replies.

"You know, my mother wants to know the bully's name who beat me up after work last week. Don't worry, I didn't tell her. I know you're tough, but I'm not sure you could go three rounds with Rosemary Devono."

Frankie eyes him from the side. She pauses for a minute, then continues writing names. "You're right about your mom. I've seen her yell at umpires. She's been thrown out of more games than anyone I've ever seen."

Tony shrugs, "She's protective of her baby boy, what can I say?"

"Maybe she should tell her baby boy to stay in his own lane." Frankie's voice becomes tighter.

"Hey, I came over to offer an olive branch, not fire you up more."

They both continue their work of labeling cups while trying to talk in hushed tones. Neither wants this family to know what is happening, or not happening, between them. Both glance around the room then back to the cups at hand.

"Look, Tony, I'm sorry I hit you. But, in my defense, it was all your fault."

"You're kidding, right?" He stares at her, shocked and confused.

"Dead serious. Really, what were you thinking? You can't come up behind someone like that and expect not to get hit." The walls are being fortified. "You're lucky I didn't hit you with a combination. You would have ended up in the ER."

Tony lowers the cup in his hand. He looks directly at Frankie's avoided gaze. "Yes, if we were in a dark alley. A parking lot. If I was a stranger. Any of those scenarios would justify me getting nailed in self-defense, but that's where your argument has holes, Frankie. I've known you my whole life. It was just the two of us in a room where we've been hundreds of times, and I tried to lay all my cards on the table." Tony shakes his head in frustration. "I don't know what happened to you, what caused you to 'change' as you said, but just so we're clear." He bends down to catch her eyes, then points to his chest. "I'm safe. I could *never* hurt you. I'm not the guy you swing at, I'm the guy who has your back when you need to swing."

Tony places the marker and the cup down on the counter and walks away from Frankie. She watches Nunnie catch his eye as he heads to his seat next to Sammy. Nunnie winks at him. *How does that woman do it?*

Sam calls everyone to the table for dinner, bringing Frankie back from her thoughts. Seats around the table are filled. Nunnie offers a prayer of thanksgiving and blessing. Since no rookies are at the table to intimidate, Maryssa and Frankie get the middle seats to expedite the dishing out of food. Plates are passed, and bread is buttered. Layers of conversation fill the room like a symphony orchestra telling a story. The sounds of clinking silverware, laughter, and children playing echo off of the high ceiling.

Nunnie chats with Tony and Beau about the kitchen remodel. Hannah chimes in with some design ideas. Frankie tentatively asks a few questions about what Tony needs from her. Nunnie determines that the two of them will spend tomorrow together, shopping for appliances, flooring, cabinets, and countertops. Apparently, she knows a guy in Washington, Pennsylvania, so it is settled. Frankie and Tony will drive there tomorrow. Beau offers to go with them, but thinks better of it and backs out after receiving a daring stare from Nunnie. Frankie spends the rest of dinner sulking nervously.

After the table is cleared and dishes are washed, they all gather around Sam's smart TV and wait. A few minutes pass before they hear ringing as Sam pushes buttons on the remote. Haddie's face pops up on the large screen. Her smile bubbles up from somewhere deep within her. She waves as everyone vies for her attention. Chloe jumps up and down as she blows kisses to her aunt. The little spitfire looks exactly like her mother, Haddie's sister Lizzie. Haddie blows kisses back and pulls on her earlobe, her secret signal with Chloe when she is on television.

"Wow, you guys are a sight for sore eyes!" Haddie wipes a stray tear as she takes in the screen filled with her favorite people.

"Hi, Daddy!" Maryssa pipes in and waves to Malik who sitting next to Haddie.

"Hi, Baby. Hi everyone. I was working on my inventory list when Haddie told me she was calling, and I couldn't resist. Mary, was it hard to let someone else host dinner this week?" Malik waits, already knowing the answer regardless of what comes out of his mother-in-law's mouth.

"Not at all. In fact, I could get used to this." She winks. Every time Mary sees Malik, her memories are flooded with thoughts of Ruthie. The family was devastated when Ruth and Lizzie both passed away from ovarian cancer months apart. Even now, their legacies are shining beacons of faith to the family. Ruth lived a good life, and Malik was devoted to her. Everyone knows that Malik Lavalier is Mary's favorite out-law, but she would never admit it to anyone. He named his flagship restaurant, Maria's Ristorante, after her, so the admiration is mutual.

"Where's Uncle Jackson?" Chloe is smitten with her uncle. She is the only person in the world who can out-talk the trivia-king president.

"He got tied up in a meeting, he'll be along soon. I wanted to call before anyone left since this request involves the whole family."

"What? Does he want to quit politics and join the family business? If he does, I'll teach him to run the tractor and dig holes." Sammy laughs at himself.

"Haha," Haddie smirks at her cousin. "No, but this does involve the vineyard and the family."

Haddie has everyone's attention now. The room is filled with looks and mumbling. The matriarch is intrigued and takes charge. "What does Jackson need from us, Sweetie?"

Haddie proceeds to explain to her family all about Jackson's documentary idea. "We spoke with Sandra, who was instantly on board. She began rattling off ideas and topics. If Sandra has her way, there will be separate episodes to cover many issues, including economics, education, healthcare, welfare, immigration, and anything else she can include. It turns out Sandra's husband won awards for his docudrama on the media's role during the Color Revolution. They have been researching joint project ideas. According to Sandra, Jackson's call was 'pleasantly serendipitous' to them." Haddie takes a breath while watching her audience for any responses. The room is silent.

Haddie continues her presentation. She explains that Jackson is working with legitimate bipartisan players from both nations to identify subjects for the documentary. Sandra will work with a casting company to aid in the search for "entertaining" characters. While they are working on story boards, Sandra will begin interviewing the Marchio Family, who are straddling both governments. Sandra wants to start within the next couple of weeks, and will come to West Virginia to film at the vineyard.

Frankie listens as Haddie continues talking to the family. Inwardly, Frankie dreads more time being filmed than she already has scheduled with Lisa. She scans the room and catches Tony watching her. She scowls at him then directs her attention back to Haddie.

"Aunt Jo, Jackson really wants to hear from you on both the topics of healthcare and education based on all of your experiences with Matty. If it's too personal, we understand. Sammy and Maryssa can cover small business and tourism. Uncle Sam and Uncle Dom, retirement issues. The goal is to show that both countries are more united on ideas than they realize. Jackson wants to quiet the shouting of the media and politicians who thrive on divisiveness. We're game to whatever you all want to cover, but it's important that you consider the ramifications carefully. If someone doesn't feel comfortable, we can find a new plan. I'm certainly not going to force anyone to participate in a reality documentary without their permission."

Groans and eye rolls fill Sam's family room. "And there it is," Maryssa groans.

"Auntie Had, you really need to move on." Chloe scolds her beloved aunt as laughter erupts from everyone, including Malik, who gets an elbow to his ribs.

"As I was saying," Haddie grunts, "Governor Marchio is working his connections to find some up-and-coming politicians to interview as well. There is one guy in particular who has really been kissing up to Jackson. It's almost bordering on harassment. The guy is on the maybe list. He's a Stanley, so I was instantly not a fan. I think his name is Chase. He's out of Morgantown but is gunning for a more national position. I don't necessarily feel comfortable with a Stanley being involved, but I wanted to run his name by you guys first. He could be totally fine and just in the same family. I mean, I'd hate to be judged by anyone based on Sammy."

Everyone laughs. Sammy smiles, "You could only be so lucky."

"We've heard all about Chase Stanley. Ben has already tried to bridge the divide between our families. I don't think any of us trust the Stanleys, but we won't take a stand one way or another at this point." Sam shares with Haddie his conversation with Ben Stanley.

Frankie walks back into the kitchen and fills her cup with water. Between the farmhouse renovation, the studio build, and her own television special, this month is getting out of control. She places a hand on her stomach as she attempts to calm her breathing. She takes a big gulp and scans the room. To her dismay, Tony is watching her, again. She carries her cup back into the fray but stands in the shadows of the room as the family hashes out details and strategy.

After the video call, everyone pitches in to clean up and put Sam's house back in order. "Many hands make light the work" is a family creed. As the afternoon fades and the family trickles out, Frankie makes every effort to avoid Tony. He makes no effort to speak with her again, irritating her more. Frankie sticks around to pull out her old photo albums. Lisa wants to include photo montages of Frankie growing up throughout the first season. Frankie isn't sold on the idea, but Lisa talked her into trying.

She pulls out a few that aren't cringe-worthy. Sam comes up behind her and looks at the chosen ones spread across the coffee table. He flips through the memories in his hands and sighs. Sitting down next to Frankie, he peeks over her shoulder and smiles.

"I love this picture. You were the cutest soccer player. So aggressive on defensive. You told your coach that you pictured the opposing player as your brother." Sam chuckles. "Well, it was true. You and Mom wouldn't let us fight, so I had to get out my frustration on the field." Frankie shrugs at her father.

"We were trying to keep the ER visits to a minimum between the two of you." They both softly laugh.

Frankie hands him another one, "Remember this one from the Italian Heritage Festival? I'm covered in sugar."

"You love those frittis. I think you could eat an entire dozen all by yourself if we let you."

"Fried dough, covered in sugar? Who wouldn't eat an entire dozen?" Frankie makes a mental note to make frittis this week.

"Look at this one from the lake." Sam's whole face smiles as he holds the photograph.

"That was right before Sammy and Tony pushed me into the patch of poison ivy. The left side of my body was covered in calamine lotion for the rest of the week. Including my scalp." She instinctively reaches over and itches her left arm.

"That's right." Sam laughs and rubs his chin. "As I recall, you rubbed your arm against his back on the way to the cabin. You both were covered in calamine. I have never known two people who are as fiercely competitive as you are loyal."

"Loyal? We would fight to the death if you let us." Frankie shakes her head thinking about her older brother.

"You can't fool me. I've watched you two. You are the worst to each other, but woe to the person who comes against the other. Remember the kid who stole Sammy's bike? You put gum in his hair and spit in his face. Your mom about had a heart attack. And what about the time you had pneumonia, and Sammy slept on the floor of your bedroom all week, just in case you needed him? I have tons of stories like that. You two may act like you hate each other, but I've seen the unbreakable bond you have."

"If you say so." Frankie sighs, deep down she knows that it is true. Sammy made her tough, but also made her feel safe. There is part of her that feels like maybe she let him down. She wasn't as tough as she thought back then, but she is now.

Sam points to a picture in the album of the two of them sharing a humongous banana split. "Here's a good one of us."

"The Poky Dot does have iconic banana splits. I wonder if Chloe has been there yet. She would love it. I need to tell Maryssa."

"Maybe we can take her. I would love to try and tackle a split with you again. That was our go-to Daddy-Daughter date destination. Back in the day, you liked hanging out with your old man. We were buddies. You went to college, and suddenly, I'm chopped liver." Sam sits back into the couch and pats Frankie's back.

"Dad."

"All I'm saying is that this is nice, Frankie Jo. I miss you being around the house."

She nervously laughs, not wanting to ruin the moment with honesty. "You just wish I was home to make dessert every night." Frankie starts to collect the photos from the table.

"Well, that would just be the *icing* on the cake. Get it?" He winks at Frankie.

Frankie shakes her head. "You can't help yourself with the dad jokes, can you? I'm sure Sammy would move back in with you. He needs someone to cook for him. Of course,

Tony would probably move in too." She stands and places the pictures she's chosen into her purse.

"You're right." Sam picks up a photo album and looks through the pages. "Speaking of Tony. I saw the two of you talking today. It looked like a serious conversation. Anything going on I should know about?" He studies his baby girl.

"No. We were talking about the kitchen. No biggie."

"You know, I always thought Tony had a crush on you."

"You're reading into it."

"He was asking about you the other night at Poppy's. He was worried about you after you dropped the tray. Your brother may be clueless about it, but I'm not." Sam flips the page of the photo album. Frankie keeps moving things in her purse to avoid eye contact or prolonging the conversation.

"He's a good one, that Tony. He's always been a hard worker and a stand-up guy. Maybe you should think about it. That's all I'm saying."

"Tony is a player like Sammy. All guys are. Guys only have one focus, and I'm not interested in being played." She grabs her purse off the table and jams it onto her shoulder.

"Hey, now! That's quite a statement. First of all, your brother is all talk. Just wait until he meets the girl of his dreams. Second of all, don't judge all men by one bad experience in college. I'm assuming that's where you picked up the generalities about guys."

She turns to leave in a huff, but adds one last dig before storming out the door. "Maybe I picked it up from you, Dad. My whole life, I judged all men by you, the gold standard. You're right about college, though. The weekend before I left for junior year, I heard you and Mom arguing about the affair. Yeah, so I know all about it. It turns out you're a player too, Dad. So, save me the 'he's a good guy' speech, I'm over it."

Frankie turns to see her mother, who has overheard the outburst. Hannah stares at her husband of over thirty-five years, waiting for him to say something. Sam sits in stunned silence. Frankie leaves, slamming the door behind her.

Great! Nice job adulting, Frankie!

Tony

Tony's truck windows are rolled down as usual. The smells of summer flood the air inside the cab. Fresh cut grass mixed with mossy humidity wafts all around him. He hears kids laughing and birds chirping as he drives through town to his parent's house. He waves to neighbors he has known his whole life as he pulls onto Gould Avenue. At the top of the hill sits the elementary school he attended and the railing where he fell and busted a tooth. Cooler evenings have all the neighbors outside in their yards and on their porch swings.

"Hey, Tony!" Mary, his cousin from across the street, yells as he climbs out of the pickup. "Your mom said you're working on a new kitchen set for the Marchio girls and their TV shows."

"You heard right. We're hard at work. Two sets in one studio. It's coming together."

"Your mom said you might get your name in the credits. I'll have to record it so I can tell all of my friends."

"We'll see. I'll probably be at the end when they cut to commercial." Tony laughs as he walks backward to the curb.

"We're really proud of you, Tony."

"Thanks, Mary." He waves as he walks around the side of the mint green stucco house. This is the house where he grew up with his sister. The house his parents will never leave.

Barbara, the next-door neighbor, yells from across the side fence. "Hey, Tony! Tell your mother, I said thanks for the tomatoes. Her garden looks great this year. I can't wait for another batch of peppers."

"I will. Good to see you." Tony waves but keeps walking. If he stops to talk to anyone, the whole street will ascend, and he'll never make it into the house.

"Rosie says you're going to be a big TV star, building sets for all the cooking shows."

"I don't know about that. I'm just helping out the Marchios, not *all* of the cooking shows."

"Well, they'd be lucky to have you. You remember where you came from, you hear?"

"Yes, Ma'am. I surely will." Tony shakes his head before ducking into the backdoor of his parents' house. The delicious aroma hits him before the door opens all the way. He takes a deep breath. He is still full from lunch with the Marchios, but he won't dare tell his mother. Italian mothers don't care how much you've eaten, when you've last eaten, or if you're even hungry. Somewhere along the way, they are told their sole purpose in life is to feed every person in the world, and they are on a mission to do just that, one stomach at a time.

"Ah, you're here, come give your mother a kiss. Anthony, Tony's here, get off that ladder and come downstairs." She screams the last part.

Tony crosses the kitchen and kisses his mother on the cheek. "Hi, Ma. What's Dad doing on a ladder?" The old kitchen hasn't changed since Tony was little. Green laminate countertops cover old painted cabinets. He has no idea what color the original linoleum was when it was installed. It's a dingy grey now. He offers all the time to remodel it for them, but they won't hear of it. He's not sure if it's more pride, stubbornness, or fear of change. He's determined to do it for their fiftieth anniversary. He's working with his sister to send them on a cruise. Darren, his brother-in-law, and Sammy can help him remodel the whole thing while his parents cruise the ocean on vacation. His mom will definitely yell, but she'll love it when it's finished.

Rosie twists her wrist and stirs the eggs and peppers around the pan. Just as quickly, she grabs a spatula to flip the fried potatoes in the second pan, careful to keep the browned part intact. "It's just a step ladder. He thinks the seal on one of the windows is cracked. He's convinced himself there's air coming inside. Keeps complaining about the gas bill. I told him it's summer and we don't use the furnace. Then he complains about the electric bill. I swear that man is going to be the death of me. Sit down. Dinner will be ready soon. I picked these peppers today. Speaking of which, I need you to come over one night this week and help us out in the garden. We have more tomatoes than we know what to do with. We need to start canning soon."

"Ma, I thought you were doing a smaller garden this year. What happened?"

"What? It's already there. Why let the ground go to waste? What if something happened and we had a bad summer? And, I like to give some to the family." She shrugs as she turns off the burner.

Big Tony lumbers down the narrow stairs wiping his hands on a rag. "Tony, we're going to need a new window in the back. You get it for me, and I'll put it in myself." He walks behind his son and kisses the top of his head.

"Pop, I don't want you up on a ladder. I can put it in next weekend. I'll measure it before I leave. I probably have one at the warehouse already." Tony knows how hard it is for his dad to ask for a window. Their family hardware store used to carry windows along with most other building supplies. As chain stores came in and took over, the ability for small shops to carry everything weighed heavily. Some items had to give. The shop focuses on tools, grills, farm supplies, and heating fuels now. They do the occasional special order, but that's a rarity these days.

"What? I'm too old to climb a ladder? Are you listening to this one, Rosie? Wiseguy over here. I can fix a window. I just need the window. Now, let's eat. Your mother picked the peppers today. I saw them on the counter and was hoping for some eggs and fried peppers." Big Tony sits down at the table and picks up his fork in anticipation. "Anthony, let him help. He wants to put in the window, let him put in the window." Rosie shovels food onto Tony's plate then her husband's, hers is last. Tony gets up to fill glasses with water and ice before she can protest. "Tony, I can get your drink. Sit and eat before it gets cold. I know you and Sammy don't cook for yourselves. Eat."

"Ma, I already got the drinks. You sit and eat."

"Where is Sammy? You could have brought him for dinner." Rosie waits for everyone else to take a bite first. She smiles at their satisfied faces.

"He had to go to the vineyard to check on a few things while it's still daylight." Tony takes another bite of spicy eggs. Delicious. The combination of different flavors explodes in his mouth.

"Rosie, this is so good. Your Ma is the best cook. If you can find a woman who can cook half as good as your mother, you'll be one lucky man." Big Tony shovels in a bite of potatoes then brings his hand to his wife's and lovingly squeezes. The crunch of the potatoes brings a crispy flavor you can only get with bacon grease.

"Listen to this charmer." Rosie smiles back at her husband. "Speaking of women. Anyone we should know about? You seeing anyone? Aunt Angie knows a girl from her church who is single. Her husband, God rest his soul, was a louse. Drank every night and ran around on her. Poor thing is very pretty, according to Angie. Anyway, he must have fooled around with the wrong girl and ended up on the wrong end of a shovel, if you know what I mean. Good thing for this girl that her husband had a good pension. At least she got something out of the marriage. Anyway, Angie says she's starting to date and thinks you'll be perfect for her.

She has a four-year-old son, and he wants to play T-ball this year. I told Angie to tell her you could help coach."

Tony chokes on his potatoes. "Ma! I can't coach some kid's T-ball team that I don't even know. What were you thinking?"

"What? You don't want to date a pretty girl? Sorry for trying to help. I only gave birth to you after two days of labor and dedicated my life to raising you. God forbid I try and help you find a woman." Rosie mumbles a string of Italian words that would have gotten a bar of soap shoved in Tony's mouth as she pushes food around on her plate.

"Come on, Ma. Not tonight. I know you want me to find a nice girl, but I don't need you and Aunt Angie signing me up to coach T-ball in another county. Okay?" He takes his mother's hand in his while looking her directly in the eyes, so she knows he's serious.

"Okay," she shrugs.

"The boy is right, Rosie. He'll find someone, just give it time. Did you make any pie? I saw you trade some tomatoes for apples with Barbara." Big Tony pushes his plate out of the way and pats his stomach. "I have room for some pie, if so."

"All right, I'll stop. I'm just saying, I'm not getting any younger. I'd like to enjoy my grandchildren before I'm too old to still play with them." Rosie gets up and walks to the counter where she's hidden an apple pie.

"Ma, you have grandchildren. How would Heather feel if she heard you talk like this?"

"Your father needs someone to carry on the family name. Heather's kids can't do that. She has a different last name. But I'll shut up. I get it. You don't want your mother meddling in your life. I only labored for three days with you and changed your diapers, but forget about all that. I'll mind my own business." She cuts slices of pie and hands them to her husband and son.

"I thought it was two days of labor?" Tony ducks before his mother can connect her hand with the back of his head.

More Italian words that would make a sailor blush come out of Rosie's mouth.

"Thank you, Ma. I love you." Tony attempts to end the conversation because he knows he won't win. He also knows he still has one more layer of the contentious narrative coming. He's hoping, like he does every time he is with his parents, that this time, it passes.

"Dad, did you watch the Pirates game yesterday? That walk-off homer at the top of the ninth was beautiful." Tony takes a bite of his mother's homemade apple pie. The crust is flaky and sweet. It melts in his mouth.

Big Tony leans back in his chair as he chews his dessert. "No. I missed the game because I was working. Not all of us have off on the weekends. Now, if my son was going to take over the family business. The business that his father and his grandfather built, maybe we could split weekends, and I'd be able to watch a few games."

There it is.

"I thought you hired someone to help on the weekends?" *God, please let this conversation end peacefully.* Tony takes another bite, trying to reduce the tension that always comes with this talk.

"You think I'm going to let a stranger open and close the store for me? What? And let him rob me blind? No, no, no. That's my store, and I'll work it."

"I can help on Saturdays if you and Mom want weekends to yourself." He offers the same olive branch he always does, more of himself.

"No, no. You have your own job. It's more important than the hardware store that put you through school and kept you clothed and fed you your whole life."

Rosie steps in as always. "Anthony, leave him be. We've been over this. Who wants more pie?"

Silence is her answer. A rare quiet moment in this kitchen. Tony uses it to shove in the last two bites of pie. "Ma, thanks. This was delicious. I need to run. I have to work on some bids and the crew schedule."

"You can't stay? You just got here."

"No, Ma, I really can't."

"All right, let me pack up some food and pie for you and Sammy. Speaking of which, how is Frankie Jo doing? Is she nervous about her new TV show?" Rosie asks over her shoulder while filling plastic containers full of food. Frankie spent a lot of time in Rosie's kitchen when she was younger.

Tony snickers at the thought, "Nothing could make Frankie nervous. In fact, she could make a bear nervous."

"Sometimes, the tougher we are, the more we're hiding. Frankie is tough for a reason. Trust me." Rosie Devono hands her son a bag filled with leftovers. "She is one tough girl, but she's had to be. Now, that's all I'm saying about that. Make sure you share that food with Sammy. You two come over any night this week for dinner and to help me in the garden. I'll give you some fresh vegetables for the Marchios. The bugs got Mary's pepper plants this year." Rosie shakes her head then pulls her son in for a tight hug. Something about Italian mothers and their hugs. They're like a soothing balm for a searching heart.

"All right, Ma." He turns and kisses his father's cheek. "Pop, send me the measurements, and I'll bring the window with me. We can fix it together."

A shower of "I love yous," instructions to drive safely, and to call when he gets home follow Tony to his pickup truck. As he drives up the hill and away from the house, the disappointed look on his father's face consumes him. Sadly, Tony sees that face more and more these days.

Frankie

Mr. Bubbles, Nunnie's rooster, crows on cue. A crack of light pierces the darkness in Frankie's room. She rolls over and places the pillow over her head. Maryssa despises that rooster and warned Frankie about Mr. Bubbles. Nunnie told Frankie she was worried Mr. Bubbles would have ended up on Poppy's menu if Maryssa hadn't moved out of the house.

Usually, Frankie is already awake and working out in the basement by the time the rooster crows. She didn't have any nightmares last night. She slept too fitfully for that. By the time she fell asleep, Mr. Bubbles was just about to start his day. This morning, she ruminates whether the demons from her dreams are worse than the lack of sleep. Between storming out on her dad yesterday and the conversation with Tony, her mind is a battlefield.

To make matters worse, she still has to drive up to Pennsylvania with Tony to meet with Nunnie's "kitchen guy." A series of excuses ran through her mind all night, but each one ended with Nunnie giving her the look. There is no saying no to Nunnie. Hopefully, the trip won't take long. Tony texted her a white flag with "truce" last night. Surely, they can manage one day without hurting each other. Well, without Frankie hurting Tony.

She finally fell asleep at one but woke up at three, all tangled up in her sheets. After kicking free of them and lying in a pool of sweat, she turned on the ceiling fan and tried to go back to sleep. An hour later, she contemplated going to the basement but knew that would raise red flags with her nosy roommates. Whoever thought living with her grandmother and aunt was a bad idea didn't warn her. Actually, they did, but Frankie wanted it anyway, and it's great until Nunnie starts meddling. Frankie obviously fell asleep at some point because here she is cursing Mr. Bubbles at six.

Frankie gets out of bed and does a few stretches. Her body is tight from the overnight wrestling. She does a few yoga poses to lengthen her muscles and relax the tension. She catches a glimpse of herself in the mirror. Bags are under her puffy eyes, and her face is blotchy. She chastises herself for not taking off her makeup and drinking water when she got home from her parents' house.

She walks down the hallway to the shared bathroom, careful to avoid the noisiest of the floorboards. Creaks follow her with every step. The bathroom slowly fills with steam once she turns on the water and grabs her towel. She avoids the mirror and the dark circles. Hot water soothes her muscles, but does nothing to cleanse her guilt.

The lavender and mint shampoo clears her airways and reminds her of high school. It's strange how certain smells can transport you. For Frankie, this minty and herbal combination fills her with calmness. It brings back the feeling of innocence, of not knowing the things she now knows. Her life is so far away from those days of virtue. She clings to this feeling before it fades away, and her past is there to remind her that she's a broken and messy person now.

Deena has been warning Frankie to talk with her dad before something bad happened, but Frankie knows Deena didn't have last night's confrontation in mind. Maybe Nunnie is right, and her temper is out of control. But how does one get their temper under control? Boxing used to be her go-to therapy. Now, it barely numbs the edge. Something triggered it, and she thinks she knows what, but why now? Frankie is excellent at avoiding her past by jumping into work. She blissfully surrounds herself with boxing and baking. Creaming butter and sugar together every day would make anyone happy.

Frankie towel dries her hair and pulls it back into a ponytail. She braids it then wraps it into a bun on the back of her head. She applies moisturizer to her face and balm on her lips. She throws on her favorite navy and white striped tee then pulls on her short overalls. She ties her bright white tennis shoes and grabs her tablet with the shopping list and idea boards. She may have to spend the day with Tony, but she will be efficient and super casual. She subconsciously touches her knuckles at the thought of Tony. She doesn't want to hurt his face or his heart. More importantly, she wants to protect herself while not hurting him.

As she bounces down the stairwell, the smells of coffee and bacon cause her stomach to rumble. She slows at the sound of Tony's voice. Taking a deep breath to prepare herself, she ducks under thick plastic barriers in the hallway to the makeshift dining room slash kitchen. This remodel is adding layers to her already stressful life.

"Good morning. No boxing today?" Nunnie fills Tony's travel mug with coffee as he eats a piece of bacon.

"No. I might go to the gym later." Frankie searches for her own mug on the dining room table that now houses their emergency kitchen items. When they were packing up the kitchen, Esther and Frankie told Nunnie she could only keep out the "necessities." Aunt E and Frankie quickly realized that Nunnie's definition of the word differed from theirs, so they went with "emergency" items instead. Even that was difficult.

"Here's your mug, Sugar. I already poured it and added your cream and sweetener. Eat some toast and bacon before you leave."

Frankie smiles at the term of endearment. Her father insists that Nunnie calls everyone Sugar so she doesn't have to worry about getting anyone's name wrong. She kisses her grandmother before grabbing a slice of thick Italian bread. "Thanks, Nunnie. Only you would cook breakfast during a renovation."

"I used a toaster and microwave. That's hardly cooking. Besides, you two have a long drive and a busy day. You need something to eat." Nunnie picks up her own toast and takes a bite.

They sit in silence for a minute before Nunnie reminds them to listen to one another and not be stubborn. She tells them, again, how the guy they're going to see worked with Poppy years ago when he built the barn and the pavilion. He's a good guy, but they need to make sure he gives them a fair deal.

They finish eating, and Tony is already standing, "You ready?"

Frankie nods. They both hug Nunnie goodbye and head out the back door to Tony's truck. As soon as Tony starts the ignition, the country station he had on blasts a song Frankie barely recognizes.

"Sorry." He quickly turns down the volume and reverses into the gravel to turn around and get going on their adventure. A catchy song fills the cab of the truck as they drive toward the main road. Tony hums along. Neither says a word.

The truck hugs the right side of the long, curvy driveway as Sammy's pickup approaches. Tony begins rolling down his window as Frankie groans.

"You two heading up the road?"

"No, we're playing a game of dominoes." Frankie sarcastically smirks at her older brother.

"Aww, it's good to see you too, Sis." Sammy blows a kiss at Frankie.

She mock catches it and smiles sardonically.

"How far off of I-79 is this place anyway? Will you be back by lunchtime?"

"It looks like it's an hour and fifteen. Not too bad, but lunch may be pushing it." Tony ignores the sibling rivalry and moves along the conversation.

"If you're back in time, I'm meeting Dad for hot dogs at T&L. He seemed weird this morning when I called about the vines. I figure we'll grab some lunch and maybe go fishing later if you're up for it." Sammy turns his gaze to Frankie, "Mom said he got into it with you last night. Do you know what's wrong with him?"

Frankie just shakes her head. She can't admit any of it. She doesn't even know what Sammy knows. They don't have many heart-to-hearts, and she's not going to start now. Frankie looks out her window, praying this conversation ends soon.

Tony picks up on Frankie's tension and wraps up the conversation. "I'll call you when we're on our way back to town. See ya."

"See ya." Sammy nods and pulls away.

The pickup drives down the winding driveway onto the main road. Frankie leans into the passenger side door and stares out the window. The stress and guilt mix into a toxic cocktail of melancholy she can't shake. The rolling hills are bathed in sunlight. Cloud shadows float across the landscape as they make their way to the interstate.

Tony fiddles with the radio until he settles on his favorite station. He hums along to the song playing before looking over at Frankie. He gauges her demeanor. Tony has been reading Frankie Marchio for years. He knows her, but he can't seem to talk to her anymore without upsetting her.

"Arguing, I would understand. Sarcasm, bring it. Anything but silence. Come on Francesca Josephine, you're better than this." Tony watches the road ahead of him, no doubt waiting for some kind of witty response from feisty Frankie.

She shakes the cobwebs. "Sorry. I just have a lot on my mind. Between the show, the farmhouse construction site, and my orders, which have blown up since the Inauguration, I can't seem to keep track of it all. I guess I'm just overwhelmed."

Surprised by her rare honesty and an even rarer glimpse of vulnerability, Tony is silent while she processes her own words and worries. The corners of her lips are slightly downturned. The lines around her eyes are deeper set. She can feel the heaviness pushing down on her shoulders.

"Not to downplay anything you've just said, but I can share a trick my mom taught me when I was a kid."

She nods, giving him the okay to enter her world.

"Take every worry, and fight it with a grateful fact. We can start with the cooking show. Be thankful that your two cousins are reality TV show pros and can help you out during the learning curve." He glances over to see if it's working. It is. "Be thankful that you have a large family who can pitch in and help you fill orders until you get your own bakery and staff. If that's what you want." Her lips have a slight, very slight, upturn. He continues, "The farmhouse is easy. Be thankful the best contractor in the area is working on the kitchen remodel and the studio for your show."

She delivers a classic Frankie eye roll in his direction, but she's smiling. "Rosie Devono is a smart lady. Too bad you didn't inherit her brains."

"There she is, Frankie is back in the building." They softly laugh as the easy banter returns.

"Now that you're smiling tell me about your ideas for the studio kitchen."

They spend the hour drive talking about Frankie's ideas for the kitchen and the show itself. She bounces her theme ideas for the series off of him. He adds in a few tweaks for the kitchen design that can be changed with each theme. Tony confesses that Lisa scares him. At the last meeting, she actually growled at him. Frankie assures him it was probably a flirtatious purr instead, which has them both laughing harder.

Once they reach the restaurant supply store, Hank the "kitchen guy" is waiting on them. Apparently, Nunnie promised him a birthday cake for his granddaughter's baptism if he gave them a discount.

Of course she did.

Hank pulls out samples and catalogs before leaving them to browse. Frankie and Tony are like sugar cookies and icing. Their ideas and choices complement each other. The easy flow helps them to pick out appliances, a sink, a state-of-the-art faucet, and some retro farmhouse light fixtures that are back in style. Surprisingly, they end the trip with a high five at the counter. Hank even throws in a free apron with the store logo.

While Tony makes arrangements for the delivery, Frankie runs next door to grab coffee for their drive home. She climbs inside the truck and hands Tony an iced caramel latte with whip cream and a domed lid. He examines the cup before taking a drink.

"The whipped cream was too much, right? Normally, I would skip it, but they made it fresh in house. I had to say yes." Frankie watches his reaction

"No, no. You were correct with the whipped cream. I'm more of a black coffee kind of guy, but I could definitely get used to this. It's like a milkshake." He takes another long drink.

Frankie's satisfied grin settles on her face. Tucking her legs up onto the seat under her, she buckles her seatbelt and gets comfy in the cab of the pickup. She hasn't felt this carefree in years. She tries to enjoy the ride for once, literally and figuratively. She pulls out a lemon square from a small paper bag and hands him half. "Taste this and tell me your thoughts."

Frankie takes a bite while watching him. Tony looks at her warily before sticking the entire half in his mouth. His black, wavy hair is highlighted by the sun streaming in from his window. His dimples take her breath away, like always. She laughs and shakes her head at his response. He makes faces while he's chewing to exaggerate the idea that he's thinking. "It was lovely."

More laughter. "Lovely? That's all I get?"

He wipes the corner of his mouth then licks the stickiness from his fingers. His broad smile makes hers bigger.

"It's a lemon thingy. What am I supposed to say? Lemons are not for dessert. They are for putting on an iced tea glass in the summer or for shoving into your Corona bottle at the beach. Desserts are supposed to be sweet, not sour. There, I admitted it. Are you going to send me to bakery jail?"

Her head falls forward in laughter, trying not to snort coffee out her nose, which makes him laugh harder in return.

"Bakery jail? Seriously?" She tries to calm herself before eating the last corner of her lemon square.

"I've never understood lemons for dessert. My mom makes lemon bars for pot lucks, and everyone loves them. Personally, I think they're terrible." He looks directly at her daringly, "Don't you dare repeat that."

She's holding her side from all the jokes, "I won't. I promise I'll keep your secret. Besides, I totally understand. I appreciate them, but I haven't found a lemon dessert I can't live without yet. I keep trying to find the one that helps me understand the hype. That's why I got this one when I saw the aesthetic of it. It looked so pretty and inviting. It tastes good, but I can definitely live without it. I keep trying to find the one that makes me want another one."

"Ah, so you're on a quest for the Lemon Grail, and I was your dispensable sidekick? I see how you are."

The fits of hysterics begin to die down as they get back onto the interstate. They drink their coffee to try and cover the lemony aftertaste of their ill-fated snack.

"Doesn't Sam like lemon desserts?"

Frankie stares out the window again, seeing something other than the green trees all around them. "He does. Well, Daddy loves Aunt Roxie's lemon cookies. He can eat a dozen at a time," Frankie sighs.

"You okay? Sammy mentioned your dad earlier. Do you want to talk about it?"

Frankie looks over at him. As much as they harass each other, he has always been honest and genuine with her. She shrugs her shoulders. The words aren't there yet. She can't even process it all, let alone explain it.

The atmosphere of the day changes, sadly. This has been a great time and she doesn't want it to end. Frankie weighs whether or not to try and get it back on track or take it deeper.

While she's thinking, Tony dives right into the messiness. "We can talk about my dad if it makes you feel better. I went over to visit them last night. Big Tony started on me again about taking over the business. I'm not sure why you and Sam argued, but you weren't alone in that department."

Frankie instinctively reaches over and touches his hand, resting on the gear shift. "I'm sorry. I know that conversation is always hard for you."

"It's just the same argument we've had for ten years." He shrugs.

She waits.

"I don't know how else to tell him no. I get it. I do. He's worked his whole life for that store. I grew up in the store. It has nothing to do with him, but he can't see that. He's so defensive about it. Honestly, I don't even know how it's still running. He used to let me see the books, but now he tells my mom to lock them up at night. I hate hurting him, but he won't let it go."

"What does Rosie say about it?"

His ironic smirk explains it all. "Nothing. Everything. She tells him to leave me alone then tells me to think of my father. She tells me he's proud of me and what I've built, then she tells me to see his side of it."

"Maybe, she's right."

He looks at Frankie like she's just punched him again.

"Think about it. You've built something amazing. You have two and a half crews working for you. You deal with payroll, benefits, insurance, bidding wars, crazy television producers," she grins. "You want your dad to be proud of you?"

"Of course."

"Well, maybe he wants the same thing. He wants to know that you value what he's built. He wants you to be proud of him. Maybe in some weird way, by you not wanting the store, he thinks you don't think it's good enough. He's not good enough."

"That's crazy." Past conversations fly through his mind as he processes Frankie's words. "I don't know. Maybe, but he knows I love him. I've never said anything bad about the store. I just wanted my own thing. I don't want to be tied to a building. I wanted to build something just like he did, but I wanted it to be my own." Tony thinks back. Has he ever said that to his Dad? He looks back at her then down at her hand, still holding his. She sees it too and pulls it back to her lap.

"Francesca with the truth bomb." He smiles at her, not wanting to lose the moment. "You've given me a lot to think about. Thank you."

They ride in silence for a few minutes. There has never been an awkward silence between them since she's known him. It is the silence between two people who feel safe in their thoughts and companionship. This isn't the first time Frankie appreciates their comfortable silences.

"I said something horrible to Daddy last night, something I've been holding in for years. I just snapped. Deena has been telling me I needed to talk to him about it, but I couldn't. Last night, I couldn't hold it in, and I went off on him. The worst part is that I didn't feel relieved afterwards. I felt sad that it was out in the open and can't be unsaid. I felt justified and guilty at the same time. Then, I saw the look on his face. I ran. I can't take it back. I can't erase it. I have to live with it." She looks down as her hands twist around the bottom of the cup she's holding.

Tony keeps his eyes on the road. "Well, one thing I know first-hand is that Sam Marchio loves his kids. If he can forgive Sammy for all the things we've done, I'm sure he'll forgive you for whatever happened last night."

"That's the point, I'm not sure I can forgive myself for what I said, but worse, I'm not sure I can forgive *him* for what he did to cause me to say what I did." She turns away from Tony as he listens. Her hand brushes away a single tear. "Like I said earlier, I have a lot on my mind this week. Plus,

Lisa is coming in to work on scripts and blocking. Whatever that means." She chuckles at herself. Tony knows it's time to change the subject, so he follows her down the Lisa hole. They fall back into their normal flow the rest of the drive home, talking about the realities of reality TV.

As Tony pulls his truck in front of the farmhouse, Frankie gathers her purse and their empty cups. She looks over to see Tony watching her. "Well, it has been an enlightening day, Francesca. In one day, I have learned that we make a good design team, that neither of us likes lemon squares, and that coffee tastes better with whipped cream and ice."

Frankie opens the door and climbs out with an ornery smile. "I've learned something today too. I now have blackmail material on you. I might call Rosie and ask for her lemon bar recipe." She winks and slams the door behind her. Frankie smiles as she skips the steps up to the front porch. She turns and watches Tony drive away as he laughs.

Jackson

Jackson stares out the window overlooking the White House grounds. A deep robin's egg blue blankets the sky. Not a cloud in sight. Several workers from the grounds crew are mowing the lawn. The steady whirring of their motors transports Jackson back to childhood. His mother was determined that he be raised like a regular kid even though his father insisted on private tutors and boarding schools.

Every year, he and his mother would spend the summer at his grandparent's home in Vermont. When Jackson was eleven, his grandfather taught him to work a lawnmower. By the second week, Jackson was mowing the lawns of every neighbor within walking distance. If the homeowner was over sixty, Jackson was expected to mow the lawn for free, unless the payment consisted of cookies or other treats.

Jackson loves his father, but his grandfather molded him into an earnest man. Once, his grandfather caught him taking a nap on the porch swing. The man gently woke Jackson up and proceeded to tell him they didn't rest until the job was finished. He would have plenty of time to sleep then. Jackson cherishes those precious summer memories. He longs for the physical labor, the sun on his back, the smell of fresh-cut grass. Losing his mother and her parents over the course of his life changed him. He spends every day trying to make them proud. He is their legacy. At their hands, Jackson Cashe learned to serve others, work hard, and to fear God. He wandered away from God after their deaths, but he is back on the right path now.

Light tapping on the door reminds Jackson that he still has a job to do. Jackson turns slowly to see Haddie and Madison walking into the Oval Office. The lift in his spirit is natural and reactive. "The two of you together can be dangerous. Should I duck and run for cover or jump on board and enjoy the ride?"

"The choice is yours, Babe, but I'd get on board before the train leaves the station." Haddie walks over and kisses her husband squarely on the lips. He surprises her by wrapping an arm around her waist tightly and dipping her backward while deepening the kiss. He slowly returns her back to an upright standing posture.

Haddie giggles, "Whoa, cowboy, what was that? You made me giggle, and I'm not a giggler."

His boyish grin has her blushing. "The memories of youth." He raises then kisses her hand still resting in his.

Madison clears her throat while scrolling her tablet. "Should I give you two some privacy?"

"No worries, Madsi. I'm back to business. We have work to do. Is everything ready for our brunch?"

Madison nods and gives him a look of annoyance, "Of course. Do you doubt my awesomeness?"

He takes his jacket from the back of his chair and puts it on while walking to the door. "Doubt you? Never."

Jackson and Haddie walk hand in hand down the hallway, greeting staffers as they pass. He needs as many people noticing him as possible right now.

The patio just outside of the Oval Office has a table set for four. It is shaded by the trees and secluded enough from prying eyes. "Good choice of eating on the patio, the weather is perfect today." Jackson gives Madison props.

"You said you wanted low key and optimal for conversation. The patio meets both criteria, plus it's not often the weather is cool enough this time of year." Madison places her tablet at her seat and looks around the space. "You know this is going to cause issues, right? Low key doesn't mean secret."

"So you've told me multiple times. I'm actually counting on that." Jackson picks up the tennis ball he has stashed behind a planter and begins bouncing it on the concrete. "If I'm being charged with collusion for having conversations with other nations, then the fundamental role of President puts me in jeopardy. Hiding only makes it worse." Jackson chuckles at himself.

"I still don't understand why I'm invited to this private meeting." Haddie pulls out a chair to sit.

Jackson leans down and kisses the top of her head. "Because, my dear, you are the smartest Republican still in Washington. All the others left the country during the Separation."

"I'm aware," Haddie grumbles.

Marcus opens the door to the patio with Governor John Marchio in tow. Jackson asked Marcus to personally meet their guest at the receiving gate. "Mr. President, Mrs. Cashe, Ms. Lyn, Governor Marchio has arrived."

"Thank you, Marcus." Jackson walks over and extends a hand to his friend, "John, I'm so glad you could make it."

Madison shakes hands with the governor before he hugs Haddie. They all sit around the impeccably set table. "I have to say, I was intrigued when I got your call. When the impeachment investigation began, I wondered if you would continue forward with reunification plans, especially considering that I am the main point of contention with the inquiry." The elder statesman ironically chortles at the thought. "Who could ever imagine that a former United States Senator for over two decades, and a retired Navy man, would be considered persona non grata as an enemy of the state? My, how things have changed."

Jackson leans over and places his hand on John's shoulder, "That, my friend, is exactly why it is so important that we keep meeting."

"Nice touch asking your aide to detour me by the press room. I have to admit, that was the first time I've been used as eye candy, and boy, were they drooling."

"Ha, you caught that, did you? My grandfather taught me to never run from a bully." Jackson takes a drink from his glass of orange juice as servers deliver their plates. The four of them catch up on personal business first. They have many friends in common. Jackson tells John all about the Bible study he is doing with Malik. Haddie fills John in on the family vineyard and her new pursuits as First Lady since postponing physical therapy school. The conversation flows freely between these simultaneous friends and enemies of state.

Madison returns after being summoned for a call and directs them back to the business of the office. "Mr. President, I hate to rush the meeting, but you have a tight schedule this afternoon."

"Sorry, Madison. It's not often I get to have brunch with a friend and mentor, but as always, you are correct. We should at least talk shop. If this meeting counts toward my alleged offenses, I aim to get my money's worth." The cynical edge in his voice does not go unnoticed as Haddie and Madison catch each other's eyes. "So, John, how are things progressing on your end? Are the Allied States still interested in reunification?"

John folds his napkin and places it on the table. His posturing speaks volumes, "Well, I wish I had better news from the home front, but I've got to be honest with you."

Jackson nods, "That's what I admire most about you."

"As you know, Congress commissioned an exploratory committee to work with you. I am the chair of the committee, but I only hold so much weight. With that said, the rest of the committee was making headway on our negotiation points. We had some big hurdles to jump, but we were working on some compromise points as well. Most of these men attended the summit and were moved by your willingness to listen. They were impressed with the US delegation. However, since the summit, there have been concerns over the infighting reported in the news. I've got to tell you that the media isn't helping your cause. You see we've gotten used to not having this type of discourse anymore, and it's been nice, really nice. Reporters in the Allied States stick to reporting the facts and leave the personal commentary to the comedians who harass everyone equally. To be honest, it's giving me stomach problems just watching you go through this inquiry."

"We talked about these concerns at the summit. John, this is just a bump in the road. Not everyone will be behind a reunification. We planned for backlash. The impeachment inquiry was a blow we weren't expecting, but we both know it is nothing more than bogus grandstanding. It will blow over as quickly as it came."

"Jackson, that's the thing, you're right. It will blow over, but it will be followed by something else in its place. If it was just the arguing, we could work with that. Things have come to light and we are facing bigger issues. I'm concerned that these new issues are insurmountable."

Jackson sits forward in his chair and leans in toward his guest. "What changed since the summit that is insurmountable now but wasn't present when we met a few months ago?"

John Marchio is a steadfast man. He is a rock. Jackson admires him greatly. John looks at Jackson with empathy. These two men both know and feel the weight of servant leadership. "The difference is the Constitution. We took it with us, and we honor it. The United States manipulates it, which is why the Separation occurred in the first place. The current document barely resembles the original."

Jackson shakes his head in disbelief. As a student of the Constitution, heck, as a lover of it and the Founding Fathers, he knows John is right. He has made compromises. He has rationalized, but deep down, he knows. In an effort to protect some, they took away the rights of others. He also knows this age-old debate did not cause the divide, it was merely the strike of the match. One country wanted bigger government, the other wanted less.

"Jackson, the minute this country abolished state rights, giving authority to the federal government over state legislatures and the judicial system, that was a shock. Then, you completely overhauled the judicial branch. Too much power for one group is dangerous. I don't care if the Republicans, Democrats, Federalists, or a high school glee club are in charge; that is too much power for one group to have over its citizens. Personally, I'm a fan of stalemates and gridlock in Congress. They encourage compromise and negotiation where both sides have to listen and work together. Isn't that a novel idea?"

Jackson hasn't seen John Marchio this intense since before the Separation. John looks like a college professor holding court. John continues, "The Supreme Court wrote a judgment last week stating that the Constitution was archaic and outdated. The judicial system in the US now has the right to overrule Constitutional Law if the court finds that a law goes against 'common and moral decency.' Who sets the mark for that? The United States government essentially abolished all of the checks and balances created by the Founding Fathers to prevent exactly what is happening. The government, which was solely created to prevent leaders from controlling individuals and states, is now controlled solely by the government it was designed to keep in check. The United States is a mockery of why America was founded and a slap in the face to those who died protecting her." John's fist comes down on the table, causing a light rattle. The other three startle at John's raw emotion. Jackson has been making excuses for months. His hand runs through his thick hair, which is rapidly turning gray. "I have people looking into the Supreme Court's decision." He looks at Madison, who nods in solidarity. She has heard similar arguments from Jackson all week.

"John, this is exactly why we need reunification. Groupthink is real and perilous. The American people are stronger together. We need differing viewpoints and voices."

John sighs, "Jackson, I know you love the Constitution. If I were a betting man, I would bet all my money that you know it better than most scholars. I would also bet that what is happening to it is eating you up inside." John gauges Jackson before continuing. Jackson's facial expression solidifies John's conjectures. "Jackson, we have seen countries all around the world fall overnight. New governments, new regimes, new ideologies throughout history. America stood the test of time because of that 'archaic and outdated document' signed by our forefathers. Those men were geniuses. They founded a government that could sustain itself based on self-governance, individual rights, and democracy. A republic of the whole country, not based on population centers. But you know all this already, don't you?"

Jackson has no words. Madison watches Jackson, as Haddie looks between the three of them. Haddie refers to them as three of the smartest people she knows. She has witnessed their deep passion and integrity and now watches an impasse that is a crater in all of their hopes.

"Jackson, one great nation split in two. The United States gives all the power to politicians and their donors. The Allied States gives all the power to the citizens. I don't trust politicians, and I've been one for over half of my life. Politicians don't play by the very rules they set for the people. The Allied States honors the Constitution and rebuilt a nation based on words that made America the world leader for over two centuries. The United States turned its back on the Constitution. They dismantled it and built a new ideology based on the 'common and moral decency' of whoever holds power at that time. Neither country is perfect because they are both ruled by sinful humans, but one has a system in place for checks and balances and the other encourages the powerful to amass more power."

Jackson looks at Madison. She is still resolved to make this work. She would follow him into battle regardless of the odds. Haddie's face holds love and compassion that moves him more than words can express. His wife, a Republican who didn't even vote for him the first time. She would support him no matter the odds.

"What can I do? My hands are tied and I'm at the mercy of the media and big tech. We were greater together. How do I get both sides to realize that?"

"I agree, but I don't think you can, at least not while all the shenanigans are still happening on your side of the border. If someone disagrees with the party line, they either have to move to the Allied States or risk being thrown in jail. This bitter infighting is caustic. Jackson, you know my feelings on peace. That only comes from Jesus. This world will always be at war. America was one nation under God, until it removed God. Now, it's one nation under a free-for-all. Your government has sold its soul to a living, breathing devil. I wish I had better news, but for now, I'm not getting anywhere as far as reunification."

"There must be something I can do to instill confidence. I've seen the Allied States argue. How is this different? Who is the devil in this scenario? Help me to understand." Jackson studies John as the elder statesman glances around the table at their guests. Understanding settles on Jackson's face. John wants to speak privately to his friend, not to the president. "Madison, Haddie, will you give us a minute, please?"

As the Chief of Staff, Madison Lyn already has reservations about this meeting. A private conversation causes her great concern. "Jackson, I strongly advise against this," she pauses, "for both of you."

"Madison, you need to trust me on this one." Jackson touches her hand.

Madison intensely studies Jackson's face before rising from her chair. "Governor, as always, it has been a pleasure."

The two women say their goodbyes and excuse themselves from the patio. As soon as the door closes Jackson is all ears, "John, talk to me."

"Jackson, I like you. You know I do. I trust you, but not your government and definitely not the outside influences calling the shots. There is more to the story, but it's classified. You just have to know where to look and who to ask." John reaches into his pocket and pulls out a slip of paper. He slides the folded paper across the table before covering his lips with a finger, encouraging Jackson to remain silent. John settles into his chair as Jackson reaches for the paper.

He reads the handwritten list of companies and individuals. Most of which are linked to the financial, academic, and entertainment worlds.

"Have you read the book Animal Farm? If you haven't, you should. It's a wonderful and enlightening tale about how easy it is for smart, hardworking, loyalists to back the wrong horse, or pig, in that scenario. I won't spoil it for you, but read it if you get the chance. My granddaughter just read it for homeschool. You know that communism and socialism are essentially the same concepts, with the difference lying in whether the movement begins with a bloody revolution versus a political movement. Both ideologies call for government-controlled societies based on equity, not equality. There is a grave difference between those two words. Hear me out for a moment. I don't intend to insult you with a history lesson. These are just the musings of an old man who has seen a lot over my career."

"I'm listening." Jackson leans back into his seat while folding the list and tucking it into his jacket pocket.

"One of the reasons the Separation occurred was over a move toward socialism and the silencing of the opposition. The very people complaining about the corruptness of government insisted that the government take complete control over every aspect of society. The irony doesn't stop there. These same 'activists' fight against the injustices in America all while accepting billions of dollars from China who runs forced labor camps with over four million slaves." John grunts in frustration.

"I'm following your concern, but I'm failing to see how this tiresome debate between socialism and capitalism is impacting a reunification. Allowing capitalism free reign holds many dangers that I can argue against. A central government that holds its citizens accountable and regulates the good of the whole from the wants of the individual, is vital. From what I've been watching, the Allied States are working to provide state-assisted programs that mirror the welfare system the Republicans railed against before the Separation." Jackson's voice sounds irritated.

A sly smirk emerges on John's face. "I love sparring with you. Yes, we are working on temporary assistance programs, emphasis on temporary. We're putting money in personnel who are job and crisis counselors to help get people back on their feet instead of continually providing money. We're tweaking the old adage by giving people fish while teaching them to fish instead of providing the fish long term. As with most of our conversations, we could debate the deep state of dependents for hours, but that is not my point. As long as money is flowing to the right people, a blind eye overlooks everything happening in D.C. Politics is a trillion-dollar business and everyone wants a piece of the action."

"In the years leading up to the Separation, all the infighting and riots, the war on terrorism, we left our doors wide open to attack. Sadly, the enemy crept right in through Wall Street without anyone noticing." John points to Jackson's pocket. "I think it would be interesting to talk to insiders who know things. Maybe those who were silenced by their backers or bosses for speaking out. I'm sure they would have a different side of the story to tell. If there is a shadow government in place, I'd look for the people who have been silenced inside those shadows."

"John, you must be joking. You're suggesting some crazy, conspiracy theory stuff. Are you pitching a novel you want to write during retirement?" Jackson attempts to lighten the mood, knowing his friend can't be serious. "I'm giving you the benefit of the doubt because of our friendship, but this is nuts. Surely you're not falling for all the propaganda."

John keeps his wry grin. "That would be great book. Maybe I need to find a ghost writer. The first chapter could start with the FBI trying to destroy documents during the beginning phases of the Separation. Maybe the secretary of a fame-hungry intelligence agent rescues intel from the shredder. She smuggles out documents and passes them along before evidence is destroyed. Chapter two would reveal a list of names from the salvaged intel of people who have invaluable knowledge to share." John lets that information sink in before continuing. "Good thing all of that is fiction and crazy talk, because if any of it is true, I can promise the Allied States would not get into bed with any business, individual, or government associated with underground backers. That would be a nail in the coffin for reunification, I'm sorry to say."

"John, no one from the United States is in bed with communist backers. I would know." Jackson is frustrated.

"Do your homework, and then we'll talk. Taking dirty money might be the only truly bipartisan effort in politics." John Marchio taps the table before rising. "Ask yourself this; How are all of these 'civil servants' living so high on the hog? Follow the money. If I'm off my rocker and none of this is true, why work so hard to silence and discredit the opposition?"

"To prevent panic and the incitement of loose cannons." Jackson is exasperated from this cloak-and-dagger discussion.

John's laughter is sad and dark, "The rhetoric goes both ways my friend. We choose to believe those whom we want to believe. When my brothers and I would fight, my mother had us sit down and each tell our side of the story. When we were all finished, she would let us know that she believed the truth lay somewhere in the middle and it was up to us to figure out where our story went off track. That was the end of the discussion. Jackson, the Separation occurred because neither side was willing to acknowledge the middle."

John studies his protégé. "I like you Jackson and I want to help you, but my hands are tied too. As always, this has been an enjoyable visit, Mr. President. Hopefully we can continue this conversation sooner rather than later." John pats Jackson's suit jacket, right above the secret list of names as Marcus arrives to escort John to the door.

The weight from this little slip of paper is pulling him down further into the abyss of politics. Jackson Cashe is drowning, right in the middle of Pennsylvania Avenue.

****

Haddie meets her chief of staff in the colonnade. Ashleigh offers Haddie her phone and schedule for the rest of the day, including a briefing for a committee she has been personally asked to chair.

"Your grandmother has been texting you for the past hour. Every five minutes a new Bible verse would pop up onto your screen. She didn't use the emergency code and I didn't want to interrupt your brunch, so I just let them pile up. I hope that was all right?"

Haddie struggles with allowing someone else into her personal world, even someone as sweet and honest as Ashleigh. She learned quickly the importance of having another person to help her juggle all of the information coming at her from every direction. Most days, Haddie feels as if she lives life on a dodge ball court and Ashleigh is the only person blocking her from getting nailed in the face.

"That's fine. Trust me, if Nunnie wanted to get in touch with me, even the National Guard couldn't stop her." Haddie laughs as Ashleigh tries to stifle one of her own. The phone in Haddie's hand vibrates as Nunnie's face pops up with another text.

Nunnie: This is the last text for now, I promise, but tell Jackson to read Second Chronicles twenty. I just can't help but feel a heaviness to pray for him today. I don't know why, but Jackson has moved to the top of my prayer list. Frankie has been at that spot for six months, maybe that means things are turning around in her heart. Anyway, I love you and Jackson. Call me when you can.

Haddie shakes her head and mumbles, "I don't know how that woman does it."

"I'm sorry, what?" Ashleigh attempts to walk, listen, and take notes.

"Nothing. Let's ask Rich's office if this committee is a good idea. I'm really intrigued by it. Also, make a note for me to call my cousin Frankie. I'm also intrigued by her right now."

Tony

A spattering of cars fills the parking lot, hours after the lunch rush. Tony pulls into Poppy's and parks at the farthest edge of the lot that he paved and painted himself. Tony knows this building like the back of his hand. Not only did he grow up on this property as Sammy's constant tagalong, but he also took the bones of a rustic barn and remodeled it into an artistic dining masterpiece. Poppy's has graced the pages of both culinary and design magazines. More than all the accolades and marketing, he loved doing it for his second family.

"Come on, Ma. I hope you have on your walking shoes because we have to climb the outside stairs to get to the studio." Tony jumps out of his truck and walks to the passenger door to open it for his mother.

"Are you sure it's okay? Will I get in the way?" Rosie asks out of politeness but doesn't really bother with his answer. She is going to experience every inch of this real life television set.

"It's fine. I have a couple guys from my crew up there working on the set, including Beau, so Maryssa knows you're coming." Tony smiles at his mother. "She said to bring you. I'm sure it had nothing to do with you mentioning it ten times after church on Sunday."

"Well it worked. You know what they say about the squeaky wheel."

"It gets replaced?" Tony laughs as his mother turns to glare at him.

"Wiseguy."

"Come on," Tony holds out his hand to help his mom.

They ascend the outside stairs to what used to be Maryssa and Beau's apartment. It spans the entire width and length of Poppy's. Tony and his crew have been set-building

141

and soundproofing for Maryssa and Frankie's television shows. They are finalizing the details this week. Lisa is in town for a visit, so he wants to check in and make sure she's happy since her company is footing the bill.

Tony opens the door to a flurry of activity. His crew has drills running and paint rolling. The production team is testing sound and lighting equipment. Lisa walks around with Maryssa and Frankie in tow, frantically poking at her poor tablet. Frankie looks up and sees the new guests, drawing the attention of the others. Frankie waves at Rosie, a smile warming her face.

"Ah, if it isn't the good-looking contractor. This spectacular woman must be your mother. We've been waiting for you." Lisa crosses the room to shake hands. "You've done some great work here, Tony. I'm impressed."

"I'm glad it meets your approval. My crew aims to please."

"Oh, how I love a man who wants to please a woman. Well done, Tony's mom. You've raised him right." Lisa steps between them and takes Tony's arm into hers as she pulls him toward a back wall where her team is working. "Frankie and Maryssa can give you a tour of the set. I just need to borrow your son for a minute."

Tony follows along behind Lisa while trying to listen to her and his mother at the same time. He's not sure which scares him more, not listening intently to Lisa or leaving Rosie alone with Frankie and Maryssa. He watches as the three women walk around, pointing and chatting. Rosie picks up a cake pan from a box and examines it. Tony cringes until he witnesses Frankie give Rosie a side hug. He wonders how he managed to love the two most stubborn women in the world. Lisa talks, he tries to listen.

After a quick tour of the studio, Tony and his mother excuse themselves from the construction site. They navigate the stairs back to the main parking lot as she sets her sights on their next destination. "We're going to see Mary, right? I brought her some homemade pepperoni rolls and pasta e fagioli since she doesn't have a kitchen. I made extra for your apartment too."

"Thanks, Ma, and yes. I called Mary this morning to make sure she would be around today." Tony is driving over the dirt road that runs the length of the vineyard, connecting the farmhouse to the restaurant.

"So, that Lisa is quite a character. All that good-looking contractor stuff." Rosie watches her son's expression. "I hope Frankie doesn't think something is going on there with you and that Lisa."

"Ma, is that your way of asking me a question? If it is, the answer is no. Lisa is just a client, and she acts that way to everyone. She's actually very nice and professional. Most of the time. I think the excitement of filming soon gets to her. They're starting next week."

"Well, I might have been digging for information, but not on Lisa." Rosie raises an eyebrow, anticipating his next words.

"If you're asking about Frankie, I don't think that's going to work out either. I'm not sure Frankie feels that way about me. She's dealing with things, and I don't think she wants my help."

"Frankie is a tough cookie. Her shell is hard, but once you crack it, she'll be worth it. Good things don't come easy. Keep working on our girl."

"What does that even mean, Ma? She either likes me, or she doesn't. I can't force someone to have feelings." He shakes his head.

"Oh, she has feelings. She's just too tough to admit it."

"You keep saying she's tough. What are you not telling me?" Tony glances over at his mother in the passenger seat.

Rosie is quick to change the subject. "Did you see the cookie sheets she was showing me? Those are the same ones I have at the house. Frankie remembers baking cookies with me that summer I helped watch them while Sam worked. She saw those cookie sheets and ordered them for the show. She might even have me make a guest appearance. Can you imagine? My sister will just die for sure if she sees me on television."

Tony watches his mother as she, undoubtedly, is picking out an outfit in her mind for the show. They pull up to the farmhouse and climb out of the truck. Tony grabs the box filled with food his mother made for Mary, Esther, and Frankie. They walk up the stairs to find Mary on her front porch swing enjoying a glass of sweet tea. The side table has a pitcher and extra glasses. She is expecting them.

"Rosie, I'm so happy to see you. Grab some tea and swing with me. You can see the kitchen after we catch up."

Rosie's face lights up. Mary Marchio makes everyone feel special.

****

Frankie

The set finally settles down after Tony and his crew leave. Lisa sends her team back to the hotel for the night as the three women sit down to talk business.

Frankie begins by holding in her snickering, "Lisa, I don't ever think I've seen Rosie Devono that quiet in all the years I've known her. I'm not sure if you scared her or impressed her with your star quality."

Maryssa laughs along with her cousin. "Seriously, Lisa, you crack me up. You don't seem like the same person who took Haddie under her wing during *Future FLOTUS?*. You have no filter."

"Oh, I'm definitely not the same person. Years in this business have changed me, that's for sure. I'm harder and louder. Sandra was an intense boss and scared the pants off of me more than once, but I learned more from that woman than any college course. She is a force. She taught me to speak up and demand what I deserve. She also told me to run if I'm ever offered a job to produce a reality dating show." They all laugh at that one. "Speaking of Sandra and Haddie, I hear Sandra's documentary company is filming your family?"

Frankie and Maryssa nod.

"She called me last week to make sure there weren't any contractual issues. Once I heard it was for Haddie, I offered to help in any way I can, so let me know. Obviously, you all should use this space since it's already wired for sound and light. There is enough room in the middle to stage a cozy interview space. I, for one, can't wait to see it. Between Rich Miller and Sandra, it will be an entertaining show for sure."

"There's that Lisa we know and love. Offering your help and ideas. You're still a softy inside." Maryssa pokes Lisa's shoulder.

"Ha-ha. I love being assertive, but I probably need to work on my filter. I'm not sure Tony's mom liked me calling him good-looking repeatedly. I hope I didn't offend her."

"Nothing offends Rosie. She was probably worried you were making moves on Tony. She's been planning on Tony and Frankie getting married since we were little." Maryssa grins at Frankie with a childish glint in her eyes.

Frankie's shocked face opens the door for more teasing. Lisa jumps on quickly. "Ooh, now that's an interesting storyline. I can work with that. I see a whole episode about you finding your perfect wedding cake. Or maybe an entire series about wedding planning. Tony is eye candy. It won't be a hard sell to the network."

Frankie swats her cousin's arm for opening this can of worms. "Don't you dare, Lisa. I see your mind working overtime, and I'm stopping it now. No, absolutely not! Maryssa Marie Baker, you are now on my list, and it's not a good list."

"Frankie and Tony sitting in a tree K-I-S-S-I-N-G." Maryssa begins singing as Lisa joins in the fun.

Frankie's head sinks the table as the women chuckle and sing.

Frankie

The bass vibrates off the stretched canvas on the platform. Laughing, grunting, and blaring music fill the space. Frankie watches Deena's footwork as her friend shuffles around the ring. Frankie came to Pounders to workout and ended up watching a sparring match between Deena and some guy who came in running his mouth. His moves were sloppy, and Deena called him out for it. Next thing Frankie knew, Deena was schooling him on technique. The match drew a crowd.

By the time they finish, the guy is soaking wet in his own sweat. Deena barely glistens as she maneuvers between the ropes and hops to the floor. She shakes her head as Frankie attempts to hide her laughter from the poor, defeated victim. "You went easy on him."

"I didn't want to embarrass the poor guy any more than I already did," Deena shrugs. "How did the meeting go today with your producer?" Deena pulls off her gloves and grabs an edge of tape between her teeth to unwrap her hands.

"Okay, I guess. Lisa talked. I listened. Maryssa translated. We start filming next week. I went through my episode themes, she talked about blocking and lighting. The only thing I understood was prep work and samples." Frankie's face twists as she contemplates the enormity of this new endeavor.

"Poor Frankie. How terrible to have your own television show. You're a successful businesswoman, and you haven't even broken a sweat. Cry me a river of tears." Deena offers a snarky grin to her friend before grabbing a towel to wipe herself down with it.

"Hey!" Frankie throws her own towel at Deena.

147

"I'm just saying, enjoy it. This is a huge break. You're acting like it's a burden. My brothers have been trying to get a reality show for years. They want to call it the *Fighting Finnegans.*"

Frankie chuckles at the thought. "Are you serious? Now that I would pay to watch. Your family is more jacked up than mine."

"I know, right? Pop thinks it will add to our business model and build on our brand. We're gaining speed in the national circuit thanks to some of our boxers. We just need a jumpstart to franchise the gym. You've been given a golden ticket. You can finally open your own bakery. Now, you can pick and choose your projects. All I'm saying is that this is a blessing, so act like it." She has a satisfied look before taking a big swig from her water bottle.

Frankie lowers her head. "I know, I know. I just don't like attention. People think I do, but I really don't. I'm worried that all of my nervous energy will spill out, and I'll end up talking more than baking. I'm a nervous talker. I talk too much."

Deena holds her sides while breaking out into a raucous laugh. "You? Talk too much? That's so funny. You do hear the sarcasm, right? From what I see, you talk about everything but what's important. You just rattle off information when you're nervous. The only thing you need to worry about is accidentally sharing one of your grandmother's secret recipes. That woman is fierce."

Frankie laughs at herself a little. "That would be dangerous."

"Look, I'm serious. I'm worried about you. You're holding in too much. You really need to tell your family some of this stuff you're dealing with. It's too much for one person. You have the group and me, but your family is your tribe, just like mine. You can't keep things from your people. Tell them, maybe they'll surprise you."

"What if you're wrong? It could be disastrous. And what is it with everyone commenting on my anger issues this week? Why can't y'all stay out of my business?"

Frankie's aggravated huff tells Deena that the line has been drawn. Deena wraps an arm around her friend, "Unfortunately, you are now part of my tribe, which makes you my business."

"And you know everything, so see, I do talk to people. Your argument is innately flawed." Frankie hip bumps Deena and bends to grab her bag from the floor.

"Not the same, and you know it, but I'll stop. Let's go, I'll hold the bag."

An hour later, Frankie is spent. Her muscles are stinging and she's covered in sweat. This was exactly what she needed. Deena hands her a water bottle with electrolytes and they start talking about weekend plans. Frankie is listening, but she can't get her mind off of their conversation earlier. It's not until Frankie opens the front doors that her mind sharply focuses. The flat tire is a kick in the gut. Shoulders slump, head drops. She pulls out her phone and quickly texts "help."

"Doh, again? Isn't that your second flat this month?" Deena, who is hanging out of the gym door, commentates.

Frankie turns and glares at her friend. "Yes, it is. In your parking lot."

"Hey, don't blame us. It's potholes. Call the president and complain, aren't you related?"

"Wrong country." Frankie spits out as Deena laughs. "I didn't replace the spare from the last time."

"Are you calling your dad?"

Frankie plops down on the curb next to her car. She covers her arms over her head, which is now resting on her knees. She mumbles, "Nope. I still haven't talked to him. I texted my brother."

"Yikes, it must be worse than I thought if you asked your brother for help." She looks over her shoulder at someone yelling for her. "You wanna come inside to wait?"

"No, I'm just going to sit out here and wallow in my self-pity."

"Suit yourself. I need to get back in there before my brothers destroy the place. Text me later."

Frankie nods. She spends the next fifteen minutes mindlessly searching her phone apps for something to keep her attention from Deena's honest advice. Anticipation crushes her each time headlights do not belong to a bright red Ram Bighorn. She lifts her water bottle to her lips, only to find it empty. *Of course, it's empty. I can't catch a break.*

Pounders is located near the interstate. It's settled back off of the main road and surrounded by offshoots of other strip malls. The summer evening air is muggy. The breeze feels good on her sticky skin as she rolls her neck back and forth. She hears Brad Paisley singing before Sammy's truck pulls into the parking lot with his windows rolled down. The smirk on his face makes her wish she walked home.

"Need a ride?" Sammy's voice oozes with sarcasm and superiority. "That's the eye roll I was waiting for. Get in." He laughs as he unlocks the door.

Frankie tosses her bag on the floor and grabs his water bottle from the console. She finishes it and smirks.

"Hey! I'm adding that to your gas usage fee." Sammy pulls out of the parking lot. "Your car okay here tonight?"

"It'll be fine. The Finnegans have lights and cameras on all night. Rough business."

"I bet. Although I'm not sure theirs is a business I would mess with, with or without cameras." Sammy looks over at Frankie, "You okay?"

"I'm fine. Thanks, Sammy," her voice is laced with gratefulness, and not just for tonight. He reaches over and shoves her shoulder. The gesture warms her heart. Her dad was right.

They ride in silence for a few minutes as he drives down a back road. "Why aren't you taking the interstate?"

"Hello? This is a windows-rolled-down-country-roads kind of night. I'm not taking the interstate. I'm taking the back road. I think Beau and Maryssa are taking Chloe to the drive-in tonight. We'll drive right by it. If you're nice, I'll take you too. We can have Tony meet us and hang out like old times. I'll twist the chains on the swings and make you dizzy." He looks over at her. "Yes! I did it! I got a smile. Well, a partial smile, but I'll take it."

She lands a jab right on his arm. "You're such a jerk," but she is still smiling.

"It's not very smart to punch the person driving you." He rubs his arm and winces. "At least we know your endless hours with the Finnegans are paying off. You gave me a stinger. Speaking of, thanks for waiting outside, that Deena girl scares me."

"She should. I've seen her take down guys twice as big as you. You should come with me to their next event. You can watch her in action."

"No thanks. I'd rather not surround myself with people who can crush me with one punch."

The air blows Frankie's hair, causing wisps to fly around her face. She breathes in the mossy smells of late summer. Pinks, yellows, oranges, and purples are scattered all over the hillsides surrounding them. Leaves dance on the branches. She closes her eyes and feels freedom. She has forgotten that feeling. It's invigorating. She takes one last long breath before leaning back into her seat.

Sammy tells his car to start another playlist. They drive with the air flowing and the radio playing. Frankie feels like herself, her old self. She feels younger and free. Then Sammy pops her bubble.

"Hey Frank, what's going on with you and Dad? He's been in a funk since you two last talked, and according to Nunnie, you have been meaner than normal."

She snarls, "Nunnie would never call me mean."

"I was trying to be nice."

Frankie's mind wanders as she attempts to answer his question without popping his oblivious bubble. "Were Mom and Dad happy when we were growing up?"

"Where is this coming from? Does this have anything to do with you and Dad?"

She just looks at him, needing answers. Needing something.

Sammy sighs in defeat. "I don't know. I guess. They always seemed happy. I mean, there were hard times, but I don't remember them fighting in front of us."

Frankie stares out of the truck window. Her brother glances over at her.

"Are you okay?" Nothing. "You know you can talk to me. I can be serious, sometimes." She returns his grin.

"I know. There are just some things a girl can't tell her brother."

"You're probably right about that, but I'm guessing you can tell me what's going on with Dad. You just don't want to."

She shrugs and crosses her arms as a chill sweeps over her skin. She shivers. "I have memories of growing up, but I feel like there are a lot of holes. I'm trying to piece everything together. Right before I left for college, I heard them fighting. I heard things I can't un-hear. Now, I'm trying to see if hindsight matches the mirage or busts it wide open."

"They had issues. I think we were too young to really see it. I remember spending a lot of time at Nunnie's house and even with Tony's family."

"That's so weird. Lately, I've been swamped with memories of baking with Rosie. I thought it was because Tony is around me so much these days, but now I'm not sure." Frankie rubs her arms covered in goosebumps.

"Are you mad at Dad because he and Mom fought when we were younger? That doesn't make sense, Frankie."

"Well, there's more to it than that. I just can't figure out if I'm missing a memory, blocking it, or making it up about them. My mind has been cloudy lately. I'm smushing things together. Have you ever wished you could see clearer? Like everything aligns, and you could see it all the way through, like a time-lapse video?"

"Like the ones you make for your cakes? The ones that show how you put them together and decorate them but faster?"

"Aww, my big brother really does care about me." A gratifying smile covers her face.

He shakes his head, "Don't tell anyone I watch cake videos."

Sammy keeps pushing her. "Look, I know something happened with you. I don't know if it's Dad or a guy, or something else entirely. I just want you to know that I'm here for you. If you need me, I'm here. We've always had each other's backs. I want you to know that I still have yours."

"I know." She sits up in her seat and wipes a betraying tear from her cheekbone. "Don't get nice on me now. Are you serious about the drive-in? You okay spending a Friday night with your sister?"

He laughs and nods.

"Let's drop by the drive-in and make a night of it."

"That's what I'm talking about!" Sammy howls out the window into the night air.

They drive in silence as the road bends and curves into the next. The sun is setting behind a wall of trees. Frankie is caught off guard by the excitement at seeing the top of the big screen. Sammy pulls onto the gravel lot and gets in line at the Sunset Drive-In.

"Remember when it only cost five dollars a carload? Those were the days." Sammy groans as he pulls out his wallet for the admission tickets. "The popcorn and sodas are on you."

"Deal." Frankie strains her neck around to look for Beau's antique, blue pickup truck. He restored it with the help of Maryssa and Chloe. It was their first family project together. Something about that old pickup made the whole family feel hopeful after a season of sadness. Every time something significant happened in the Bible, someone built an altar. That truck was like an altar of some sort. The thought makes Frankie smile from deep inside, a place that hasn't felt warmth in a while. "They're over there, in the back row."

"Good. I hate being too close to other cars."

The truck inches slowly through the drive-in lot to the back row. The sound of gravel under the tires reminds Frankie of childhood. Soft music, muted conversations, and a cricket symphony provide background ambiance as the customers wait for the first movie to start. Sammy eases into the spot next to Beau's truck, careful to make it between the two poles holding the speakers. Sammy jumps out to open the tailgate for the chairs and blankets. Frankie digs through her bag to find deodorant and a hoodie. By the time she steps out of her brother's truck, coolers are opened, and food is dispersed.

"I feel like I've been had. You obviously planned on coming whether I said yes or no."

"Technically, I didn't trick you, but you are right about coming. I was on my way when I got your text, so you were either coming by force or free will." Her brother's grin elicits a shake of her head and resigned chuckle.

"At least we came with Chloe, she always picks the best snacks." The curly-haired firecracker runs into Frankie's arms as the words are coming out of her mouth.

"We made three types of popcorn. There is butter. Over there is spicy southwest popcorn, yuck. And here is my favorite, caramel." Chloe points to each bag. Her facial expressions let you know her opinion of each flavor. She holds out the bag of caramel for Frankie to grab a handful.

"You're talking my language, Miss Chloe." She leans down and kisses her cousin on the head and squeezes her with her popcorn free hand.

"Hey!" Maryssa comes over and kisses Frankie's cheek. "We also have some trail mix and homemade pizza rolls. I'll bring out the cookies later. Fair warning, they're yours, I pulled them from Poppy's dessert stash." Maryssa pops Frankie in the hip before walking back to their truck.

Frankie peeks her head over the side of Beau's pickup to find baskets filled with food, napkins, and cups. The bed itself is a fortress of pillows and blankets fit for a princess. Chloe and her best friend, Rachael, are cozy in their cloud seats. Their giggles are the cherry on top of the evening.

Frankie picks her seat from a row of camping chairs that span the tailgates of the trucks. She takes a blanket from Sammy and settles in for the movie. Blinding headlights turning down their row cause Frankie to shield her eyes. She immediately recognizes the truck as it reverses into its spot next to Sammy's. Chloe and her friend jump out of the truck as a little girl with braids and hot pink beads runs to them with open arms. A round of squealing and jumping ensues. Tony appears with a blanket and a chair. He shakes hands with Beau and hugs Maryssa. Turning back, he offers her a nod, which everyone seems to notice but Sammy.

"Francesca."

"Anthony."

"Harmony, put this on, or your mom will ground both of us." He tosses the little girl her sweatshirt as the three girls climb back into the pillow kingdom.

"Babysitting duty?" Frankie looks up at him.

"I prefer to call it winning the best uncle award, but yes, my sister was grateful for the night off. My mom has the baby. I think they're going out to dinner." Tony grins as he sets up his chair right next to Frankie's.

"Ha! I saw your sister at the grocery store the other day. The baby has colic. They probably fell asleep on the couch and missed dinner all together," Maryssa jokes.

Everyone startles as the speakers come to life. The crackling sound reminds them all of childhood summers. Beau takes a wired speaker box from the pole and places one in the bed of the truck for the girls to hear. He pulls the others as far as they will reach and places them on the ground for the chairs. The lights around the parking lot dim as pictures flicker on the larger-than-life screen. Music fills the air as cheers erupt from the crowd when cartoon characters begin dancing across the screen. Frankie takes a deep breath and recalls all the times she's been here with her parents, Sammy, Maryssa, Haddie, and Tony. Something about being here feels magical. Frankie becomes lost in the movie, the night air, and the memories.

As the first movie ends, the girls ask if they can go to the playground at the edge of the lot. Tony offers to watch them and looks at Frankie with a nod in that direction. She notices Maryssa pretending not to notice the interaction. Frankie takes a breath and stands up to follow the girls. "I'll go with Tony while you guys pack up the trucks."

Sammy feigns shock, "What? The girls don't want to stay for the slasher second feature?"

Maryssa tosses a pillow at Sammy's head. "No, now help me fold this blanket."

Frankie sits on one of the swings as the girls take turns spinning the merry go round. Tony gives them a warning before taking the other swing. He stares at Frankie while the wind dances in her hair. She took it down at some point during the movie. The thought of what it might look like now crosses her mind, but Tony's deep eyes are distracting.

"Is Lisa happy with the final sets?"

"I think so. I can never tell with Lisa. She shifts thoughts so fast. I can barely keep up with her. I'm terrified of actual filming. Maryssa keeps telling me that Lisa is silent during taping, but I'm having a hard time believing that Lisa is ever quiet." They both laugh.

"Are you nervous?"

"A little. I know everyone thinks I'm fearless, but this is way out of my comfort zone. I just don't want to let anyone down. Lisa and Maryssa did a lot to make this happen." Frankie shrugs and looks down at her feet, swaying above the mulch. The nostalgic night is making her talkative and relaxed. It feels eerily comforting.

Tony leans toward Frankie and tucks a stray hair behind her ear so he can see her face. "I wouldn't say you're fearless." He pauses as she quickly looks up at him, defensively. He loves feisty Frankie. "I know that look. Wait until I'm finished. Being fearless isn't always a good thing. I think fear is a natural reaction to danger. You aren't fearless, you are brave. You don't let fear stop you. You let it strengthen you. I've always admired that about you. You have this way of forging on no matter what is happening around you."

"Be careful, Anthony Devono, I think you just gave me a compliment."

"I have nothing but compliments when it comes to you."

His words take her back as she draws in air to steady her beating heart. Frankie isn't sure if it's the summer air or wistfulness, but something is different tonight. Tony inches his swing closer to hers. His eyes ask a question that she has waited since her teenage years for him to ask. Now she's anxious and excited and ready. She feels his breath as he slowly reaches her face. His lips very gently lower to hers. They are soft and taste like caramel popcorn. The long-awaited kiss lasts only a second before the sweetness and silence are pierced with a scream.

"What are you doing? That's my sister!"

Tony

Ringing from the bell above the door alerts Tony to oncoming traffic. A customer walks out of the hardware store as Tony holds open the door and stands to the side.

"Mr. Bakewell, how are you?"

"Ah, Tony. I didn't see you. Your dad ordered a special tool for me. Just came in. How's the contracting business?"

"Doing good, thank you for asking. Tell Mrs. Bakewell I said hello." Tony nods at his father's friend and favorite customer.

"I surely will. Have you read the papers? The Gators are looking to have a stellar year. Mark my words, you'll see them in the championship game this year." Mr. Bakewell walks to his car with his back to Tony, but Tony is positive there is an ornery grin covering the man's face.

"Mr. Bakewell, those are fighting words around these parts. You keep your Florida Gators to yourself. We both know it's the year of the Mountaineer."

Mr. Bakewell laughs and waves his hand in the air as he opens the car door. Tony is still smiling when he heads into the hardware store.

Tony's big sister rushes over to intercept him. She pulls him around the end cap of aisle one and looks around suspiciously.

"What's happening? You realize you're terrible at playing spies, right? Are you hiding from Mom or Dad?"

"Be quiet, brat." Heather offers a quick kiss on his cheek before launching into her plan. "Listen, Darren and I are taking Mama and Daddy to dinner tonight. We're pitching our idea for the store. I think Daddy finally realizes that you aren't taking it over and might actually listen. We need a reboot if the store has a chance to make it over the big box stores. Darren and I think we have a unique idea. I need you to watch Harmony tonight."

"What about the baby?"

"My mother-in-law is watching him, but Harmony specifically requested you. Which reminds me, we need to discuss the amount of sugar you allow her to eat," she gives him a warning look.

"That's no fun," he counters. "Of course, I will. Beau and I have to work on Mary's kitchen, but Harmony can tag along and probably play with Chloe."

"Good, because I already wrote a note to her teacher that Uncle Tony is picking her up from school," she smiles sweetly.

He rubs his chin. "Do you need my help with Dad?"

"No. No. We've done the research and have a game plan. I think it will work. You don't want the store and Darren wants out of the auto body shop. The store won't last much longer without some major changes. We have a business plan that will keep the name on the store and give Darren and me our own business. You don't want the store, right? You're sure?"

He kisses her on the head. Heather might be older, but Tony has a foot on her. "No, I don't want the store. Besides, it's just as much mine as it is yours. In fact, you've worked here longer, so really, it's all yours."

"You are so cute. Daddy is an old Italian man at heart. We both know the firstborn son gets the business."

He looks square at her. "You know this store backward and forward. He knows that. He loves Darren and knows he's a good businessman. This has always been your store. You've got this."

Tony gets choked up as Heather hugs him tighter than usual. He's chalking it up to the events that transpired over the weekend. He escaped a fist to the face at the drive-in thanks to the presence of three eight-year-old girls, but that didn't stop Sammy from nailing him at the apartment later that night. One punch and two beers later, a handshake agreement was forged. Tony can continue breathing as long as he doesn't hurt Frankie. Sammy is not happy. They watched baseball in silence all day Sunday.

"What happened to your face, by the way? First a shiner, now a busted jaw? Something is up. Are you in some kind of crazy fight club?" She touches his cheek as he winces in pain.

"Long story, but hopefully it will be my last. Is Ma here? I don't want her to ask questions. I just need to pick up extra grout for floor tiles I'm installing tomorrow."

"I already pulled it off the shelf for you. Daddy is in the storeroom. If I were you, I would take it and run. They aren't going to be happy about that bruise." She walks along the aisle and ducks behind the counter to pull out the heavy bags. "Here you go, pick up Harmony by two-fifty."

"You got it. Thanks, and good luck." He winks and heads back out the door to his truck. Successfully avoiding a Rosie Devono inquisition.

Tony has back to back appointments all morning for bids. Thankfully, he's done work for these clients before and can easily explain away the bruised face. By lunchtime, he needs to stop at the apartment for aspirin and an ice pack. Tony texts Beau and asks if Harmony can hang out with Chloe for a couple of hours while they work. They make plans so the girls can play while they finish Mary's tiled backsplash.

As three o'clock rolls around, Tony and Harmony drive through town with orange sodas and french fries. They stop at his two job sites where the guys all comment about Tony bringing by his pint-sized boss. She giggles while wearing her custom-fitted hardhat Uncle Tony bought her for Christmas. By the time they make it to the farmhouse, Harmony asks for real food and a bathroom.

Tony pulls his truck around to the back porch, where Chloe is impatiently waiting for Harmony. The girls run and hug each other like they haven't seen one another in days, even though they were just in school for eight hours together.

Esther bounces down the stairs with her purse in hand. "I'm going to take the girls to Poppy's for dinner, then for some ice cream. Is that okay?"

"That sounds perfect. Harmony, what do you think?" Squealing girls give him his answer. "Thank you so much." He hugs Esther and helps to round up the girls.

"My pleasure. Beau will be up in a minute. He's eating dinner with Maryssa. He's just waiting on me to relieve him from baby duty. Anyway, the girls and I are off on an adventure."

Tony walks to the bed of his truck and pulls out what he needs. Scaling the steps, he knocks on the back door before opening it. "Nunnie?"

"Come on in, Tony. I'm just trying to heat up water in this microwave. I hate this thing." Mary grumbles as she slams the door shut with her mug in hand.

"Coffee at this hour? You'll be up all night," he teases.

"No sir. This is Tally Tea. Helps me to relax."

Tony smiles. His grandmother also used to call Chamomile Tally Tea. You'd think it sailed over from the old country with them.

"It sounds like you could use some too. From the stories I heard, you had quite a weekend." Mary sits at the table, expectantly. The woman can make anyone talk.

"I'm afraid to know what you heard. You still let me inside your house, so it must not be too bad."

"Not bad at all, just interesting. In fact, a little overdue if you ask me." Mary takes a sip of her tea.

"Well, I'm not sure Frankie would agree with you."

Mary rubs the handle of her mug with her thumb. "You know Tony, it's hard to see the sunlight when you're in the forest. Frankie Jo has been wandering in the tall trees for a while now. I think she's finally starting to follow the crack of light to get her out of the darkness. Now, tell me all about your sister's plan to transform the hardware store."

Tony shakes his head in unbelief. "How do you know everything?"

"I listen, sweetheart, I listen. You can't become this wise by talking too much, I'll tell you that."

Just then, they hear tires on gravel pulling up to the back door. Beau walks in with two take-out containers. "I come bearing gifts."

Mary gives her lumberjack looking grandson-in-law a big hug. "Just in time for Wheel of Fortune. Well, boys, get to work. I want my kitchen back!"

"That woman is a force of nature." Beau rubs the back of his neck. "Maryssa has the girls making their own pizzas. She wanted to make sure you ate too." He hands Tony the container then points at his face, "It looks like you and Sammy worked everything out."

Tony gently touches his jaw. "I don't want to talk about it."

"You got it, boss." Beau chuckles to himself before reaching for the bag of grout and a bucket.

Three hours and one completed backsplash later, Tony and Beau start cleaning up the kitchen. "We could have this wrapped within the week if Mary would let me bring in some finishers." Tony washes his hands in the new sink.

"A week ago, I would have said fat chance of that happening but I think the woman really wants us out of her kitchen. I'm still surprised she let the crew help install the cabinets." Beau looks around at what still needs to be finished.

Tony begins collecting tools as the sun sets over another summer evening. He sees headlights cutting through the property, and his heartbeat picks up a little when he realizes its Frankie's car.

A few minutes later, two little girls bound up the steps and into the kitchen. They are both talking so fast and loudly. No one can make sense of what either is saying. They finish and burst into fits of giggles.

"For the record, Aunt E loaded them up with sugar, not me," Frankie says as she holds up one hand in surrender. Her other hand has car keys and a small potted succulent. "I just offered to bring them here, so blame her for the craziness."

"Well, I'd ask if you had fun, but I think I already know the answer." Tony beams at his niece as she buries her head into his side. A yawn escapes her lips. "I think it's time to get you home."

Beau gathers up his things and directs the girls outside, "Come on, girls, help me get my tools in the truck."

As the room quiets, Tony leans up against the counter. Crossing his arms and feet. Last time he was alone in this room with her, it didn't end well. This time he's using all the restraint he has in his body not to kiss her.

Frankie holds out the succulent, "Thank you. Are flowers too cliché for you?"

A nervous laugh escapes his lips. "No, Ma'am. You told me one time that flowers dying in a vase made you sad. So, until I can plant you real flowers somewhere, I thought that would be a good placeholder."

She places the small pot next to her keys on the counter. "How's your jaw?"

He shrugs. "A small price."

"Sammy told me not to break your heart and ruin his friendship."

He laughs, "It sounds like we both got the same speech."

She looks down at her feet.

"Uh oh, I don't like that look."

"Tony, I don't know what this means with us. Nothing has changed. I still have a lot of baggage. I don't know if I'm ready for this." Frankie waves her hands between the two of them.

Tony's natural instinct is to wrap her in his arms, but he can't risk spooking her. He knows that would have her building more brick walls. "I'm not asking for anything but a chance. Can we start with a date? One date, that's all I'm asking." He watches her mind race.

She nods. Tony smiles and breathes a sigh of relief. "I'm leaving before you change your mind. Go water your succulent."

He watches a small smile bloom on her face. He grabs his tools and skips down the back stairs where Beau is shaking his head and laughing at him.

Nunnie Mary

Every morning for Mary Marchio begins on a porch swing. Unless it's winter. Even then, she sometimes manages it with her favorite blanket and hot coffee. Today is no exception. The swing sways beneath her. She is comforted by the creaking of the chains as she reads down through her prayer list.

Mary reaches the bottom of the list as her eyes skim over the page and land on Frankie's name. She takes a sip of coffee and looks out from her front porch. The morning sun breaks through the branches causing shadows to dance around the yard. Mary used to watch dancing shadows from her bedroom window as a child. Her parents barely survived the Great Depression as children. Mary imagines how living through that would change a person forever. Her father was called up to the Army right after he married. When he returned from the war, her father worked two jobs, but his second income usually went to the bottle.

Her father was a good man, but he came home with a limp from the war and never recovered. He worked for another Italian man in town who owned a grocery store. The Italians in town always looked out for one another. They had to. At night, her father swept up at a local pool hall. There was a secret backroom where all the action took place. Gambling and moonshine were the commodities. Mary and her sisters used to run numbers from bookies to their father. The police never thought to stop teenage bobby-soxers.

Mary was the oldest and soon stopped the running when a high school teacher caught her sleeping in class one day. Sister Jane saw potential in Mary. Soon enough, Mary was helping Sister Jane at the orphanage across the street from the high school. That is where Mary found her calling to serve others. She even considered becoming a nun herself.

Then she met Salvatore "Salvo" Marchio. The rest was history.

Mary's youngest sister wasn't so lucky. Connie continued running numbers for the bookies even after their father had passed. With Mary finishing school, her sisters Roxie and Thelma started helping their mother with sewing and laundry to pay the bills, but Connie kept making her way back to the pool hall. Without her father's protection, the rules changed.

Connie took up with a musician who blew all his money on blackjack every night. They ran off and got married before she finished high school. Mary and Roxie knew Mack McGovern was trouble, but Connie convinced them she was okay. Little by little, the bruises couldn't be hidden, and Connie's dresses were stitched together to cover tears by the zipper.

Connie became harder and harder to reach. She stopped going over to Mama's house and she whittled down to skin and bones. Connie flinched any time a door slammed, or a man yelled. Salvo and Guy, Roxie's husband, paid Mack a few visits. They tried to help him get clean, but he didn't want to.

Mack loved whiskey, gambling, and women, just not Connie. Mack would go missing for days on end. Connie usually could find him at his girlfriend's house if she needed him, but one night he didn't come home, and it turned into a week. His body was never found, but everyone in the pool hall seemed to know where he was, and it wasn't above ground. No one talked about it, and no one mourned his death.

Connie lost their house, what was left of it. It was a shack of a place anyway with cracked windows and missing floorboards. Connie moved back in with Mama. She started sewing for ladies in the neighborhood and found a following as a seamstress. Mama told the sisters about Connie's nightmares. The screaming had Mama lighting candles at church every morning. Mary hears the same screaming at night from Frankie's room. Frankie is a locked chest like Connie was all those years ago, but Mary has no doubt that Frankie ran across the wrong man, just like Connie.

She prays for Frankie every day. She's close to all of her grandchildren and loves them equally, but Frankie reminds Mary of Connie. She is strong, stubborn, and fiercely loyal when she lets you into her world. Frankie needs healing, and Mary knows there is only one place Frankie will find it.

The creaking of the front door triggers her focus back to the front porch. Esther gently closes the door behind her then makes her way across the space. She sits beside Mary on the swing and reaches over for her mother's hand.

"Frankie went upstairs to take a shower. She made cinnamon rolls from scratch for the production crew today and made extra for us. Did you see them? They are delicious."

"I saw, and I ate one. Frankie brought me out a fresh one when I started my Bible time."

"She made me a plate to take to the warehouse too when she found out her dad would be there with Sammy."

Mary is surprised to hear that, and Esther seems to notice.

"Do you know what's going on with her and Sam? He hasn't been himself. One of the girls at the office overheard Dom and Sammy talking about a fight with Frankie."

"It's not my story to tell, but I'm praying for a resolution. Your brother asked me to stay out of it. Misunderstandings can destroy a family. You know that all too well. If someone doesn't clear it up soon, I'm going to start educating people." Mary drinks her coffee.

"Mama!" Esther chortles at her mother's passion. "I haven't seen you get so riled up about something since I was a teenager."

"I know, and I shouldn't get involved, but this is getting out of control. I might be a forgiving Christian woman, but I'm also a Mama Bear. That is all I'm saying about the matter. For now, at least."

They rock for a few moments in silence.

"The leaves will start changing in a few weeks. That is my favorite time on this porch. I'll miss it," Esther sighs.

Mary looks over at her daughter with a wry smile. "Why would you miss fall on the front porch?"

A smile that Mary hasn't seen on Esther in years spreads across her face. Esther came home as a broken and bitter woman who had lost her daughter, sister, and husband in a very short span. The joy and peace on her face today is contagious.

"Well, Mama, Wes Anderson has asked me to marry him. I just got off the phone with Haddie. She's excited for me, so I'm going to tell him yes."

Mary reaches over and touches E's face. "My sweet darling girl, it's about time. That boy has wanted to marry you for over forty years."

"Funny, those are the exact words he used when he asked. Oh Mama, I can't believe this. What a crazy journey."

"Have you two discussed details or a timeline?"

"Nothing concrete, but I'd like something quick and small. A bride at my age. What am I thinking?" Esther shakes her head, an unmistakable smile is etched on her face. "Oh Mama, I can't believe this. I'm marrying Wes Anderson." Esther giggles like a silly school girl.

"Well, I'm glad you two aren't running off to Atlantic City like you'd planned after your high school graduation." Mary knowingly looks at her adult daughter.

"You knew about that?" Her mother nods. "Why didn't you say anything?"

"Mothers know everything. We were letting it play out a while before we said something, hoping you two would wait. Then all the drama happened and you broke up with him. There was no need to say anything at that point. I always wondered what we would have done." Mary pats Esther's knee. "I think a wedding in the gazebo Beau built would be lovely. If we work quickly, you could have it as the trees turn colors."

"That would be perfect. I always wanted to get married in the fall. John's mother insisted on that stuffy family cathedral in June. That wedding never felt like me at all, but I had John when it was all over, so I didn't care what his uptight mother did."

"I remember it like it was yesterday. Daddy asked if John was related to the Kennedys with all the pomp and circumstance."

"This wedding will be nothing like that one." Esther giggles like a blushing bride. "Listen to me. I can only imagine what John would say."

"You know what I loved most about John? He treated you as more precious than gold. No parent can ask for more. He was a good man. He would be very happy for you."

"Thanks, Mama." Esther wipes a tear running down her cheek. They both look up as the screen door opens.

"What's going on? Everything okay?" Concern crosses Frankie's face.

"How do you feel about a wedding at Poppy's?" Esther smiles at her niece.

"Good grief! I only agreed to one date! This family has some serious issues." Frankie sees the puzzled looks on Aunt E and Nunnie's faces. "This isn't about me, is it?" They shake their heads no. "Then, who is getting married?"

Esther pats the swing next to her. "I am, but now we have some questions for you."

Frankie lowers her head and walks toward her interrogation.

Frankie

By the time Frankie escapes the great inquisition on the front porch, she is exhausted and hasn't even dealt with Lisa yet. Filming starts today along with preparation for the family's busiest marketing season. Regional fairs and festivals ramp up from now throughout the fall. They have back to back festivals coming up and Labor Day weekend is their biggest event. Frankie's mind races as her to do list grows out of control.

She drives along the back road from the farmhouse to Poppy's. She sees Sammy's truck parked beside an access road to the vines. He loves this place. Her brother drives her crazy, but she loves him more than he'll ever know. She's so proud of how he runs the company. Some people were worried when Daddy wanted to retire, but not Sam. He knew Sammy could do it. Sam has always trusted his kids, always pushed them, and always knew they would succeed, even in their mistakes.

Frankie has seen her father a few times, but they've managed to avoid any conversation longer than basic pleasantries. That actually breaks her heart the most. There was a time she talked to him every day on the phone. He was her rock. She's buried so many things, but lately, everything is coming to the surface. It's making her anxious. Frankie doesn't like anxious.

Knowing her dad, he is giving her space until she is ready to talk. Eventually, she will have to face him. She feels guilty about being upset with him. He didn't cheat on her. He cheated on her mother. Obviously, her mom forgave him. Why shouldn't Frankie? These and many other thoughts tumble through her mind daily. She answers each nagging question against a punching bag.

On top of everything else, there is this date with Tony looming in the near future. They agreed to wait until after Labor Day Weekend. The West Virginia Italian Heritage Festival takes up the entire weekend for her family. Tony has always been there to help in the family tents. Frankie agreed to dinner on Monday evening. Butterflies fill her stomach just thinking about it. She'll see him all weekend, but they will be too busy to even sit down, let alone talk. Monday is better. She has a week to push their date out of her mind, and not enough free time to stress about it.

There are two vans parked on the side of Poppy's restaurant as Frankie pulls into the parking lot. The morning is still quiet. A light haze hovers over the lush green landscape. Poppy's is framed by hills on one side and the vineyard on the other two sides. Frankie watches the crew hoist boxes and wires onto the outside lift system that Tony designed. She wonders how all of this happened. Six months ago, no one knew her name. Now she is getting ready to shoot a much-anticipated television special with a waiting list of sponsors.

After parking her car and taking a deep breath, she gathers the container of cinnamon rolls and makes her way to the set. Maryssa and Lisa are pointing and talking as the crew busies themselves around the studio. Frankie places the gooey rolls on a table off to the side with the water bottles and a coffee station. She strolls to her kitchen set and sees a bouquet of purple wildflowers.

She opens the card, "There is a myth that Aster leaves were burned to fight off evil. Their name means star. They symbolize patience. I chose these because they remind me of you. You are a fighter and you are beautiful. You, however, are not patient, but I am. -T" Laughing out loud, Frankie grabs her phone and sends a quick text to Tony.

Frankie: The cheesy smiley face at the end of the card doesn't help your case. You can't tell a girl she's impatient with a smiley face.

Tony: Do I get bonus points for the mythology? I did a lot of research.

Frankie: I'm not sure. I don't want to rush my answer. I will patiently consider my response and get back to you.

Tony: Then, I shall patiently await your answer.

Frankie leans down and smells the simple purple flowers. Their faces look like stars. She sends another quick text.

Frankie: Thank you.

Tony: Good luck today. Don't focus on the cameras and the crew. Just do what you do best.....own the room.

Frankie hasn't owned a room in a long time. Her confidence is shaky at best. She wonders what he sees in her and if she has any of that left to pull out for the cameras today.

"Frankie, what do you think?"

Frankie shakes the cobwebs. "I'm sorry, what?"

Lisa leans down and smells the flowers. "Mmm, I see we have a distraction. Interesting. Who sent the beautiful flowers?

Frankie tucks the card inside her back pocket.

"They're from a friend. No biggie. Now, what are we talking about?"

Maryssa sees right through the act but, as always, has her cousin's back. "Lisa was thinking about filming our prep work for the festival and including the footage with voice-overs and festival coverage. I need to contact the festival office and make sure they're okay with it, but it will give them national coverage, so I'm sure it will be fine."

Lisa jumps in on Maryssa's explanation. "I've already talked to the execs. They love the idea. We can launch your show in front of Maryssa's season premiere. We'll market it like a spinoff with a crossover episode. We'll promote the night as 'Fairs, Festivals, and Family Fun' or 'Family Traditions, Festival Edition' well, you get the idea. I'm still working on the theme."

"Whatever you think will work. I'm game." Frankie hopes her anxiety is hidden.

"I told her that filming all the cousins and aunts baking cookies together would be reality TV at its best." Maryssa laughs at the thought.

"You might need to bring in the censors. We can get a little wild when everyone is baking."

"I'm counting on it." Lisa beams with ratings anticipation. "Do you think we can get Haddie to participate? Having the First Lady of the United States would be huge."

"I'll ask, but I wouldn't hold my breath if I were you. Haddie is camera shy, as you well know." Maryssa shrugs, already knowing that Haddie will give them a hard pass on that request.

"Trust me, I know. I've never met anyone like Haddie. The audience begged for more of her, but she hid in the background of every shot. Honestly, I think Haddie is the reason Sandra left reality TV altogether." Lisa shakes her head, "Ask Haddie anyway, let's see what she says."

"In Haddie's defense, that was my fault. She was so mad at me for signing her up to do the show." Maryssa glares at Frankie, "Don't you dare repeat my confession."

Frankie holds up both hands in defense, "My lips are sealed."

Lisa's expression changes instantaneously as she grabs one of Frankie's hands and examines it. "Um, what is all this?"

Frankie attempts to pull her hand back, but Lisa's vise-like grip prevents it.

Lisa speaks very slowly, "Frankie? What is up with your hands? Did someone slam a trunk on them, or is there something I need to know?" Lisa looks back and forth between the two of them. "You do realize that a baking show will focus on your hands, right?"

"Frankie's workout routine revolves around boxing," Maryssa attempts to explain, but Lisa holds up her hand.

"I understand the discipline of exercise. I allow a sadistic spin teacher to scream at me every morning. I don't so much as have a callous on my hands. You need a new workout." Lisa is seething.

"I can wrap my hands better. I'll wear gloves always and not spar." Frankie begins over-sharing, her go-to nervous response. "My trainer yells at me when I don't use my gloves. It's not the workout, it's me. Sometimes, I get a little anxious and start before properly preparing. Whew, that's a tongue twister. Scout's honor, I'll do better. They'll be better by filming."

"No. Absolutely not. We cannot have your hands bruised and cut up during filming. This is non-negotiable. Tell me you understand?" Lisa studies Frankie's face severely. "Frankie?"

Frankie nods.

"Okay then. Well, let's get you two set up for initial interviews. I'll make sure the camera stays away from those hands today." Lisa turns and begins barking orders at the crew.

Maryssa squeezes Frankie's arm and smiles reassuringly. "There is a sadistic part of me that wants to

meet the spin instructor who gets to tell Lisa what to do."
They both laugh as the room bursts with activity.

As the day unfolds, it is even more exhausting than
Frankie had anticipated this morning. All she wants is a hot
shower and a good night sleep for once, but she has to be
back at Poppy's in an hour. She hopes to squeeze in a
minute alone before dinner. Frankie finally makes it to her
car, only to realize her window for down time is short. When
Nunnie calls a family meeting, everyone attends. It doesn't
matter that someone has been scrutinized under lights and
cameras all day.

Frankie is delirious from answering questions about
herself for hours on end. Lisa and the crew sat off-camera all
morning, firing questions and baiting Frankie. It was so
surreal. She has watched these types of shows for years and
always wondered how they conducted the interviews. Now
she realizes that every word is a potential soundbite that can
be used at any moment. Her head is spinning. She spent the
afternoon rethinking every answer.

Beau and Tony stopped by the studio at lunchtime.
Maryssa took them to Poppy's and fed them while Frankie
finished her interview segments. As Tony was leaving the
studio, he paused to smell the flowers and gave her a cheesy
thumbs up and a rotten grin. He made her so flustered that
Lisa called cut and restarted the segment. That made him
laugh harder, which earned him a massive glare from both
Frankie and Lisa.

Tonight is the family planning meeting for the Italian
Heritage Festival. Tony will probably show up for directions
and dinner. That makes Frankie want a shower even more.
She quickly darts into the house and up the stairs to the
bathroom, relived to find it unoccupied.

The bathroom fills with steam as warm water soothes
her tense muscles. Eucalyptus lather refreshes her foggy

thoughts and leaves her nose tingling. She turns off the water and grabs her towel. She swipes the mirror so she can see, but her eyes fall onto her hands. The shades of purple and yellow on her knuckles make her wince. For the first time, Frankie sees her hands as others do, marred. Ironically, her coping mechanism has left as many marks as the violation itself.

Nunnie knocks on the bathroom door, no doubt to hurry along Frankie. Frankie quickly wraps her curly hair into a messy bun, then swipes on lip balm and does a final mirror check. She grabs her favorite jean shorts and WVU t-shirt. She ties her tennis shoes and grabs her phone before heading downstairs to drive Nunnie back to Poppy's.

By the time they arrive, the family is ready to set the large farmhouse table located by the kitchen door. Water and tea glasses are filled. Big bowls of spaghetti are placed in the middle of the table. Nunnie immediately herds everyone toward their seats as hugs and kisses are passed around between family. Once the prayer of thanksgiving is spoken, conversations erupt as plates are passed. Frankie is equally relieved and disappointed that Tony is absent from dinner.

Aunt Jo takes charge as she passes out copies of the schedule. One page for setup and take-down of the tents, detailed by person and supply list. Another for the work schedules, which are non-negotiable. All hands will be on deck Friday morning before the festival begins for prep work and last-minute issues.

"Everyone is expected at the farmhouse this week to help make pepperoni rolls and strombolis and to bake and package cookies. Mom has assured me that her new kitchen is up for the task." Aunt Jo looks at Nunnie, who nods to reaffirm any concerns. "We all have our marching orders. Let me know if you have any questions. Any complaints should be written on a piece of paper then promptly tossed in the garbage." Everyone laughs, but they know it's true. Festival weekend is a great family rally event, but it is exhausting.

Frankie flips through the schedule as Aunt Jo answers questions. Equal portions of butterflies and irritation erupt in her stomach when she reads that her scheduled work times correspond with Tony's.

Haddie

The online shopping cart is filled, t-shirt sizes are verified, and checkout is now complete. With a satisfied grin, Haddie closes her laptop and checks her phone to read the latest text message. She settles back into the leather couch and responds to her mother's fiftieth text in an hour.

She hears footsteps walking down the center hallway. Jackson's habits warm her heart. He kicks off his shoes and tosses his jacket on the bed. His favorite pen is placed on his dresser. Haddie smiles, picturing him and his rituals in the adjacent room.

"Had? Where are you?"

"I'm in here, Babe."

She can read his demeanor by the way he enters a room. When she met Jackson on the set, she thought he was a player and a flirt. She didn't vote for him, and she certainly didn't want to date him. She had a successful ballet career and was in her last year of college, on the cusp of physical therapy school. When he took the oath of office as the youngest president in American history, he was otherworldly, with boundless energy and positivity. Haddie couldn't stand him.

His boyish charm and sincere heart wormed his way into her good graces. Once she allowed him in, she saw the man he is and the leader he wanted to be. The man who once annoyed her now inspires her each and every day.

Jackson gives Haddie credit for his new outlook on politics. He has always had a gift for seeing both sides of an issue. She just happens to be the voice of the other side. Sometimes she feels guilt over that fact. The more bipartisan he becomes, the more his party turns on him. His platform hasn't changed, but his ability to compromise has.

The impeachment is a painful blow to Jackson. Haddie sees it weighing him down more and more each day. The pep in his step is waning. Lines are forming around his eyes and lips. He isn't sleeping, and he's lost weight. Somedays she wishes he was just a guy she met at a coffee shop, but deep down she knows they were both called for such a time as this.

Jackson walks over and kisses the top of her head before maneuvering around to sit on the couch next to her. He pulls off his loosened tie and lays back into the couch. His feet plop up onto the cherry coffee table. Haddie snickers, "Do those socks have unicorns on them?"

Jackson wiggles his toes. "They sure do. When the cutest eight-year-old niece in the world sends you unicorn socks, you wear them."

She gently places her hand on his cheek. "I've missed that smile. It's so you, pure and hopeful."

Jackson turns to press his lips into the palm of her hand. He squirms closer to her and wraps an arm around her shoulder. They sit cuddled up together. It's cathartic.

"How was your afternoon?" His thumb rubs her shoulder.

Haddie turns her attention to her next project as First Lady. "It was good, actually. I met with the Coalition of Community Centers. I'm going to sit on a committee that will get history and literacy programs into the centers through community outreach. I'm specifically tasked with brainstorming ideas on how to get local businesses involved."

"It sounds like you've been talking to Governor Marchio. Didn't he spearhead a similar program for the Allied States?" Jackson eyes his wife suspiciously. "You know, the First Lady usually just serves as the ambassador or image-bearer for groups, right? You aren't expected to man the trenches of the committee. However, this new Eleanor Roosevelt side of you makes me want to debate your Republican status again," he winks.

"I appreciate your concern Mr. President, but I care very deeply about this program. And if you recall, I am a Republican at heart. I'm a fan of Governor Marchio, and I like what he's doing. It's working. Their crime rate is two-thirds lower than ours, and their educational models are fascinating."

Her heart sinks as soon as the words leave her mouth. Their relationship began with sparring, or as Madison calls it, debate dating. Jackson may be too raw for that now. "I'm sorry, I was making a generalized statement. I'm just excited about this program. This has nothing to do with your programs, which truly are making a big difference. I just want to find a way to help too."

"I know, I'm just tired of fighting for every initiative. Every positive change is met with opposition and bargaining. I feel more like a broker than the president. The politics of politics are killing the country."

"Says the career politician." A sarcastic smile crosses her face.

"The irony, right?" He shakes his head and rests it on the cool, soft leather of the couch. "I love your passion, and I love that you are working on this project. It's not even your admiration for John Marchio that frustrates me. It's the fact that I can't get everyone on the same page. Why can't grown adults choose to look at each concept based on face value? I feel as if every topic is hyper sensualized into identity politics. Common sense is out the window and both sides of the aisle are slamming and barricading their doors. Moderates are thrown under both buses and seen as weak. It's like living in the *Twilight Zone*." Jackson rubs his chin, deep in thought. "I'm sorry, Babe. I completely hijacked your story. I just can't believe the Allied States representatives are refusing to consider another reunification summit. Everything is so fractured."

Haddie nestles into his embrace and snakes an arm around his waist. "Sweetheart, the country was fractured for a long time before the Separation. At least now the riots have decreased."

"Great, my own wife is against reunification. I can't even convince the one person who hears all my inner thoughts." He rubs his temples with one hand.

"I'm not against reunification at all. I'm an old school patriot. I'm devastated that visiting my family involves the Secretary of State being consulted." Haddie looks up at Jackson. "No one wanted to separate, but no one wanted to listen either. Remember how bad it was before the Separation? The middle was phased out, while opposite sides were polarized and demonized. People were afraid to say anything for fear of being canceled, defriended, fired, or even splitting up their families. Madison's aunt completely disowned her. It wasn't pretty. The riots, the fires, the devastation. It was too much, and neither side backed down from the rhetoric. Both sides felt vindicated and justified in their cause."

"Haddie, I can't. Not tonight," he says, exasperated.

"I'm sorry. You know I'm on your side. I'm just trying to give you another outlook. You've spent your presidency trying to be President Lincoln, but maybe you need to go about it from a different angle. Maybe instead of expecting a thriving garden, you start with planting seeds and building bridges? You might get farther with both sides and both countries. Instead of trying to be Lincoln, focus on being Jackson."

He leans down and softly kisses her lips. "Haddie Marie Robinson Cashe, you are one wise woman."

"I must get it from Nunnie." She chuckles, "That woman…"

"Spent a lifetime praying on her knees." Jackson finishes her sentence from memory.

They cuddle together, enjoying a rare moment of quiet. Haddie's phone breaks the silence. She grunts.

"What's with the groaning? Who is texting you?" Jackson peeks at the cell phone screen.

"My mother. She keeps sending me pictures of wedding cakes and dresses and flowers and anything else she sees. Then she texts telling me she shouldn't use any of them because it's just a small wedding. Then she'll text that she should just run off and get married. Then she asks if I'm okay with her getting married. Then the cycle starts all over again. It's exhausting."

"*Are* you okay with it?" He twists one of her curls in his fingers.

"I totally am okay with it. She was so sad after Dad, and Lizzie, and Aunt Ruth. Wes has given her a new spark. I mean, I wish my dad was still here to do that, but he's not. Wes seems like a really nice guy, and he makes her happy, younger." Haddie rests her head on his shoulder. "Not to mention, his security investigation came back clean," Haddie snickers.

"She's just excited to see you. She wants you to be a part of the planning."

"Ugh, I know. I've never seen Mom so indecisive, though. It's, I don't know, odd."

"It's sweet. She wants everything to be perfect."

"I hate it when you're right."

"In that case, I'm stopping while I'm ahead. You just admitted that I am right about something. I want to end this day on a high note. First Lady Cashe, are you ready for bed? I have a long day tomorrow."

She stands up first and holds out her hand to him. "Aren't all of your days long?"

"Touché, wife."

Jackson wraps his arm tightly around Haddie's waist as they walk back into the master bedroom in their borrowed White House. "For the record, I'm glad you're working on the committee. I think it will be good for you and the committee, even if you are a Republican."

Haddie elbows him in the ribs. "Hey! Maybe you should switch sides. You know that Abraham Lincoln was a Republican, right?"

Jackson Cashe, the trivia king of North America, sighs, "You don't say."

Frankie

Frankie pulls her car around to the back of the farmhouse. She parks and pops her hatch. Tony is descending the backstairs before she closes her door. "Need any help?" Tony's boyish charm exudes from his face.

"I thought you were finished with the kitchen."

"I am. Mary wanted to ask me a question about the dishwasher, but I'm pretty sure she timed it with you coming home." He flashes his boyish smile.

Frankie's eyes automatically roll upward. "That's why she kept asking when I was leaving the grocery store. Well, as long as you're here, you can help me carry in these boxes. I have the ingredients for all of the festival cookies."

"It should be an interesting weekend. The Secret Service brigade is already inside doing their thing. I wasn't sure they were going to let me talk to Mary."

"Oh, that's right. I forgot Haddie will be here soon. Usually, when she comes to visit, I stay at my parent's house to avoid the secret suits. I can't do that now."

"You know, you're going to have to talk to your dad at some point." Tony's stare pins her to her spot.

"I know, just not right now. My life is out of control. I can't add anything else to it. I can't even go to the gym."

"You mean you can't punch people?" He ignores her glare, "Why not?"

She juggles a box on her hip while opening the screen door on the back porch. She places her box against the wall by the kitchen door. "Lisa said they couldn't film my hands with boxing bruises. I need to lay off and heal my knuckles."

"That makes sense." He places his box next to hers. "By the way, why *do* you have bruises on your knuckles? I know plenty of guys who box and don't bruise. Do you need better gloves?" he asks, but he already knows the answer.

"I don't always wear gloves. I just tape."

"Mm-hmm, and why is that?"

She looks up at him defensively. "Why do you care?"

"Hey, try to remember that I'm not the enemy." Tony gently reaches for her bruised hand and turns it over in his, examining it closely. He lifts it to his lips. "And you know why."

Frankie pulls her hand away and tucks an errant strand of hair behind her ear. She looks at the ground. He lifts her chin with his finger.

"You can't keep everyone out, Frankie. You spend all your time fighting. One of these days, you need to tell those of us who love you what you're fighting so we can have your back."

"I think you've been spending too much time with Nunnie. You're getting all philosophical on me." Frankie offers a hollow laugh.

"Maybe." He smiles back at her, "She's a pretty smart lady."

Frankie stubbornly wipes away her tear with a fist. "Yes, she is. Let's move on, you're really getting on my nerves."

"I try." He touches her face. "I need to run. We're having a family meeting about Darren and Heather taking over the store."

"Wow, that's great."

"I know. Heather loves that place. I had no idea Darren was also interested in the store. They'll take it to a whole new level. I'm relieved. I'll find out tonight how Big Tony feels, but according to my mother, he's happy. We'll see."

They stand together, cocooned in the quiet of the screened-in back porch. Both have been here countless times, but the air feels different now. It's electric. Rays of late afternoon sun dance around them in this space. The heat of the day, warming them. Tony wants so badly to kiss her, but he doesn't want to scare her off more. She breaks the moment.

"I need to get inside and set up cookie stations. Mi familia should be here soon to help bake."

"Yeah, I don't want to be late for dinner at Rosie's. I'll see you Friday."

"Okay."

"Okay." Tony turns to leave the porch and Frankie.

A coldness fills her the closer he gets to his truck and the farther away from her. The kitchen door opens behind her. Nunnie stands in the doorframe with a dishwasher instruction booklet in her hands. "Frankie, you just missed Tony."

"Give it up, lady. I'm on to you." Frankie kisses Nunnie's cheek as she squeezes past her grandmother into the kitchen.

"I'm not sure I know what you mean," but the ornery look on her face contradicts her words.

"Sure, you don't." Frankie hangs her keys on a pegboard by the phone and starts pulling pans and bowls out of cabinets. "What time is everyone coming for cookie duty?"

"Soon." Mary places the booklet in the drawer where she keeps all of her instructions. "In my defense, I couldn't remember how to change the wash cycle." The woman shrugs.

Aunt E walks into the room and looks at her two roommates. "It looks like I missed something good."

"You didn't miss a thing, sweetheart. Frankie is accusing me of interfering in her relationship with Tony. I'm just an innocent old woman trying to run her new dishwasher."

Aunt E laughs. Frankie gasps. "I don't have a relationship with Tony!"

"I have no idea what happened, but I fully believe Frankie on this one." Her voice trails to the front of the house as Frankie huffs and gathers her tools.

The calvary arrives in shifts. Aunt Jo puts Frankie in charge, but only for the night. Frankie has the younger cousins lining cookie sheets with parchment paper. Nunnie, the oven-boss, has a notebook, pencil, and a timer. Cooling racks are arranged across the dining room table. A card table is supplied with clear pastry boxes for packaging. They have stickers designed with the logos from all three family businesses, Rafaluzza Vineyard, Poppy's, and Frankie's Confections.

Ingredients are lined up and labeled in bowls on the large island. Measuring cups are scattered beside the bowls. Everyone is assigned a task for each cookie. First up is the galette batter, which will sit in the refrigerator until tomorrow night. They are making snowballs, anise cookies, and Aunt Roxie's lemon cookies tonight. Tomorrow they will attack thumbprint cookies, nut rolls, mini-biscotti, and galettes.

Baking with her family symbolizes everything Frankie loves in life. Happiness is unending. Conversations are educational and riveting. Memories are emotionally charged. Knowing these recipes have been passed from generation to generation and crossed an ocean, not once, but three times to end up in this kitchen is overwhelming. She remembers watching her great-aunts making these exact cookies as a child. Every Christmas, wedding, baptism, shower, and special occasion started with these same sugary staples. Baking erases the worries around her. It is everything in her life that is good.

Nunnie wraps an arm around Frankie's waist. "They're all here helping, for you. This family is a gift from God. Most people don't have this. You have it and keep us at bay. You didn't always do that."

Frankie looks at her grandmother. Nunnie's words feel worse than a punch from Deena. She stammers but can't say anything. She knows that Nunnie is right.

"You're not alone, you know that, right? The Bible tells us to bear one another's burdens. It's hard to do that when you don't share anything. This family has been through a lot. We can handle your burdens too, if you let us." Mary plants a kiss on Frankie's cheek and walks back to the oven.

Uncle Dom's voice rises above the others. "Sam, remember that time when Daddy let E drive the car up the road to pick you up from practice?"

Frankie watches her dad's face light up with the memory. "That was the best ride home from school I've ever had."

Aunt E picks up one of the dud cookies from the table and throws it at her brother. "I had to miss the school dance for that stunt."

Uncle Dom tells the rest of the story. "E just got her license. Daddy let her drive the car to pick up Sam at baseball practice. E was too busy flirting with Wes Anderson to realize that Sam took the car and drove it around the block."

"I would have gotten away with it if Mrs. Pascella hadn't see me and called Mama."

"What do you mean? You didn't get into trouble, I did!"

"That's not true, I had to wash Daddy's car," Sam protests.

"To take it to the dance that I missed!"

"Esther, you didn't miss the dance because of the car. You missed the dance because Daddy heard you were flirting with Wes. The car was just an excuse." Nunnie joins into the laughter now. "Daddy loved Wes as Sam's friend, but not flirting with you."

"Well, that explains a lot. Daddy never let me drive his car. As usual, the older kids ruined it for me," Aunt Jo laments while glaring at her siblings. The whole room bubbles with mirth.

As they mix, roll, cut, and bake, love surrounds them. Frankie looks around at her imperfect family and sees love and acceptance from every angle. Even Sammy and Dom are covered in powdered sugar. Nunnie's words float around her brain. Everyone showed up for her tonight, just like they always do.

Tony

The streets of downtown are completely blocked off with barrels and sawhorses. Both sides of the road are lined with wall to wall booths, standing picnic tables, speakers, and bleachers. Rows of folding chairs are placed in front of the main stage, which takes up the entire courthouse square. Italian folk music pumps through the speaker system and can be heard all throughout town. Garlic, sizzling ribeye sandwiches, and frittis frying in oil permeate the air. A travel magazine once described the West Virginia Italian Heritage Festival as a street fair meets Little Italy.

This is Tony's favorite weekend of the year. Not only do friends and family come back to town to celebrate together every Labor Day weekend, but he spends all three days in the Marchio booths as part of the family. His sister served on the festival court, along with most of the Marchio girls at one point or another. This weekend Harmony will be a minor court princess. Her green silk gown with the white sash has been hanging on her closet door for weeks. She is excited to walk on the big stage with the queen. Heather had Harmony begin primping this morning at the crack of dawn.

Tony was up until midnight constructing the booths with Sammy, Dominick, their dads, and Beau. They arrived early this morning to make sure the ovens, coolers, and fans are working. Temperatures are predicted to reach eighty-four degrees, but with the tents sitting on black asphalt in the middle of town, it will feel closer to one hundred.

The area is bustling with vendors stocking up and volunteers checking off task lists. The festival officially kicks off at noon with the coronation of Regina Maria and her court. Tony set up camping chairs for his parents, his sister and her in-laws in front of the stage. He'll sneak over to watch Harmony when she is introduced. She called him this morning to make sure Uncle Tony would be there and told him all about the curlers she had to sleep in last night. He loves that little girl.

For now, he focuses on his responsibilities in the tents. He'll help Sammy with wine sales once they open. He finds a rare moment with nothing pressing to do, so he leans against the makeshift counter until someone needs him. This allows Tony to watch the family in action. Mary and Frankie arrange the containers of assorted cookies while Maryssa, Haddie, and Esther post the prices for stuffed pepperoni rolls and tomato salad. Sammy and Dominick talk with a festival official about ID wristbands and colored cups. Jo walks around with her clipboard looking over everyone's shoulder.

Sam walks over and hands Tony a water bottle from the cooler. "The key is to avoid eye contact with Jo. She's the baby of the family, but she runs a tight ship."

Tony has no idea if Sam knows about his upcoming date with Frankie. Sam Marchio is like a second father to Tony. He's been debating whether he should ask permission to date her or wait until it gets serious. How does one handle a situation in which you're in love with your coach's-slash-best-friend's-dad's-daughter? He takes a swig of water then takes a breath of courage. "Sam, I need to talk to you about something if you have a minute."

Sam looks straight ahead, not even glancing at Tony, and holds up his hand. "I know. If it has to be someone, I'm glad it's you, but I don't want to know anything. It goes without saying that even though I love you like a son, I have a shotgun, a lot of land, and a big shovel."

"Yes, sir." Tony is equally relieved and nervous by Sam's statement.

"Okay then, good talk." Sam drinks his water then pats Tony on the back. "I noticed how you boys positioned most of the fans so that your tent get the best cross-ventilation."

"That was Sammy's idea."

"I have no doubt." Sam points out to the crowd, "You better get a seat, or you'll miss Harmony."

Tony turns to Sam square on and shakes his hand before walking over to the stage. He thinks he saw a small sliver of a smile on Sam's face, but can't be sure. Tony watches Harmony walk across the stage with her white gloves and basket of flowers. She blows him a kiss from her chair in the front row. He arrives back in time to help with the lunch rush at the booth. His family stops over to sit behind the tent and eat with whichever Marchios are on break. Chloe and Harmony are connected at the hip. Tony's heart is full today.

As the day wears down, the crowds get bigger. A big country act is coming on later tonight, so the numbers will double soon. After the dinner rush, they enjoy a lull before the next wave of people.

Tony takes a seat beside Haddie and Nunnie at the back of the booth. He whispers into Haddie's ear, "I think your wig is crooked."

She glares at him. "I already punched Sammy for making jokes about this stupid wig I have to wear. I would watch it if I were you."

"Mary, what is it about your family? They all like to punch people. I'm starting to wonder about how they were raised." Tony jokes with the matriarch of this empire.

"Why don't you come over here. I'll show you where they got it from, Anthony." Haddie spits out her water, trying to contain herself. Tony shakes his head. No one ever knows what will come out of Mary Marchio's mouth.

"Seriously, Haddie, did the wig fool anyone?" Tony tries to contain his laughter.

"Well, I stayed in the back the whole day with this stinking wig. Jackson had a fake calendar leaked to reporters. It gives the appearance that I am in D.C. all weekend. Everyone here who knows me will keep it quiet."

"Where is your team of agents? Did you give them the slip again? I've only seen Travis." He looks around the tent.

Haddie triumphantly beams, "I bought them all WVU t-shirts. Now, they will blend in all weekend. Travis played four years of college ball against WVU. He isn't happy at all with me."

"Man, you are one sneaky celebrity. I'm impressed."

"Thanks, Tony. I'd like to think I'm resourceful, not sneaky," she winks at him.

Tony leans across Haddie and looks at Mary, "I'm assuming she gets her 'resourcefulness' from you too?" His air quotes elicit a chuckle from Travis.

"Anthony, don't make me call Rosie." Mary is always one step ahead.

"No, Ma'am. We don't want that." Tony straightens up in his chair as Haddie snickers at him.

Their conversation is interrupted by the sound of a crashing pan on the pavement. Travis jumps in front of Haddie in addition to four other agents wearing blue and gold t-shirts. By the time they realize Haddie is safe, Tony is on his feet, helping Frankie pick up a tray of empty plastic wine glasses. She is pale and shaking. He takes her hand until she looks at him. "I've got this. Go sit with Haddie and the G-men over there. You've been on your feet all day."

Frankie nods at Tony and walks over to take the seat he just vacated. He cleans up the tray and brings her a bottle of water and bag of peanuts they have stashed with their supplies. Tony watches Frankie intently.

"Thanks. I didn't realize how dehydrated I was."

"It was a hot day. You need to rest more tomorrow in between breaks in the crowd." Nunnie pats Frankie's leg.

"Who are those people chatting up Maryssa and Sam? They are definitely politicians. I can spot their breed a mile away." Haddie's voice drips with annoyance as she whispers to her grandmother. "Do I need to hide?"

"The one on the left is Ben Stanley. I think the other two men are his brother and nephew Chase, the one running for congress." Mary answers while monitoring Tony, who is monitoring Frankie.

"Ugh, that guy is ah-noy-ing. He keeps trying to contact Jackson through multiple channels. I don't want him to see me." Haddie turns her back and looks around the tent, making sure she isn't recognized just as Travis leans down to speak with her.

"Mary, this family definitely gets their unexplainable gift of forgiveness from you. After what the Stanleys put their business through two years ago, I certainly wouldn't help them." Tony doesn't take his eyes off of Frankie while the words come out of his mouth.

Mary pats Frankie's knee again and looks at her as she answers Tony. "Forgiveness isn't for the other person, it's for us. To forgive someone isn't saying that the offense is acceptable, it takes the power away from the offense. Forgiveness acknowledges that we are all sinners who fall short of the glory of God. We extend the same grace that has been extended to us. Oh, it's not always easy, but with God's help, it's possible."

There seems to be more to this conversation, but Tony is missing it. Haddie leans in and kisses Mary.

"The fun police said I have to go home. One of my narcs called Jackson to tattle. Apparently, it's getting too crowded," Haddie sulks.

"Travis, I don't envy you one bit." Tony isn't sure but thinks he sees a lopsided, hidden grin on the man's face.

"Nunnie, do you want to ride home with me? Mom is there with Chloe and baby John already."

"That sounds like a plan. I'm pooped." Mary Marchio kisses Frankie and then Tony. "You two look out for one another tonight."

Tony steps behind Frankie and rubs her shoulders. Mary, Haddie, and the faux mountaineer gang turn to leave just as Haddie's phone rings. She answers it as they exit the tent. "Hi Babe, I would like to know the procedure for defecting." She pauses to listen. "Don't tell me what I can't do. I don't care if you're the President, I can defect if I want to."

Travis looks at Tony and unmistakably shakes his head.

Frankie

The weekend was a huge triumph. Frankie sold out of cookies by Sunday morning. The vineyard had success with their newest line featuring a hops infused white wine. Aunt Jo finally put away her clipboard, and Haddie did not cause an international scandal.

They all danced in the streets Sunday afternoon while Amici played out another festival as they do every year. Tearing down was faster with all hands-on deck. "Many hands make light the work," as Nunnie always says. By Sunday night, the streets were clear, and they were all exhausted.

Frankie soaks in a long hot bath. Her muscles ache, and her feet have blisters. She feels as if she spent the weekend at the gym, but she hasn't gone in almost two weeks. Deena expects her back this week. Hopefully, she'll be ready. Deena chewed her out when she heard about the bruised hands and Lisa. Frankie assumed Deena would understand. She definitely wasn't expecting Deena to agree with Lisa.

"I don't want Pounders to get a bad reputation. Your self-destructive behavior is not normal." Those words from her friend stung worse than Frankie's hands.

Frankie stocked up on good hand wraps and found better fitting gloves. Now, she can box, and everyone will be happy and get off her back. Frankie pulls the drain chain with her toe and waits for the water to recede before climbing out of the tub. She wraps her long, curly hair into a towel then rubs rose oil moisturizer onto her face and neck. She ignores the black circles.

After changing into her comfy sweats and favorite piggy slippers, she goes downstairs for tea. As she hits the bottom of the staircase, she hears voices coming from the kitchen. Hesitantly, she peeks around the corner to get a better idea of who is visiting the farmhouse on the Sunday night of Festival weekend. Calmness and curiosity sprout as she recognizes all three voices.

"Well, this is a surprise." Frankie crosses the kitchen and kisses her mother, then her Aunt Jo.

"They claim they came over to talk, but my guess is they came to eat the dud cookies that didn't make the cut." Nunnie points to the open container on the table.

"Not me. I've been living off of sugar and caffeine all weekend. I need to detox. Well, maybe not from coffee." Aunt Jo winks at Frankie.

"You are just in time for tea, Frankie Jo," Nunnie rises from her favorite chair and goes to the stove to retrieve the whistling teapot. Four mugs are filled with boiling water, honey, and tea bags. Frankie pulls out the chair next to her mother and sits in between her mom and her aunt.

"Where is Haddie? Did Jackson make her return to D.C. already?" Frankie settles into her chair.

"Ha! No one tells Haddie what to do." Mary Marchio raised tough daughters and granddaughters.

"Except Travis, Mama. She trusts him with Jackson's life, so she listens to him."

"That is probably true. I'm sure that's why Jackson sends Travis with her when she travels." Nunnie places two mugs in front of Hannah and Frankie. "Haddie and Esther went to Beau and Maryssa's house with Wes. They are working on wedding plans."

"So, you're telling me Travis went to the only place where an eight-year-old girl can tell *him* what to do?" Jo chuckles at the thought.

"Isn't that the truth? It's hard to resist Chloe. She is adorable, like her Mama." Hannah stirs her tea.

"Jo, grab your mug and come up to my bedroom for a minute. I have something I need to show you."

"Yes, Mama." Jo dutifully takes her mug and follows her mother out of the newly renovated kitchen, but not before offering Hannah an encouraging smile.

Frankie watches Aunt Jo and Nunnie leave the kitchen. Her mother twists the mug in her hands. She has no idea what's happening, but the air in the room has changed. Frankie's body tenses as her heart rate increases. She holds the warm mug between her hands.

"Is everything okay? Why did you come visit without Daddy?"

"Mary has been my mother-in-law for over thirty-five years. I don't need your dad with me to visit her." Frankie bristles at the defensive tone her mother uses.

"I didn't mean it that way, I was just curious," Frankie stammers.

Hannah reaches over and cups Frankie's hand. "I'm sorry I'm a little nervous. I asked Daddy not to come with me."

"Okay Mom, something is up, just spit it out. You're making me nervous. Are you sick? Is Daddy? Did Daddy send you?"

"No, no, nothing like that." Hannah squirms a little in her seat. "I'm here because I overheard the conversation between you and your father a few weeks ago, and I wanted to talk to you about it."

Frankie's stomach feels like it is lined with concrete. "I'm sorry, Mom. I didn't mean to drag up anything between you two. It's just been eating at me. I had to say something. It didn't make me feel better, but at least he knows that I know, I guess. None of it makes sense. It's not really any of my business. It's between you two, I just can't believe he did that to you, to our family. He always acts so perfect. I was mad, and it came out." Frankie looks down at her tea, concerned for her mom. "I'm rambling, I'm sorry."

"That's why I'm here. You said you overheard an argument between us about the affair. I need you to know something."

Frankie interrupts her mother. "Mom, don't be embarrassed. This isn't your fault. His selfish decisions have nothing to do with you."

"Well, that's what I need to clarify, actually." Hannah inhales slowly and deeply before exhaling the truth. "I'm not sure what you heard that night we were arguing, but Frankie, your father never had an affair on me."

"He didn't?" Frankie studies her mother's face. "I don't believe you. Why didn't he defend himself then? You don't have to lie to protect him, Mom."

"I'm not, honey. You see, your father has been protecting me." Boom. A brick from Frankie's brain drops to the pit of her stomach. She sucks in air.

"I-I-I don't understand. Why would Daddy need to protect you?"

"I'm the one who had the affair you heard us arguing about."

Frankie's voice shakily stammers out a whisper, "What?"

"A few years after you were born, I met a man, and well, you know the rest."

"Umm, no. I don't know the rest. I can't even begin to know the rest. You have two small children at home, and you 'met a man,' that's it? That's your explanation?"

Hannah resigns herself because she needs to share the story. Still, Frankie sees her mother warring inside between telling and running. "I don't know how to explain it."

"Then start at the beginning. Who was he? How did you meet? When did it end?"

Hannah leans back into the kitchen chair and rests folded hands in her lap. "I was struggling. I was very young when you two were born. You were so close together. I didn't know how to be a mother. I didn't have the best role model. I didn't have a Mary Marchio raise me. I had Grandma Dinah. Daddy and I tried for years to have a baby. I had two miscarriages, then nothing. We saw a specialist. When I finally got pregnant with Sammy, we were ecstatic. When he turned one, we started trying for another baby, thinking it would take a while." The sardonic laugh chills Frankie. "I got pregnant right away. Next thing I know, I have two kids under three, and my husband is working all hours trying to build a warehouse with his father and brother with nothing more than a dream and a prayer."

Frankie intently watches her mother. Ready to jump on any word she says, but her voice is silenced. She can't formulate words. Her entire world is upside down.

"Your dad encouraged me to take some art design classes at the community college. He knew I always wanted to be an interior designer, and he thought it would help get me out of the house. They say hindsight is twenty-twenty, but we think I may have been suffering from post-partum depression. Not that that is an excuse, but it explains a lot of what led me to that point. Anyway, I enrolled in a class. He was the professor. He was much older than me, and his kids were grown. He was intriguing and made me feel special. He spoke of far off travels and exotic works of art. I don't know what else you want me to say. I was young, not thinking right, and in over my head. Not to mention, your dad is a great man. He was hovering over me while I was depressed. I felt suffocated, and this man felt like freedom."

"Let me get this straight, you cheated on Daddy with an old creep because Daddy loved you too much?" Her face is tight and angry. "Are you kidding me?"

Hannah stares down into her lap. "I don't expect you to understand, Frankie."

"Good because I don't. So, what happened? Was it a one night stand or a fling?"

"It lasted for a few months. I broke it off and never told Sam. Later, I found out that he knew, but was afraid I would ask for a divorce so he never said anything and then it ended. We both tried harder after that, but we never addressed the problems, just painted over them. A couple of years later, I went back to school to finish my degree and ran into the same man on campus. I'm assuming you don't remember, because you never talk about it, but I actually left your father for him. After three months, I missed you all. I realized that his life was empty, and mine was full, but I didn't see it until it was gone. Your dad and I started counseling and I moved back home."

"That explains all of my memories of Rosie. I remember spending the night with Heather and baking in their kitchen."

"Your father was working on the regional distribution. Poppy was sick. Sammy was spending so much time with Tony. Rosie figured it out. She called your dad and offered to help with you. No questions, no judgment, just the outstretched hand of help. We've always been grateful for her." Hannah tries to read her daughter's face.

"Frankie, I'm not making any excuses. I've learned a lot about myself with the help of a Christian counselor. My father left when I was a baby. Grandma Dinah taught me growing up that all men cheat. I heard every day that I needed to provide for myself because no one else would. I spent my life trying to feel loved and accepted by others. I jumped through hoops and worked hard to be who everyone else wanted me to be. I masked my insecurity with fake outward confidence. This man made me feel wanted, needed. He provided me with the things I'd seen on television growing up. I wanted that until I realized I'd already had what I wanted. I love your dad with all my heart. I'm so grateful that he extended me forgiveness. I surely didn't deserve it, not even one bit."

A monumental shift occurs in the mother-daughter relationship. It was shaky beforehand, but Frankie never could remember why. Now she knows. Hannah's thumb rubs the handle of her mug. Frankie squeezes the bridge of her nose, warding off the headache that is trying to engulf her.

"Francesca, I know what you must think of me. I spent years hating my father. I know how hurt you are, but I needed you to know that the affair we were fighting over was not your father's. He *is* the great man you've always thought he was, and I needed to clear the air. I was selfish. I left a lot of pain in my wake, but without that pain, your dad and I wouldn't have the marriage we have now. Mary always talks about beauty from ashes. I know what that means. Without the ashes, we wouldn't have the beauty."

Hannah hesitantly reaches over and wraps her hands around Frankie's. She waits for Frankie to look up at her.

"Does the family know? Sammy?" Frankie's voice sounds as shaky as her insides feel.

"We were never sure how much you two remembered, but I don't think he knows everything. Mary and Jo know. Mary let me stay here with them while we went through counseling. Jo was still living at home. That's how Aunt Jo and I became so close. Obviously, Rosie and Big Tony know. If we made the rumor mill circuit around town, I wouldn't know." Hannah wipes her eyes with a napkin. "I understand if you hate me. I hated myself for years."

Frankie holds onto her mother's hands. "I don't hate you, Mom. This is just a lot to process. I need some time."

"I understand. I'm going to go and give you time to sort out your thoughts. Sam is probably wearing out the carpet at home. He didn't ask me to do this, but you needed to know the truth. It kills me that you thought less of him. He's been devastated since your fight." More tears stream down her cheeks. "I'm here if you need to talk. I love you, and I'm so sorry."

Hannah stands and hugs Frankie tightly before kissing her head. Frankie watches her mother walk out the door as Jo follows her, signifying those two busybodies were listening the whole time. After a minute, Nunnie walks in the kitchen and opens her arms. Frankie walks into them and sobs.

Tony

The door opens to the sound of a baseball cracking off of a wooden bat. Tony knows that sound well. The cheering crowd alerts him that it's a base run. Initial excitement cut short to routine clapping. The announcer in the background confirms the play Tony sees in his mind.

His keys clank on the side entry table where he drops them. He picks up the stack of mail and flips through it quickly. Sammy's head rests above the top of the leather couch, his feet resting on the coffee table with a box of pizza.

"Hey, I brought home pizza from Poppy's. We're up by two runs. Grab your own drink."

"Not tonight." Tony braces himself for this conversation.

"Do we have plans?" Sammy turns a little in his seat.

"I have plans."

"Work?"

"Nope. Date."

"With who?" The question comes out of Sammy's mouth before it computes.

"Who do you think?" Tony sees Sammy's jaw clench as he answers.

"That's tonight?"

"Yep."

"Who plans a date on a Monday? Seems desperate."

"Someone who has been waiting fifteen years for the date to happen."

"I don't know whether to punch you for being a sap or punch you for talking about my sister." Sammy sulks as he takes a swig from his drink.

"If my sister wasn't already married and didn't hate you, I would let you date her," Tony counters.

"I thought *my* sister hated *you.*" Sammy is full on scowling.

"Good for me, you were wrong. I'm going to jump in the shower. I helped my parents today. The hardware store was packed."

Tony walks down the hallway to his bedroom and pulls out clothes for his date. He quickly showers and attempts to tame his unruly black wavy hair. He dabs on a cologne that Frankie likes. He knows this because he wore it one day in high school, and she made a comment that someone smelled good. He's worn the same scent ever since.

Sammy gives Tony a once over as he passes by the couch. "I swear, you better be back here by eleven. Alone!"

"Yes, Mom."

"Laugh all you want. I'm serious. She's my sister!" Sammy throws a pillow in Tony's direction.

"I know." Tony ducks before the pillow hits him. He collects the items he needs for his date from the kitchen and heads for the door. "Don't wait up, Mom."

He hears grumbling as the door closes behind him. Tony reminds himself during the drive over that he's too old to be this nervous. He's been on hundreds of dates over his lifetime, but this is the first knot he's ever had in his stomach. He pulls up to the farmhouse and sees Frankie sitting on the front porch swing. He feels the smile rise up inside before it hits his face.

Typical Frankie is in her jeans cuffed at the bottom with a dark green t-shirt. He said casual, and she did it. Usually, if he tells a girl casual, she wears a dress or jeans with high-heeled shoes. Frankie has on her tennis shoes. She bounces down the stairs before he even parks and grabs the handle of the truck door.

"You know, you're supposed to let the guy ring the doorbell and open your car door. Didn't your brother teach you better?" He tries to subdue his frustration. He wants this date to be perfect.

"What, and let the five busy bodies inside talk to you? No thank you. Remember when I had a date pick me up during a family dinner, and y'all kept calling the guy the wrong name on purpose? I learned my lesson in high school, don't bring boys home."

Tony picks up the bouquet of wildflowers and daisies resting on the console. "Here, these are for you. Don't worry, someone else picked them, so they were going to die anyway. Now you can say you gave them a good home before they wilt." His sly grin makes her blush. "You look great, by the way. I was worried you would come out in one of your fancy dresses."

"I've been on plenty of dates with fancy dresses. You promised me a carefree, casual, no stress date. So, show me what ya' got, big talker." For a brief moment, Frankie's face is lighthearted and innocent.

"Ah, there's the Francesca Josephine I know." He reverses his truck and heads back down the winding driveway to the main road.

Frankie rolls down her window and fiddles with the radio. He's not sure what's come over her, but this is the first time she's seemed like herself since she left for school. She squeals when she finds "Fishin' in the Dark" and turns the radio up loud.

He smiles at the irony of song, rolls down his window, and sings along with her. The wind is whipping through the car. Wisps of her hair fly around her face as she holds one hand out the window to catch the last of summer. The smell of fresh hay and wildflowers fill the truck. They drive for a while before she turns down the radio and looks at him.

"Where are we going, by the way? I haven't been this way in ages."

"Hang on, we're almost there. Just a few more turns. I thought you would have guessed by now."

"I don't think I've been out this way since we were kids. Wasn't there an ice cream parlor on this road? I loved their swirl cones with sprinkles."

He smiles. He definitely picked the right place for dessert. "Here we go, Buffalo Creek Reservoir."

She sits forward in the truck and stares over the dashboard. Her mouth opens in surprise and memories. "Oh my goodness, Daddy used to take us fishing here all the time. I can't remember the last time I was here." She turns back to him, leery, "Are we fishing? Not that I don't like fishing, but I would have dressed even more casually."

"No fishing tonight, just a picnic. We can come fishing here another time if you want." Satisfaction and relief flood his knotted stomach. "Come on."

He jumps out of the truck and pulls a cooler and a blanket from the bed. He walks around the tailgate and takes Frankie's hand. Tony leads her down a path to the bank of the reservoir. He picks a spot near a tree and lays out the blanket.

Once they settle down on the blanket, Tony docks his phone in the cooler with speakers and starts a playlist. The first song is "Fishin' in the Dark." She looks at him and laughs. He begins unpacking the cooler and hands her a bottle of her favorite Rafaluzza blackberry wine to open. A charcuterie board filled with meats, cheeses, and bread is set before her. Kalamata olives and red grapes are the cherries on top.

"Impressive. Did you have help putting this together?" Frankie eyes him speculatively.

"Not with the idea, but Maryssa did help me get all the ingredients. Let's go back for a second, I want to make sure I heard you correctly. Did you say impressive?"

She rolls her eyes and hands him a glass of wine. She holds hers up and out to him, "To first dates."

"Salut!" The tinkle of glasses touching trails through the trees.

The calm evening breeze is light and refreshing. A stubborn, late summer sun dances across the water, playing hide and seek with the tree branches. A symphony of crickets, birds, faraway chatter, and fish skimming the water's surface serenades them. They fill the evening recounting the weekend's funniest moments. Haddie's wig and security detail make the top of the list. Their conversation is light and free-flowing.

Frankie eats the last block of brick cheese as she swirls the dark liquid in her glass. "Do you know why the blackberry wine is my favorite?"

Tony shakes his head.

"I'm the youngest grandchild. Well, except Aunt Jo's kids, but they're all still young. The youngest grandchild of the older group, I guess. Anyway, I grew up hearing stories about Poppy. The garden, the games, the blackberry picking. I was so little when he died. I only have a few memories of him. My favorite is when I'm sitting on his lap, sipping blackberry wine. This wine is my connection to him, how I remember him. When I taste it, I taste childhood. Is that silly?"

"Not at all. I think that's the best reason." He breathes a sigh of relief that the walls are down for now. He picks up a focaccia bite. "My turn. Do you know why I picked this spot?"

She shakes her head.

"One summer, Sam brought us out here with my dad. I remember asking Big Tony why Sam brought you with us because girls don't like fish. My dad just laughed at me. We set up our chairs and got our poles ready. I looked over at you expecting to see you cringing. Instead, you were digging your hand into the white Styrofoam cup, pulling out a worm, sticking it right onto the hook, then perfectly casting your line into the water."

"You picked this spot because I touched a worm? You have issues, Devono," she chuckles at him.

"Are you laughing at me?"

"I am." Her smile grows exponentially.

"That's fine. I won't finish my story." He leans back on his arms and eats another olive.

"No, tell me. I'm sorry for laughing, but you walked into that one." She pushes on his shoulder. "Go ahead. Finish your story"

"I knew you were different that day. Special. You've always walked to the beat of your own drummer. Isn't that the saying? You fascinate me, you always have. I knew right then that I wanted to spend every day seeing what else you could do."

Frankie's parted lips are letting out air and sucking it in, but her face looks surprised. Her hazel eyes are locked on his until they close, and she regains her composure. "I don't know what to say. That was, well, perfect. Thank you."

"You're welcome." Tony reaches over and tucks a stray piece of hair behind her ear. "So, how am I doing so far?"

She pauses, making him sweat, "Pretty good."

"Would chocolate-covered strawberries help, or should I skip right to the swirl ice cream cone?"

"Let's see how you do with the strawberries first."

Frankie helps him clean up dinner while he pulls out a container from Poppy's. She sees the intricately dipped and drizzled strawberries. She closes her eyes in astonishment. "I can't believe you. Maryssa asked me to make these for an anniversary reservation tonight. You sneaky sneakerson."

"Hey! I'm trying to bring my A-game tonight, and you make the best. I had no other choice." His boyish grin and unapologetic shrug have her entire face smiling. The strawberries are perfect, but he already knew they would be.

"Hey, how are things with Big Tony? Is he okay with your sister taking over the store?" Frankie takes a bite of the strawberry she hand-dipped in dark chocolate then swirled with white.

"I took your advice and talked with him. He was hurt but understood. The next day Heather and Darren made him an offer. No one saw it coming since Darren had the auto shop with his brothers, and Heather was just part-time at the store. It's perfect. They plan to update the inventory and make it some kind of boutique hardware store. Either way, they're happy, my parents are happy, and I'm free from guilt over the whole thing. Apparently, my mom has been fasting from chocolate. She knew God would work it out, but didn't know how He would do it. The night they signed the papers, she ate a pan of brownies."

"Wow. That's quite a story. I'm sure Heather is excited, and Rosie and Big Tony."

"How about Sam? Did you work things out with him?"

Frankie takes a deep breath and lays back on the blanket. He can see the wheels turning in her head.

"Frankie, if this is going to work, you have to trust me. I know there are things in your head you need to sort out, but I'm safe. Talk to me, please." He leans down beside her and rests his head on his hand.

She looks over at him and searches his face before inhaling a fortifying breath. "I overheard a fight between my parents. I thought they were fighting over an affair my dad had. I was devasted. I thought Daddy was a fraud and that if he could cheat, any man could. I went back to school that fall and made a series of bad decisions because of this knowledge I thought I knew. I don't necessarily want to go into details about my stupidity and ruin our night, but needless to say, that one overheard conversation and the depression that followed changed the course of my life."

Tony can't help himself. He reaches over and strokes her cheek with his thumb before playing with her hair between his fingers.

"It turns out that I heard wrong. Sam Marchio is still the same great guy, but I have harbored anger at him for years over something he didn't do. My mother is actually the one who had an affair. I guess your mom knew about it and helped out with us kids while my parents sorted out things."

That's why Ma keeps making cryptic comments about Frankie's baggage.

"After that Sunday dinner when I snapped at you, I'm sorry for that by the way." He smiles sweetly at her apology. "I confronted my dad then stormed out of the house. He never corrected me because he was protecting my mother. Last night, my mom came over and told me everything, and before you ask, I don't think Sammy knows any of this. I talked to Daddy this morning and his hug healed a lot of wounds, but I'm still processing everything."

He nods. "Wow, that's a lot of family skeletons to rearrange. How are you feeling?"

"Honestly, I don't know. Relieved. Confused. Angry. Sad. I guess I'm a swirl cone of emotion." Frankie tries to laugh, but Tony sees the profound confusion in her eyes.

"See, you never stop amazing me. You're taking this massive bombshell in stride like it's just another day at the office." Tony watches her thoughts dancing around her.

"Trust me, it looks a lot different on the inside."

"I want to see the inside too. Mess and all." His breathing deepens as she glances over at him. Her deep green eyes stare right through him. "Can I kiss you?"

Frankie slowly nods once. His hand reaches over for her face. He leans down and lowers his mouth to hers. Her lips are soft and full. He wants to spend the rest of his life kissing these lips. He pulls back and gazes down at her face. "Thank you for telling me."

She nods again slowly. "Thank you for listening."

The sun is setting as the darkness unfolds around them. Their orchestra only gets louder as the park empties of people enjoying its beauty and the last days of summer. The breeze has picked up, causing them to shiver a little in the evening air.

"We better go." This is the last thing that Tony wants to do, but he doesn't want to push his luck. Their date has been perfect so far.

"Yes. You're probably right."

He leans down over the blanket and sweetly kisses her once again before sitting up and offering her a hand. They pack up their picnic in silence and hold hands on the walk back to his truck. This time, she allows Tony to open the door and help her inside the cab. When he gets into the driver's seat, he turns around to dig out a sweatshirt and hands it to her. "Here, you look cold."

She examines the article of clothing. It is so soft from years of wear and care. The cuffs on the sleeve and the neckline are slightly frayed. It smells like him. She pulls the sweatshirt over her head and snuggles into it.

"You got this sweatshirt on signing day. The college brought one for you and Sammy both. I've wanted to wear it since that day."

Her words fill his entire body with warmth. He reaches over and takes her hand in his and lifts it to his lips.

They listen to the night as they drive to get ice cream. The chocolate and vanilla swirl is better than they both remember. The last bite is finished as they reach the turnoff for the vineyard.

As the farmhouse comes into view, the moon is high in the night sky. Stars fill the darkness with not a cloud in sight. Tony parks the truck and turns in his seat. Frankie's face is highlighted by the light of the moon. An ethereal glow illuminates her face. He reaches over to touch her cheek. "I had an amazing time tonight, thank you."

"You definitely brought your A-game, Anthony."

"I'm glad you approve, Francesca. Can I see you again tomorrow?"

She nods. "I'll see if I can fit you into my busy schedule."

He peeks over her shoulder. "I should have stopped alongside the road to kiss you goodnight. I think we have an audience."

"Duh. Downstairs or upstairs window?" She keeps her gaze on him as he peeks around her.

"Both." He laughs.

"Were you serious about complete honesty? I can tell you anything?"

He nods, getting nervous.

Frankie smiles, "I'm keeping the sweatshirt. It smells like you." She jumps out of the truck and bounces up the stairs, taking his heart with her.

Frankie

Music envelops the space around Frankie as she sways to the rhythm section's deep melody. A cake plate spins in front of her as she smooths cream cheese icing along the sides of her creation. A handful of chopped pecans are sprinkled on top of the carrot cake. Frankie stands back to look at the beautiful work of art. Finished. Perfect.

All of her tools go into the sink just as the timer rings. Frankie leans down to pull out cookie sheets. The sweet aroma wafts around her as it infuses the kitchen. Each cookie is perfectly round and very large. Bits of pretzels peek out of the salted caramel cookie. Baking pans rest on cooling racks as she checks her fudgy chocolate cupcake batter.

"Frankie? I'm here. I don't want to scare you." Maryssa's voice, from the back door, pulls Frankie from her focus.

"Hey, Maryssa! Yeah, I'm in the kitchen."

Frankie uses an ice cream scoop to fill cupcake liners. Large chocolate chunks are suspended in the decadent batter. The consistency is thick and silky smooth. Maryssa looks over her shoulder and groans next to Frankie's ear.

"Those look sinful."

"I know, right? I might have one for lunch." Frankie beams at her masterpiece.

"Sign me up for that lunch date." Maryssa walks into her office to drop off her keys and purse. She grabs her apron and attempts to stealthily extract information. "Speaking of dates, didn't you have one last night?"

Frankie snickers over her shoulder with a "seriously?" look. "Smooth."

"What? I'm just making conversation," Maryssa feigns innocence.

"Uh-huh. Sure. Didn't you get recon from the three window lurkers? I thought for sure Haddie would have called you as soon as I went to bed."

"According to my sources," Maryssa clears her throat, admitting she's being nosy, "there was a brief conversation in the truck before you emerged wearing his sweatshirt. No kiss. No walking to the door. You kissed the three of them goodnight, refused tea, and went to bed."

"See, you already know how my date went. Tell Beau to ask Tony if you're so interested."

Now Frankie gets the "seriously?" look from Maryssa. "I did. Beau won't ask and Tony won't talk. All Beau said is that Tony has been singing all morning." Maryssa studies the subject of her interrogation.

"Tony always sings." Frankie smiles back at Maryssa, who is leaning against a prep counter, staring. Waiting, impatiently. "All right, all right, it was nice. It was *really* nice, and there was a kiss, just not in front of the looky-loos." The grin on Frankie's face makes her cheeks ache.

Maryssa squeals, "I knew it! Gimme details."

"I promise I will tell you everything tonight. I need to run as soon as these cupcakes are out of the oven. I'm going to change while these are baking. I want to hit the gym before taping this afternoon. Don't tell Lisa. I promise I'm not boxing, just a light workout."

"All right, we can pause this conversation, but I do need to talk to you about something before you leave."

"Okay, shoot." Frankie listens as she bends to place the cupcakes into the oven.

"You're fired."

Frankie laughs. "Okay."

"No, I'm serious. Your services are no longer needed at Poppy's." Maryssa looks all business.

"Wait, you're serious? What's this all about?"

"It's about you, Frankie. Our agreement was that you would work as the manager while you built your bakery business. You've done that. Now, you have your own baking show and a booming business. It's time to fly the coop. No more managing a restaurant. You've trained Amanda well. She runs this place better than the two of us combined. It's time for you to open your own bakery."

Panic floods Frankie's body. She wrings her hands and thinks of every excuse in her armory. "We don't know if the network will even air my show. What then? Are you going to hire a pastry chef to replace me?"

Maryssa snorts at the ridiculous question. "No, silly. I'll contract my desserts out to your bakery. The show will only grow your brand. I can advertise Frankie's Confections at Poppy's. Your business is big enough to go out on your own now with or without the show. You can rent or buy in town or build on the property." Maryssa crosses over and rests her hand on Frankie's. "It's scary. Trust me, I get it, but it's time."

In a rare moment, Frankie drops her guard. She tries hard to keep the tears from overflowing her eyelids. A whisper escapes, "I'm scared."

Maryssa wraps her arms around her cousin. The same cousin who followed the older kids around like a puppy dog. Frankie was always the tough one trying to prove herself and fight her way into playing with them. She holds the back of Frankie's head. "Are you kidding me with this? I should have fired you last year. You are ready for this. Plus, you have an army of family to help you. Not many people have that."

Frankie pulls away from Maryssa and wipes her face. "I know. I just wasn't ready. Are you giving me two weeks?" Frankie sarcastically asks.

"I'll give you as long as you need, but I'm interviewing an assistant manager today. Amanda knows someone looking for a job."

"Thanks," Frankie wisecracks.

"You know what Nunnie says when you see an open door. Run for it. That's God inviting you to the next level."

"I just didn't realize you were letting the last door kick me in the rear," Frankie's voice cracks with emotion.

"Stop, you know I'm not doing that. I'm gently nudging you off the high dive."

"It feels like a shove."

"Shove? Nudge? It's all the same in this family." Maryssa shrugs.

The cookie timer on the oven dings, alerting Frankie that her final batch of cookies is finished along with her time at Poppy's, her safety net.

The parking lot at Pounders is crowded for a weekday afternoon. Frankie finds a spot and parks. She grabs her duffel with the new gloves inside, and heads into the building. Two guys are sparring. Three bags are being used, but the speed bags are all open. She heads to the locker room to store her bag. She grabs her towel, water bottle, and hand wraps. Deena comes over as soon as she sees Frankie.

"I saw your car pull in. Here, I have something for you." Deena takes Frankie's hand to pull her over to the office. "I got a new liniment from my homeopathic guy. It smells awful, worse than the last one, but it works." Deena starts rubbing a thick, opaque oil into Frankie's knuckles.

"Ugh, that is horrific." Frankie coughs and gags at the smell.

Deena chuckles. "I know, but it works."

There is a hint of hyssop and lavender, but the tea tree oil is potent. "Well, if it doesn't help my skin, at least it's working to clean out my sinuses."

"Suck it up, buttercup." Deena moves on to the next hand. "Take better care of yourself, then I won't need to use this." The warning, slash, threat is heard loud and clear. "I'm glad you came today. I'm dying to hear more about your parents and the big date. Have you talked to your dad?"

Frankie runs through her memories from yesterday. After being fired this morning, yesterday seems a million miles away. "I drove out to the house. I tried to apologize, but he stopped me. He just hugged me tightly. All the guilt and burden I'd been carrying just fell off of me. We had coffee and cinnamon rolls, like nothing had happened."

"What about your mom? Are you mad?" Deena begins the process of wrapping Frankie's hands, making sure to apply an extra layer over her knuckles. The wraps will heat the oils and help the healing process.

"I'm not mad, but I am hurt if that makes sense. I'm trying to understand. My mom didn't have a father in her life at all, and my Grandma Dinah was a whackadoo. I never really knew her, but now I know why. Mom was young and didn't know what a good marriage looked like so she got spooked, I guess. I don't understand, but I'm trying to make sense of it. It's just weird. It's like I blocked out that entire time period. It makes me wonder how many other things I've blocked out. I just wish I had more clarity these days. I feel like I'm walking in fog all the time." Frankie inspects the second hand. She opens and closes her fist. "It's too thick."

Deena rolls her eyes. "No, it's not. It's protected. Deal with it. Now for the real scoop. How was the date?" She wiggles her eyebrows.

"What is it with everyone? It was just a date." Frankie tries to hide her happiness.

"It wasn't just *a* date. It was *the* date. Now spill." Deena finishes and leads Frankie out of the office to the heart of Pounders.

Frankie gives Deena the abbreviated version of the date as she jumps rope. Then they move on to burpees and Frankie's recent firing from Poppy's. Frankie is frustrated when Deena responds with a "Finally."

Frankie heads to the shower when they finish. Deena is training her new client when it's time for Frankie to leave. They wave to each other and Frankie moves on to the next portion of her packed schedule.

Frankie spends the drive lost in thought. Her parents. Tony. Sammy. A new business. The most worrisome is the missing memories. She's astonished how she could have blocked out an entire chunk of her childhood. It explains more than she cares to process at this time. Some things might be better left forgotten. By the time she reaches Poppy's, Lisa's crew is finishing Maryssa's segment. Frankie heads to the makeup station and reads through episode notes.

Today is the first actual baking segment. Up until now, Frankie has only taped interviews and background segments. The first recipe is a family favorite, tiramisu. This is the same recipe Haddie used to stop the criminalization of Christianity, so it's kind of a big deal. Frankie's goal is to take away the intimidation that surrounds Italian delicacies. This is the best place to start, plus it's Tony's favorite dessert.

After many takes, cuts, and makeup refreshes, Frankie is in the homestretch. Lisa goes over a few notes as the crew moves cameras and works on still photos. Frankie walks back on set and gets ready for Lisa's order of action when she notices two friendly faces lined up against the wall. Her heart overflows as she finishes strong like she's been taught her whole life to do.

When Lisa calls the final cut, applause explodes throughout the room. The crew congratulates her as Maryssa is the first to offer a hug, followed by her dad.

221

"The set isn't big enough for all of us, but we wanted to be here for your first wrap. Everyone is downstairs waiting for you," Maryssa explains.

Frankie is engulfed securely in her father's embrace. All is right with the world. "I'm so proud of you," he boasts. Frankie relaxes and deeply breathes in her father's familiar scent.

Frankie gathers her things and follows her cheerleaders down the stairs to Poppy's. By the time she turns the corner of the restaurant, the entire Marchio clan is on their feet, clapping and hugging Frankie. She is overwhelmed. Even Sammy tells her he's proud. He follows it with a snarky comment, but she'll still count it as a win. Frankie scans the room, taking in her entourage. Maryssa tilts her head toward the bar area where Tony is standing, waiting.

As everyone scatters to help with dinner, Frankie makes her way over to Tony. He takes her hand and pulls her behind the wall separating the bar area from the dining room. "I waited over here for you. If I got too close to you, I knew I would do this. And I don't think Sam Marchio would approve." He tilts her head up to him with his finger and kisses her with longing. She melts into him.

Frankie wraps her arms around his waist. "Very wise of you."

"Congratulations on your first segment. How do you feel about it?"

Tony is the only person to ask how she feels. "Good, I think. I'm glad you came. I was hoping."

He pulls her closer into a hug and holds her. "Are you getting soft on me, Francesca?"

"Maybe." Frankie breathes in the herbal smell of his cologne. She looks up at him, "Are you wearing Polo?"

A blush crosses Tony's face. "Maybe. I heard you say once that you loved that smell."

She laughs at him. "What, like in high school?"

"Maybe."

Frankie is mesmerized by the layers of this man. "That is so cute," she whispers before stealing another kiss.

Their quiet moment is interrupted by Beau clearing his throat and Maryssa making a gagging sound. Tony and Frankie reluctantly pull apart but stand close to one another. Their arms still touching.

"Okay, you two. We have guests." Maryssa moves around them. "Frankie, help me get the flutes for this champagne."

Beau carries two bottles to the bar while Maryssa pulls out a server's tray. Frankie picks flutes from the back shelf to help load up the tray. Behind them, Beau pops the champagne cork. Glass breaks. Frankie is as white as a ghost. Her hands are empty.

Tony reaches Frankie in seconds, inspecting her. "Are you okay? Did it startle you?"

Maryssa picks up broken glass as Beau holds a bottle of overflowing bubbly liquid, not knowing what to do with it now.

"I think I just need to sit down. I'm not feeling well." Frankie's voice trembles.

Tony grabs a towel from under the bar and wraps Frankie's hand tightly, where blood oozes from her palm. He lifts Frankie into his arms and carries her to the front door. "Party is over, we're going to the ER."

Jackson

The West Sitting Hall reminds Jackson of the formal living room at his grandparent's home, the Cashe side of the family. It appears warm and inviting, but stiff. His mother used to call it the "breakable room." Jackson and Haddie feel more comfortable in the private living room, but tonight he is sitting in the room closest to the stairs. He is anxiously awaiting Haddie's return from West Virginia.

The upholstered chair is stuffy looking but sturdy. It dates back to the nineteen twenties. Jackson chose this chair because it has a direct line of sight to the landing off of the Center Hall. He knows Haddie landed, so she will be home shortly.

Madison suggested multiple times that he call it an early night since his mind was too focused on the clock, but he insisted he could keep working. After repeating herself three times, she called it quits for the night. He didn't argue. Jackson had Marcus order him a copy of Animal Farm by George Orwell a week ago. The last book John Marchio suggested Jackson read changed his life. If John thinks he should read it, he will.

Jackson hears footsteps pitter-patter up the stairs. He stands in anticipation. Haddie turns the corner as their eyes meet. Haddie walks across the expanse, not taking her eyes off of him for a second. "Mr. President, you are a sight for sore eyes."

"As are you, Mrs. Cashe." He meets her halfway with wide-open arms. She melts into him. Jackson's racing heart relaxes, and he breathes in the vanilla and gardenia lotion she loves. "I've missed you so much. I'm just not myself when you're not here. I need you, Haddie."

She looks up at him. The lines are deepening around his eyes. The grey around his temples and hairline keeps growing. Her fingers brush his cheek as she studies his face. "Are you okay? I'm worried about you."

He takes her hand and walks her through the master bedroom and into their living room. She sees a pillow and blanket on the couch. He moves them to the side and sits down, pulling her onto his lap.

"There are at least ten different beds you could have slept in around this place. Why the couch?" She wearily watches him.

"I don't sleep well when you're not with me. The bed is too big."

"You weren't sleeping well before I left either. I'm worried about you." Haddie counters his argument.

"It's a lot of hard work running the country," he answers sardonically.

Her sneer lets him know she doesn't appreciate the snarky reply. "You have been leading the country ever since I met you. This is different." She wraps her arms around his neck and snuggles in close to him. "I'm only trying to help. The pressures of your job aren't the issue. It's something else, and you know it."

Jackson tosses thoughts around in his mind, debating whether or not he can express his worries without Haddie thinking he's crazy. She rubs her thumb across his furrowed brow.

"Jackson, talk to me."

"Remember when Hayman had me sign the act that would restrict the movement of Christians and the spreading of evangelism?"

Hayman Barnes was Jackson's Chief of Staff before Madison. He was born a bureaucrat and was deeply entrenched in the party. He convinced Jackson to sign into law the deportation of all evangelical Christians if they didn't follow restrictive guidelines. Haddie almost left Jackson to live in the Allied States. Jackson thought he was protecting the country from radicals who tried to assassinate him and kill Haddie in the process. Jackson had no idea he was being duped by his closest advisor as part of some sinister plot.

"How can I forget? Hayman was one evil man. Sorry, I know he was close to you at one point, but he was scary. You know under that law it would be illegal for Uncle Malik to teach Bible studies?"   •

"I've thought about that many times." Jackson rests his head on her shoulder. "I signed the order because I had been having nightmares about losing you, about losing everything. I wasn't sleeping. It's as if I knew something was coming. A change, but I didn't know what or who was coming at me, just that something was coming. I can't explain it, but I've been feeling it again. Last time I reacted out of fear, and I let Hayman manipulate and cultivate that fear. I don't want to do that this time, but I don't know what I'm facing."

"I'm so sorry, Jackson. Thank you for telling me." Haddie lifts his face to hers and convinces him with her gaze. "God has gotten us this far. We can't doubt Him now. We'll call on our prayer warriors and ask for discernment for you. We'll get through this together." She leans down and kisses him gently and longingly. "I've missed you so much. Just for the record, I don't sleep well without you either."

Jackson buries his head in Haddie's embrace and holds her tighter. "Tell me everything about your trip. Don't leave out anything."

Haddie makes a groaning sound. "Sometimes I feel like my family should have its own reality TV show. You just can't make this stuff up. Mom's wedding is pretty much set, just our family and his. His ex-wife is even invited, which is weird, but they both like her, so it's okay, I guess. The festival was so much fun, until someone dropped a pan, causing you and Travis to lock me down, which I'm still mad about by the way. I'm proud to say that my t-shirt idea worked. My security team blended right in and didn't draw any attention to me. Bonus, I enjoyed watching a Pitt grad wearing WVU letters."

"Yes, I heard that Allison wants hazard pay for your t-shirt stunt. She told Travis that you tortured her," Jackson laughs. "Anything other than taunting your security detail?"

"Frankie went on a date with Tony, then filmed her first segment today. Maryssa just texted to tell me that somehow Frankie cut her hand at the afterparty and is at the ER."

"Is she okay?"

"I'm guessing, or else Maryssa would have frantically texted me to come back for the funeral. Maryssa has a tendency to exaggerate, as you well know. Anyway, Tony is with Frankie."

"Finally, those two have been flirting since I met you."

"Much longer than that. We all agree. Hopefully, Frankie lets down her guard and gives him a chance."

"Hmm, a stubborn Marchio woman making sure her man is worthy. That sounds familiar."

Haddie swats Jackson. "I don't hear you complaining now."

"Never, sweetheart." Jackson kisses her. "Are you hungry? Malik made lasagna for you. It's in the refrigerator."

"I love that man." Haddie's stomach rumbles in anticipation.

"Your entire family shows its love with food," Jackson taunts.

"Again, I don't hear you complaining," Haddie grins.

"Never, sweetheart. Let's eat." Jackson takes Haddie's hand and leads her toward the kitchen and leftover lasagna.

Tony

The country station seems to be playing all of his favorite songs today. Big Tony was in a good mood this morning. Rosie is planning a retirement trip to Florida. Heather and Darren are working on a new website and social media presence. Tony won two bids today for big projects. Today is a good day.

Tony pulls into the parking lot at Poppy's. The late afternoon sun warms the asphalt while a breeze from the surrounding trees cools the heat of the day. Lisa's production vans are still filling the outer parking spots, so Frankie is probably filming. Tony heads into the restaurant and looks for Sammy and Dominick. The two of them are supposed to meet with Maryssa and Beau about the upcoming Wine and Jazz Festival. Tony is only here for Frankie.

He spots the four of them at a back table eating bruschetta. "Looks like I got here in time for food." Tony grins as he joins the family meeting.

Beau stands and pulls over a chair for Tony. Tony slaps Dominick on the back before bending to kiss Maryssa on the cheek. She passes him a plate, "Mangia, there is plenty. I have tiella coming out soon. I made it with sweet Italian sausage crumbles."

"I definitely came at the right time." Tony eats in silence as the four of them talk about logistics for the upcoming event. The main focus will be on the vineyard, but Maryssa and Frankie will have food items available. Tony will help set up and work both days. The things he ends up doing with this family.

Sammy's phone rings, and he excuses himself from the table. "It must be a girl, or else he would talk loudly in front of us," Maryssa jokes and elicits laughter from the table.

Dominick takes the opportunity for a bathroom break and Tony takes another forkful of tiella.

"Tony, do you know what's going on with Frankie?" Maryssa's voice is like a needle across a record. Everything stops.

"Going on with what?" Tony starts to get nervous. He finally has Frankie taking down some bricks from the impenetrable wall she's built over the years. He doesn't want anything to help her rebuild them.

Maryssa sounds annoyed, "Oh, I don't know, let's see. She punched you in the face. Keep denying it if you want to, but we all know. Her unhealthy and excessive boxing obsession. Busting up her hands weekly. She barely missed Beau with a roundhouse kick last week for startling her in the kitchen. Aunt E told Haddie that Frankie has night terrors and ends up in the basement working out all hours of the night. To top it off, she heard a champagne cork pop and literally broke a glass by squeezing it in her hand. Shall I continue?"

Tony takes a long drink of water. Of course, he thinks about these things constantly. Red flags and worry for her run on a loop in his mind. He tries to level his voice, "Have you asked her?"

"Yes, I asked her, and then we rolled sugar cookies together as she told me everything." Sarcasm oozes off her smirk. "Frankie isn't Haddie. She's never been a talker. She's a doer. I just didn't know if you knew anything. The whole family is baffled. We know something happened, but we don't know what. Anyone who asks gets their head taken off by her. It seems to be getting worse."

"Look, whatever it is she'll tell us when she's ready, or she'll work it out on her own. That's how Frankie works. She's always been that way. Let's give her some space." Tony doesn't want someone to spook her now when she's actually

229

making headway and opening up to him. "If you're so worried about her, why did you fire her? Why now?"

Offended and surprised, Maryssa spits out a rebuttal, "Technically, I didn't fire her, I just pushed her along."

"Oh, okay. If that helps you sleep at night." Now it's Tony's turn to vent his frustration. Tony and Maryssa are in a standoff of icy glares.

"Drop it. You're both worried about her. Don't make it about something else." Beau settles the matter then stands quickly and turns toward the door. His arms are open wide. Tony hears the pitter-patter of feet behind him. He turns in time to see Chloe bound up into her daddy's arms. She is buried in his bear hug as she giggles and coos like a little girl.

"How'd it go, sweetheart? Are you going to be the next rising star in the family?" Chloe turns Beau into mush.

"It was so much fun! Miss Lisa was a little scary like Mommy said, but she was mostly mean to Aunt Frankie, not me. That was funny. She said I can do it again on Mommy's show or Aunt Frankie's. She said that maybe I can have my own kid cooking show. Ooohh, that Jen Z. would be so mad if I had my own show. Maybe I should do it." Chloe is a chatterbox, like Harmony.

"Slow down there, chief. We don't do anything to make other people feel bad. Even if it is Jen Z.," Beau mumbles the last part. "Let's get second grade under our belt before we sign any television contracts. Geesh, this family is unreal with all the television specials."

"Are you ready to eat? I saved rigatoni and meatballs for you." Maryssa slips into mom mode and forgets about Tony.

"Yummy!" Chloe and her head of ringlets bounce into the kitchen with Maryssa. She chatters the entire way.

Beau quickly realizes that Tony only has eyes for Frankie and vice versa. He abandons his plate and quietly turns to follow his girls into the kitchen. Tony pulls out the chair next to him as Frankie comes over and sits down. She holds up his glass, and looks at him questioningly. He nods as she takes a drink of his water. He smiles at the intimate act. *God, please don't let her pull away, again.*

"Francesca" he croons at her.

"Anthony," she nods back at him.

"I heard you had a helper on the show today." Tony gently lifts Frankie's bandaged hand and turns it over in his, inspecting it while pondering the conversation he just had with Maryssa.

"It's fine. I just have to keep changing the bandages." He waits for her eyes to return to his face instead of her wound. Somehow, it feels as if he is staring at all of her wounds right now, especially the invisible ones. She closes her eyes and breathes in and out, steadily. "Chloe is a natural, definitely better than me."

"I doubt that. Was it planned? I didn't know you were having guests already. If you want, I can make an appearance. I make a mean PB&J."

"It wasn't. Lisa saw my hand and called an audible. We changed the segment from Italian buttercream icing to homemade ice cream. The simplicity of the recipe made Chloe the perfect co-host. I was able to wear a glove while touching the cold ingredients. Chloe did all the barehanded mixing, stirring, and eating. I suggested calling the episode 'Smoke and Mirrors,' but Lisa didn't find that funny." Frankie shrugs at her half-hearted joke.

Tony watches her. "Are you hungry?"

"Starving, but I'll wait and eat at home. Nunnie is making me fried potatoes with peppers and sausage. This is the last batch of fresh peppers before we start canning. You should come, you know she has plenty."

The invite surprises and encourages him. "I can't. Sammy and I are hitting up the batting cages. He's upset we're not spending enough time together." They both chuckle at that one. "But I'd like to drive you home if that's okay?" She nods. Tony rubs his hand across her back and shoulders.

A growling sound comes from behind them. "Don't touch my sister. I'm begging you. Not while I'm in the same building." Sammy kisses his sister's cheek before picking up her hand and inspecting the bandage. He then sits back down at the table to finish the rest of his tiella. "How's the hand?"

"Fine."

"Good. Is this clown bothering you?"

She smiles back at Tony. "Not at the moment. I'll let you know if it changes."

"Good," Sammy grunts in annoyance.

"I'm going to drive her home. Is that okay with you, Mr. Marchio?" Tony struggles not to laugh.

Sammy's hostile look lets Tony know it's not okay, but he has no say in the matter.

"Bye, Big-Brother." Frankie kisses the top of Sammy's head on the way to the front door.

Tony takes Frankie's non-injured hand in his as they walk out to the parking lot and to his truck. He opens the door for her. She's getting better at letting him. Once he explained it wasn't a chauvinistic tactic, but a gesture of honor and respect, she appreciated the effort.

The engine roars to life. Tony plays with the radio and finds their first date playlist. She looks over and smiles. For the first time, Frankie reaches over and holds his hand first. He chooses to take the main road instead of the shortcut through the property. Anything to prolong their drive.

"How was your day?" Frankie asks as the wind kisses her hair.

"It was actually really good. The family is transitioning like players taking the outfield. You never would've known there was a great divide last month. Big Tony is chipper. Rosie is relieved. I owe it all to you, you know." He glances over at her.

Puzzled, "What did I do?"

"You gave me another insight into how my dad was feeling. I told him how proud I was of him and that I wanted to be like him and start something for myself. I talked to him honestly, which gave my sister the nerve to ask for the business herself."

"Sometimes, it takes an outside perspective to see things straight." Frankie stares out at the acres of grapes and blackberries growing.

Tony steadies himself before asking the next question. "How is your hand, really? Remember, I saw the cut and all the stitches. It can't be *okay*."

"It's not great. The anti-inflammatory medicine helps, but it still throbs. I need to ice it."

Her honesty today is moving him more than anything else she has done. "Thank you for telling me."

"Thank you for not coddling me."

"Can I ask you another question?" Tony plays his odds.

"You can ask, I'll decide if I want to answer."

"Fair enough." He pauses as he reaches the turnoff for the farmhouse driveway. "What happened that night? It wasn't a startle, you didn't drop the glass, you squeezed it." The fear on her face scared him more than the blood. He had never before seen that emotion from her.

Frankie closes her eyes and drops her head back onto the seat. She breathes in as much air as her lungs can hold before exhaling. "Nunnie and Deena keep telling me to be honest and take chances. To forgive and all the other piles of advice they dump on me daily. You've been so patient with me." She peeks over at him, a look of contemplation flashes across her face. Her facial expression verbalizes an inner turmoil. "I hope you can handle this."

He squeezes her good hand in his. "Try me."

"Something happened to me at school. I'm not ready to talk about it yet. To be honest, I only remember bits and pieces. I've blocked most of it out. Memories have started to come back in splotches like I'm watching a movie in my head, but I'm starring in it. I have recurring nightmares that stop at the same exact place. Not that I want to get to the end, but I don't *not* want to get to the end either, if that makes sense. Things trigger me lately. It wasn't so much as the cork popping as it was the sound of the air pressure releasing as it came out before the cork. I know that sounds weird, but it reminded me of that night. I froze and I don't remember anything after hearing the sound. That's all I'm ready to share."

Tony parks in front of the farmhouse and studies her face. "Thank you, I know that wasn't easy. I'm glad you trust me enough to tell me. I'm assuming no one else knows but Mary?"

She shakes her head. "Nunnie doesn't know the story, but she knows something happened. I just can't tell them."

"Does Deena know?"

"That's actually the reason we met, but that's a story for another time. I'm hungry and tired."

"I understand." Tony reaches over to pick up her hurt hand and gently kisses it. "I want to kiss you so bad right now, but Mary is sitting in her porch swing pretending not to watch us."

They both laugh. "I'll take a rain check. Have fun with Sammy. Make him buy the first bucket of balls."

"Oh, I think I'll be footing the bill for the entire night since I'm dating his sister and all."

"I hope she's worth it," a mirthful smile crosses her face.

"She's priceless." The look on Frankie's face is all he needs. He winks at her before she climbs out of the truck. He watches her wave through his rearview mirror as he drives away.

Jackson

"All right people, I think we have a plan. Everyone will work on their individual section of the proposal. We'll reconvene tomorrow afternoon. I want each team to provide Rich with specific talking points for the media. We can't risk anything being off message. I'll brief the House and Senate leaders later today."

Jackson drops his pen on the coffee table and relaxes into the silk couch. Top-level White House staff begin collecting their items to leave. Conversations trail as pairs and groups of people leave the room. Madison stays seated and waits for the last person to exit, including Rich, their college roommate and third musketeer.

"That went well, don't you think?" Jackson sighs as he waits for Madison's next agenda item.

Madison Lyn is distracted. "Yes, I do. We'll need to keep tabs on the technology aspect, but other than that, I think this will work."

"Great, what's next on your list?"

"Jackson, I actually need to speak with you about something important."

"Oh no, Madsi, I can't take any new fires. How bad is it? Just break it to me. Is it about the impeachment?"

"Well, sort of, but it's mostly personal." Madison Lyn sits forward on the opposite couch of Jackson. She rests her elbows on her knees. "After the impeachment dust settles, I'm going to resign."

Jackson bolts upright in his seat. "Madsi? What? Why? Did something happen?"

"I want you to know that your confidence in my ability to do this job means the world to me. I've loved every minute, even the stressful ones. This has nothing to do with you or the job itself, but I'm finding it increasingly difficult to stay on this course." Madison pulls out her tablet and opens a folder for Jackson to see.

Jackson watches her intently, trying to figure out what is happening. Madison and Rich have been his right and left hands since his first campaign. When he had to fire Hayman Barnes, replacing Madison as his new Chief of Staff was a no-brainer. Surely, he can figure out a way to make her stay.

"Jackson, what I am about to tell you is going to sound completely crazy. Conspiracy theory, off my rocker, crazy. I've heard these stories my entire life and chalked them up to folklore and family tall tales. Then, a series of events transpired recently that caused me to pay attention and ask questions. Normally, I would have ignored them, but in collection, they are alarming. So, I started to dig deeper, but it might seem like I've lost my mind."

"Madsi, you know I trust you. Spit it out." Jackson's nerves are standing on edge right now.

"You know my grandparents and father immigrated after escaping from China during the Great Proletarian Cultural Revolution?" Jackson nods, she continues. "My grandfather was a principal. They left at the beginning of Red August. They had to sneak out of the country after my grandfather and ten teachers in his school were severely beaten by their own students under the guidance of the Red Guard."

"That's awful. I knew about your heritage, but not what pushed your family to come to America. I had no idea, Madison. I'm so sorry."

"I'll be honest, I didn't either. Some of their friends and family left before 1966, but it was hard to get out. My grandparents stayed, hoping the class discrepancy would improve, and they would continue living as they did. Sadly, like most of their friends, they were wrong. I knew something happened to my grandfather, but no one spoke about the disgraceful event. I never bothered asking beyond what they told me. I grew up in southern California and had no concerns about communist China. When my family opted for citizenship in the Allied States instead of supporting me, I was hurt, but not surprised. Between the impeachment and Governor Marchio's confidential information dump, things started lining up in ways I hadn't anticipated and I noticed some trends." Madison shifts in her seat, preparing for the next part of her story.

Jackson worries about where this conversation is heading. "Madison, how far are we going with this? I thought we agreed that the list of names was a tactic from the Allied States to stall reunification. I'm not putting weight on theories about shell corporations from China."

"Jackson, I warned you this was going to sound crazy. May I continue?" Madison's voice has an edge that Jackson has never heard from her.

Jackson wearily nods.

"*As requested by you,*" she glares, "I quietly made a few calls to inquire about the shell companies. My notes and unofficial report are in this file. All of the information is on my personal tablet and not saved to any drive. This is the only copy of my notes. I wish now I'd actually used a pen and notebook, but that's another issue." Madison hands Jackson her tablet before continuing.

Madison closes her eyes in deep thought before continuing. "After tracing the information and tracking the money trail, which sadly, wasn't all that hidden, I found out that the governor had missed the target."

"Wait, are you telling me that you proved Governor Marchio wrong, or right?" Jackson's confusion is etched on his face.

"Both," she shrugs. "There is definitely a system of shell companies working in tandem, and this is truly the most bipartisan effort in the history of the country. He was correct on both of those points. They aren't tied to China, but China is reaping the benefits and enjoying the show."

Madison moves across the room to sit on the couch next to Jackson and points to the graphics she's pulled up on her tablet. "Shell corporations, working under an umbrella organization have donated over half a billion dollars into our political and educational systems. The money is mainly filtered through non-profits and universities. In the three years leading up to the Separation, they funded and supplied 'anti-fascist' groups with military grade weapons, emergency medical equipment, legal funds, and financial support. These were the same groups leading all of the riots. They essentially funded a network of secret revolutionaries who fought a war against the old republic. And well, they won. The United States is no more."

Madison opens another file on the tablet in his hands. "What bothers me the most is this umbrella group of shell companies financially supported eighty percent of media and entertainment companies before the Separation, and one hundred percent of them currently. This spreadsheet charts when and where strategic stories were leaked on which platforms before the Separation. The next set of charts show the usage and repetition of the exact same keywords and talking points on those same platforms. The patterns are undeniable. It is statistically impossible for a narrative that consistent to not be organized. It was an underground coup that caused the momentous shift in the country not underlying issues between the left and right. When you look at the Separation through a different lens, you see similar patterns that occurred in Russia, China, Germany, Cuba, and Venezuela before their revolutions."

"These are incredibly high numbers. Did you verify these statistics with anyone else?" Madison's offended and annoyed look serves as Jackson's answer.

"I'm only getting started. Remember during the latest flu season? China's gross national product tripled because they manufacture ninety-five percent of all medical and health supplies. The Allied States was the only nation not impacted because they began manufacturing their own medicine and equipment two years ago."

"I'm getting tired of talking about how great the Allied States is this week. First Haddie, now you. I'm starting to get a complex." Jackson rubs his temples. A knot is forming in his stomach. "Tell me how this relates to us and how we can fix it."

"Jackson, we have been fighting a silent war that no one knew was waged, and it all revolves around money. A two percent minority of elites have taken over the government one subgroup at a time. Think about it. Leading up to the Separation, the small business market was decimated. People had to rely on big corporations for every staple. Riots, inflation, food shortages, strikes, government shutdowns, off the chart crime rates were daily staples. You name it, the world faced it. Now, use your annoyingly vast history knowledge base and think back over every socialist revolution. Without a public face and campaign to rally against, we totally missed the attack because they didn't fight with guns and war machines. It came as more of an undercurrent than a revolution. Identity politics pit everyone against each other. The Separation occurred, giving them exactly what they wanted. They slowly deconstructed the greatest republic the world had ever seen."

Jackson takes a deep breath as he studies her. "Madison, I want to believe you. I know your facts must be correct, but you are expecting me to believe that shell corporations, funded by some type of international communist network, are the puppet masters of our government? The government over which I am the head, and you are my Chief of Staff. This would all be impossible without our knowledge."

"Hold on to your hat, it gets worse."

"I doubt that." Jackson surrenders back into the settee. "Lay it on me."

"Something Governor Marchio said didn't sit right with me. So, I started asking questions and tracking down people on the governor's list. One name kept rising to the top of every conversation." Madison takes a breath before hitting Jackson with the hammer, "Hayman Barnes."

Jackson's eyes pop as his jaw drops. He shakes his head before rising to pace. "Madison, you can't be serious!"

"Think about it, Jackson. You were handpicked by the party to run as the first president after the Separation. Don't get offended, but Hayman totally handled you from the beginning and none of us questioned it because he is your father's best friend. You fired him and made him persona non grata for a while, but his name has been circulating again. Next thing we know, we have a target on our backs."

"You're telling me that Hayman, a man I have known since I was born, the man who mentored me throughout my career, is the greatest mastermind of all time?" Jackson's head is spinning.

"No. Hayman Barnes is a highly connected soldier in a network of spider webs. The real enemy is the Global Organization and Defense Alliance, or the G.O.D. Alliance as they ironically call themselves internally. I don't even share your faith and I'm offended by their arrogance. Externally, they are known as the Global Alliance, a coalition of 'philanthropists' made up of Big Tech, Big Pharma, and old money elitists. They provide resources and aid to countries who agree to adhere to their globalization and peace ideals. They are touting themselves as the saviors of the world. They are controlled by a clandestine group of ten people. I can speculate on who they are, but no one will verify or deny anything about 'The Board' as they're known. Jackson, people were genuinely terrified to speak with me."

Jackson sinks back down onto the settee next to Madison and slumps into the cushions. "I can't believe what you are telling me. This can't be true. This is science fiction, blockbuster movie, make believe lunacy."

"I know. I thought the same thing." Madison takes the tablet from Jackson and swipes until she finds another file. "Here are the most recent civil unrests and revolutions that have taken place in the past thirty years. Below this chart, you will find the money trail that ties the shell corporations involved in each of these coups to the Global Alliance."

Madison drags and opens a folder containing lists and video clips. "Wait until you see their marketing. Rich is amateur hour compared to the alliance. Their messaging is nothing short of inspirational. It is fodder for humans who want peace, love, and joy. I mean, who doesn't want those things, but come on people, use some common sense. Alliance marketing is set up so that anyone who speaks out against them must want world hunger, war, racism, environmental catastrophes, and anything else they can pin on you. Their plan is brilliant and fool proof. As you will see from the news clips and following charts, they leave destruction in their wake. Those who question alliance methods are silenced and their careers destroyed. According to an ex-husband of one of their lackies, phase one is to name the villain so everyone knows the enemy. Next, they use their network of shell companies to advertise and proclaim the enemy's many alleged transgressions. Then, they sell fear as their weapon. This fearmongering has close neighbors and family members turning on one another. The disruption and destabilization of the government structure is easy once they make everyone a 'soldier' for the cause. Much like the Hitler Youth and the Chinese Red Guard, they radicalize people with fear and lies. Remember the Eco Youth group Hayman wanted to start?"

"I think I'm going to be sick." Jackson sits up and rests his elbows on his knees and his head in his hands. "That is why Hayman pushed so hard for the Extremist Religions Act targeting all evangelicals in the second year after the Separation?" Madison nods. Jackson walks to the window and stares.

"Think about it, Jackson. You were America's Sweetheart. The first President of the 'new' United States. Star of *Future FLOTUS?*. You hosted a peaceful and groundbreaking reunification summit. You were riding high until the Allied States offered suggestions that were against the global messaging of the alliance. The machine wanted you to turn the Allied States, not the other way around. Next thing you know, polls showed you trailing, the media turned on you, you barely won your reelection, and now they are seeking impeachment."

"This sounds like a movie. A book that George Orwell wrote." Jackson looks at Madison, his eyes pleading with her to admit this is a prank.

"He did write it, twice. They're called *Animal Farm* and *1984*. You should also try reading *When Twilight Breaks, Next Year in Havana,* or *Red Scarf Girl.* My mom sent me a copy of that one last week. Reading it felt oddly familiar, and not in a good way. Jackson, I know this is a lot to take in and process. Keep my tablet tonight and read my notes. We can talk in the morning, or call me tonight. I haven't slept much in the past two weeks. I think I'm getting an ulcer." Madison rubs her stomach.

"You realize exposing this is political suicide."

"Try actual 'suicide,' and by that, I mean murder. Don't get me started on what these groups do to dissenters and truth-tellers. Most of the people on the list Governor Marchio gave you are dead or missing. This is scary movie stuff." Madison walks over to Jackson and hands him the tablet. "Jackson, I don't know how I got onto this course of discovery, but I can't unsee it, and I can't support it."

"Thank you, Madsi. I know this must have been difficult for you." Jackson's mind is reeling. "I still don't understand why you are resigning. What are you going to do? Why won't you stay and help me fix it? The Madsi I know has never backed down from a fight."

"I'm not. I spent my entire life appreciating the sacrifices of my grandparents by trying to live the best American life I could. This reminded me how precious my history is to me. Even the darkest stories taught me how important it is to fight for freedom." She bows her head, dreading Jackson's reaction. "You're not going to believe this, but I actually already have a job. During my research, I have had several phone conversations with Rhett Paulson. I'm going to work with him once I leave the White House."

"Madison Mei Lyn, that is by far the most shocking piece of information you have shared with me today. You absolutely hate that guy. His underground podcast decimates us on a daily basis. He was run out of Washington by a media lynch mob that used to tout him as the golden child. Not to mention the fact that, oh, I don't know, he dumped you and tried to sabotage us the week before the election! How on earth can you work for that jerk?"

"I realized that maybe he was right."

Frankie

Music fills the kitchen as food is prepared for the festival this weekend. Poppy's closed early for the night, so they could prep. Frankie checks the timer on her first batch of cookies. Maryssa ladles homemade tomato sauce into small plastic cups with lids while dough rises for strombolis and pepperoni rolls. The kitchen smells heavenly.

"Knock-knock. Need some extra hands?" Aunt E pushes the swinging door open, trailed by Nunnie. "Sam, Hannah, and Jo are on their way."

"Just in time. I'm getting ready to roll out dough. I need a station for stromboli stuffing and one for pepperoni rolls. I'm making veggie strombolis, sausage strombolis, and loaded strombolis." Maryssa wipes her hands and turns to welcome their incoming helpers.

"My mouth is watering. Do you pay in food?" Frankie's back is to the door, but she instantly recognizes her father's voice.

"Does our family pay in any other commodity?" Maryssa laughs at her uncle before giving him a big hug.

Sam walks over and kisses Frankie's head while she scoops out cookie dough then rolls it in cinnamon sugar. "Are those my favorite?"

Frankie giggles at her father's childlike spirit. "Yes, snickerdoodles. I made an extra dozen for you. I also have peanut butter chocolate chips in the oven, and my next batch will be oatmeal scotchies."

"That's why you are my favorite daughter." He takes the filled cookie sheet and hands her the next empty one.

"I'm your only daughter." She laughs as he winks and walks to the oven.

Aunt Jo arrives next with her daughter, Olivia. Poppy's kitchen is busy, busy, busy. Frankie makes her way across the room to retrieve more supplies when she notices the assembly line all around her. Music is replaced by laughter and conversation that has aged like a fine wine.

It is a work of art how they dance around one another like it's second nature. Frankie has heard Maryssa and Haddie compare family cooking sessions to the ensemble of ballets they performed. Uncle Malik says it reminds him of a symphony, everyone playing their individual instruments together in harmony. Frankie sees it now. She watches the seamless transitions and harmonic balances of their strengths and weaknesses. Her dad is rolling out the dough while her mother cuts it into pieces. Aunt E and Aunt Jo work on stuffing strombolis. Olivia boxes the cookies. Maryssa constructs pepperoni rolls while Nunnie mans the timer and ovens. Frankie's heart warms.

"Are you slacking off, or do you need a break?" Maryssa looks over and notices Frankie standing in the middle of the kitchen, staring.

Frankie snorts at the thought of slacking off with this crew. "Just admiring your dough stuffing abilities."

They all laugh and continue with their conversations and assignments. Frankie appreciates the interpretations given by her cousins and uncle, but she sees their family as a cookie recipe. Different ingredients, important staples on their own accords, whipped together into a decadent batter, refined by fire into a chewy goodness of perfection. Separate, they're fine, but together, they're stronger and cohesive. Her strength doesn't come from her fists. It comes from this.

The evening rolls on as they work in unison. Sammy and Tony call from the festival grounds to ask if the kitchen crew needs help. They already set up tents, tables, chairs, portable appliances, and signage. They'll pick up the food tomorrow. Frankie finishes scooping the last of the cookies.

Maryssa thanks everyone for their help. Nunnie and Maryssa clean the space as the others store the food items.

"Ma, do you need a ride home?"

"No, Sam. I'll get a ride with Frankie."

"Girls, do you need anything else from me before I leave?"

"I'm good, Daddy. Love you." Frankie kisses her father and accepts his bear hug on her way to the oven and beeping timer. She hears her father's voice as she opens the oven, the heat hitting her like a brick wall. She realizes she hasn't drunk much water today.

"Oh, Maryssa, before I forget. Ben Stanley called me today. Apparently, he and his nephew will be campaigning at the festival tomorrow. He was hoping to get a photo op with a celebrity chef. I wanted to tell him to shove it, but my mother taught me to extend grace to those who offend me." Sam winks at his mother.

"Those Stanleys are like a wooden nickel. We can't get rid of them, and they keep ending up in our pockets," Nunnie sighs.

Frankie is dizzy. She hears the words spoken around her, but everything else is fuzzy. The heat from the oven feels like it's sucking the air from her lungs. Her body tingles. The room begins to move around her. She feels her father's arm around her waist as he growls out a potty word.

"Frankie!"

She breathes in and out like Deena taught her.

"Frankie?"

More breathing. Frankie's eyelids close to block out the blur. Her breathing is slow and steady.

"Should we call 911?"

She tries to shake her head. *Please hear me.*

"Francesca Josephine, can you hear me?" Nunnie's voice cuts through the fog.

Frankie opens her eyes and looks at the faces around her. She takes one last steadying breath. "I'm fine." There is a collective sigh of relief.

"Here is some water. Drink this." Frankie watches her mother push her dad out of the way. "Sam, let your mom look at your hand."

Frankie gulps down the water and rests the glass in her lap. "What happened?"

"You tell us. You took a pan out of the oven, then turned pale white and started to droop." Hannah studies her daughter's every movement.

"No, I mean to Daddy?" Frankie's voice is barely a whisper. "Why is Nunnie looking at his hand?"

Hannah sighs, "Your dad went to catch you before you fell, but you had a hot cookie sheet in your hand. He grabbed it so it wouldn't land on you."

"Is he okay?"

Maryssa redirects her attention. "Frankie. Hello! You passed out on us. The more important question is, are you okay?"

"I'm fine. I'm just dehydrated. I didn't eat much today. I'll be fine. Seriously. Help me up, please."

Maryssa eyes her questioningly before helping her up from the floor.

"Daddy, are you all right?" Frankie peers around the mother hens hovering around her. Nunnie has the first aid kit opened on the counter. She cuts a final piece of tape for the gauze and inspects her work.

"Nothing a little lavender oil and ointment won't heal." He walks over and inspects his own child just as Nunnie did to him. "You sure you're just dehydrated?"

Frankie nods. "I'm fine, Daddy. It's been a long day."

Hannah continues to hold Frankie's arm. "Well, we have a big weekend ahead of us, so you should get to bed.

You go back to the farmhouse with Mary. We'll help Maryssa clean up and box these last cookies. Before you try, don't argue with your mother. I said go."

"Yes, Ma'am." Frankie kisses everyone goodbye and heads home with Nunnie. They ride in silence and walk the stairs to the back porch. As soon as they enter the kitchen, Nunnie begins pulling items from her cabinets.

"Go take a shower. I'll make a snack."

"That's okay, I think I'm just going to bed."

"I wasn't giving you an option. Shower, then back down here for a snack."

"Yes, Ma'am." Frankie doesn't have it in her to argue with Nunnie tonight. Food is probably a good idea.

Frankie shuffles upstairs to her room. She takes out her ponytail and unwraps the bandage on her hand. Her finger traces the stitches. She heads to the shower and lets the steam wash over her tired bones. Her mind runs through the last few years of her life. So much has happened since college.

When she gets back to her room she finds her favorite pajamas are lying on top of her laundry basket. Nunnie must have washed her clothes today. She's been so busy they were piling up quickly. Grateful, she slips them on and heads back downstairs to the kitchen, more fittingly called the family counseling center.

Nunnie slathers peanut butter on bread as Frankie enters the kitchen. Her world-famous raspberry preserves spread like icing on top of a cake. Two tall glasses of milk wait on the table. Nunnie nods, directing Frankie to sit.

"Milk instead of tea? This must be a serious conversation." Frankie pulls out a chair and sits at a table that is older than her.

"That depends on how much you want to talk."
Nunnie places both sandwiches on the table and settles in
beside her granddaughter.

"That depends on what you want to talk about, I
guess."

Even as an adult, Nunnie's "don't give me that sass"
look still works. Frankie straightens in her chair and quickly
places food in her mouth.

"Francesca Josephine, I have lived through wars,
feasts, and famines. I have buried a husband, a daughter, a
son-in-law, and a grandchild. I have seen heaps of ashes and
the beauty that comes from those charred remains. I know
PTSD when I see it. We didn't call it that in my day, but it
certainly existed. The question is, what is the source of
yours? I know the information about your parents was
difficult for you, but I don't think that is the whole story."

A cold chill rolls over and through Frankie. She can
feel her heartbeat rapidly increase. Her skin turns pasty
white. Her voice is shakier than she would like it to be,
"Nunnie, I don't have PTSD."

"Behavior and mood changes? Not being able to sleep,
and when you do, it's filled with nightmares? Pushing
everyone away from you? Physically assaulting people who
startle you? I could go on and on, but I think you get the
picture. Frankie, you are letting fear and anger rule your life.
If you don't let those go, they will consume your every
minute. I suspect they already do."

Frankie feels the tears welling up in her eyes. She is
determined not to cry. This is too much. Everything is too
much. She quickly swipes at a tear that forcefully escapes.
Then another. "Nunnie, I..."

Nunnie reaches over to hold Frankie's hand in hers.
"Frankie, the Bible tells us to bear one another's burdens for
a reason. Sweetheart, some burdens are too heavy to bear

alone. The weight will crush you under itself. There are no medals for bearing the weight of the world on your shoulders. You have to let it go before it destroys you."

Nunnie leans over and wraps her arms around Frankie's trembling body with tears streaming down her face. Even newly remodeled, this kitchen works its magic. The epicenter of the Marchio family, this room has seen countless tears and hugs over the years. Christ is the foundation of this house. Every sickness, every blessing, every sorrow, and every joy. Tonight will not be the exception. Nunnie holds Frankie until she is ready to talk.

Frankie pulls a napkin from the holder and wipes her face and nose. She takes deep breaths as she attempts to get herself together. Her face feels red and blotchy. She has to deal with this before she hurts anyone else. First Tony, now her dad.

"Frankie, we're going to take this one step at a time. Start at the beginning. We'll work our way through this, but we need to get you out from underneath this weight. Nothing is too big that we can't handle together." Nunnie rubs Frankie's back as she attempts to compose herself.

"I don't know where to start because I don't even remember most of it. I only know fragments, but I do know that it was my fault, I was careless. Reckless."

"I doubt that, but tell me what you do remember."

"You have to understand that I just found out about my dad. Well, what I thought Daddy had done. I thought all men were cheaters and players. I wasn't going to let anyone get the best of me. I wasn't about to allow another man to let me down. I was away from home, and I was careless."

"Oh, sweetheart, you wouldn't be the first person in this family to go wild, and you certainly won't be the last."

"It was more than that. I was out of control, partying every night. There was a string of Roofie rapes in town. The university kept it quiet, but the school paper was reporting about it all the time. There were at least ten women during my first year at school. A few more the other two years. I knew better. We were all warned repeatedly by school administrators. My friends all made pacts, none of us accepted drinks from anyone. Until one night. I was out with kids from home. We all knew each other, so I let my guard down. Chase Stanley was there with his younger brother. I think that's why I panic when I hear his name. He reminds me of that night. There was a keg at the party, but we started with a bottle of champagne. I forgot that detail until Beau popped the cork the other night." Frankie rubs the healing cut on the palm of her hand.

Nunnie watches her with one hand on Frankie's back, stroking it.

"I remember the people at the party. I can see all of their faces perfectly, but I don't remember anything else about the night. I woke up the next morning with the worst headache I've ever experienced in my life. It felt like knives were stabbing the back and top of my head. Everything was blurry and fuzzy. When I swallowed, it felt like I was swallowing broken glass. I remember feeling so dizzy that I rolled off a couch and vomited all over the floor. I had never seen the room before, and no one was around me. I scrambled around to find my clothes and get dressed. I left as soon as I could. I raced back to my apartment. When I opened the door, my roommate was crying to her boyfriend. She had no idea what happened to me. She told me we were all at a bar and then she lost me. We always go home together, so she knew something was wrong. She was ready to call my parents when I walked in the door. I spent the next two hours vomiting until her boyfriend picked me up and carried me to her car. They drove me to the ER. I had bruises on my arms and legs. The doctor administered a rape kit and took a full blood panel. The police interviewed me, but they never arrested everyone."

"Oh, my precious Frankie. I am so sorry, my angel. Why didn't you tell us?"

"Tell our family?" Frankie huffs, "So Daddy, Sammy, Uncle Dom, and Dominick could go and murder every male in Morgantown? No. I wanted to put it behind me. I didn't want them to see me like that. Weak. On top of that, I hated my dad at the time."

"You listen to me. You are not weak. This was not your fault. I don't care what you did or didn't do that night. No one ever has the right to do that to another human being. Let's clear that up right now, young lady. You're probably right about the family. God says revenge is His, but we're not perfect." Shaking her head, Mary hopes they would have allowed justice to prevail and trusted God, but their flesh would have put up a really tough battle. "What did the police say?"

"The DNA they collected matched the other cases, but they never found the guy. That's how I met Deena. The police brought in an analyst from the FBI. They asked the victims to participate in a group discussion in hopes it would jar someone's memories. Deena handed out the self-defense pamphlets that day. She looked so fierce and scary. I wanted to look like that. We made fast friends."

"Thank God for Deena. She has definitely helped you. We didn't know what happened that year, but we knew it was something. I thought it might have to do with a boyfriend, but I was way off the mark. After you started working out with Deena, we saw your spark start to come back. It was just a flicker, but it was still lit. Blessings do come out of trials."

"Nunnie, stop. I know you'll be mad at me and probably wash my mouth out with soap, but I'm furious at

God. He could have stopped it. He could have protected me that night, but He didn't. This is all God's fault." Frankie spits out the last words. Words she has held back from even herself. They came out of the pit of her anger. Her look challenges Nunnie to make a counter-argument on His behalf. The Godly matriarch of the family.

"Soap? Seriously? Do you think you own the market on being mad at God? Do you think I haven't uttered those exact words in this very kitchen?" Mary Marchio settles back in her chair and crosses her arms. "You try burying a child or a grandchild who has just given birth to a baby. Little Miss, you have no idea the depths of my sorrows, but He does. Oh, He does. I have spent a lifetime on my knees with my Father. Let me tell you one thing I know for sure, God is big enough for your anger. There is a big difference between questioning God and asking God questions. The latter requires a relationship. If you have that relationship, everything comes out in the wash. He already knows how you feel, and He'll be there when you're ready to deal with it. Not one time does the Bible tell us that life will be easy and pain-free, not once. It does, however, tell us repeatedly not to be afraid. The Bible is a love story from Him to us. It's riddled with war, murder, pain, and yes, even rape. God never lets us suffer just to suffer. He is good and just. He uses every pain for our good and His glory, if we let Him."

Frankie stares open-mouthed at her grandmother. She has seen Nunnie upset and passionate before, but not like this. She watches as Nunnie crosses the room and walks over to her bookshelf in the other room. She spends time looking for something, finds it, then returns to the kitchen table.

"This book is written by an amazing missionary, Dr. Helen Roseveare, who worked in the Congo. I have no earthly idea of how you are feeling, but she does, and she writes about it. When you're ready, you should read this. You should also go talk to Aunt Connie."

Mary sits back down and takes both of Frankie's hands in hers. "Francesca, in my lifetime, when I have found myself in the deepest sorrows of life, those crevices where even darkness flees, that is exactly where God was waiting for me. Not one time has God ever left me alone and broken. Not once. Our family has seen our share of beauty from ashes. The thicker the ashes, the more beautiful the blessing. Romans twelve, twenty-one, tells us to 'not be conquered by evil, but conquer evil with good.' Sweetheart, how can God make something beautiful when you are clutching the ashes so tightly? It's okay to be angry, but give your anger to Him and watch Him transform it into something magnificent."

"I don't know if I can," Frankie whispers the words as a few straggling tears creep down her rosy cheeks.

"You've been doing it your own way for a while now. How is that working out for you?" Nunnie grins warily. "All you have to do is talk to Him like you just talked to me. Be honest and tell Him how you feel. He already knows. I promise He'll meet you where you are." Nunnie reaches over and wipes Frankie's tears. Frankie nods in understanding. "Instead of assuming you know who He is, try getting to know Him."

They both glance toward the window where headlights reflect off the glass. Gravel crushing under tires confirms what they already know. Nunnie gets up from the table and kisses the top of Frankie's head while squeezing her tightly. "We'll talk in the morning. I love you so very much, sweet girl."

"Wait, where are you going?"

"I'm pooped, I'm going to bed."

Confused, Frankie calls to Nunnie as the woman leaves the kitchen for the front stairs, "What about your sandwich?"

"Oh, honey. That isn't for me. I made that for Tony."

"Tony?"

"That boy has it bad. Surely you didn't think he wasn't coming here to check on you the second he heard you fainted." Nunnie winks, "Good night, Francesca. I love you."

Frankie turns as soon as she hears knocking on the back-screen door. Nunnie yells without looking, "Come on in, Tony."

Tony appears in the doorway with a worried look on his face. "I heard you collapsed at Poppy's? Are you okay? Frankie, this is crazy. I can't take you getting hurt anymore. I'm going to stick you in bubble wrap. You need to tell me what's going on. I can't help you fight something if I don't know what it is we're fighting."

Frankie marvels at her grandmother's insight. She pats the vacated seat next to her and points to the peanut butter and jelly sandwich. "Sit down, it's time to talk."

Haddie

The streets of Washington, D.C., are speeding past as the Beast careens toward the White House. Street lights shine through the windows, flittering across Haddie's face. Ashleigh frantically fields texts and calls blowing up both of their phones. The rest of the car is eerily silent.

"Travis, can we go any faster?"

"Ma'am, we'll get you there as soon and as safely as we can." Travis offers Haddie a reassuring smile.

Travis and his wife have become part of their family. He is a very stoic man, but Chloe melts his heart, which endeared him to Haddie right away. Haddie admires how loyal and steadfast he is, always one step ahead of everyone else. She feels better knowing that Travis is in charge of their safety. Sadly, this is something Travis can't protect Jackson from this time.

They approach the White House. Haddie asks to be delivered directly to the West Wing. She knows that's where Jackson will be tonight with Madison, Rich, and their teams. As they pull around to the door, she jumps out without having her door opened, garnering her a scolding reproach from Travis. He really is a good man.

"I know, Travis. I'm sorry," Haddie yells over her shoulder.

She heads unswervingly to the Oval Office door then looks for approval from Jackson's executive assistant and unofficial sentry, Mrs. Pennington. After a quick buzz to Jackson, Haddie gets the nod of approval and discreetly slips into the room to stand off to the side. The last thing she wants to do is disturb this briefing. She watches Jackson command the room and remembers all of the speeches and meetings she has witnessed. He was born for this role.

Haddie is brought back to the moment by movements and Madison's voice. "All right, let's work up some plans and meet back here in two hours. Grab some food and caffeine. It's going to be a long night, ladies and gentlemen."

Jackson crosses the room and wraps Haddie in an emotional hug. This is taking a toll on him. Things seem to keep getting worse instead of better. She feels his need as he holds her tight. His breathing begins to calm. He lets go but takes Haddie's hand and leads her back to the couches where Madison and Rich are waiting.

"Haddie, do you remember what news agency the reporter represented?" Rich stares intently at her.

"It was Jim, I think that's his name. The one who asks a series of questions, but never wants an actual answer because his question is the answer? That one." Haddie is trying to hold it together.

Madison laughs, "That describes the majority of the press corp."

"Okay. That's what I thought based on Ashleigh's account. Now, what exactly did he ask you?" Rich holds his phone like a weapon. Haddie hasn't seen him this attentive in a long time.

"I was leaving my committee meeting. I thought it was odd when the press was outside, so I was guarded." This is why Haddie hates the press. It's like they want to make her look bad.

Rich interrupts, "You are always guarded, that's why they like to fluster you."

"Rich," Jackson's voice conveys a warning.

"He's right, and Haddie knows it." Madison referees, as always.

Haddie rolls her eyes, a mix of defiance and acknowledgment. "He asked why I was serving on a committee that promotes the agenda of the Allied States while two current US states were holding emergency hearings on secession."

"And how did you answer?" Rich is on high alert, further raising Haddie's concern.

"I told him the work of the committee will complement our strong educational system. That the committee was made up of business, community, and educational leaders from across the United States. I avoided the Allied States question and directed it back to Jackson's programs. I didn't give the appearance of shock or confusion that he obviously wanted. Then Ashleigh whisked me away, saying I had another engagement." Haddie awaits the reaction from the gallery.

Rich leans back into the silk settee and folds his hands behind his head. "I have trained you well."

Haddie tosses a pillow at Rich's head.

"Enough, kids. Put your grown-up hats back on so we can focus." Haddie turns her attention to Madison, who, in typical fashion, summarizes the situation concisely. "Haddie responded perfectly. She remained calm and unphased by his surprise attack. The press has no idea we didn't know about the secession votes. The majority and minority leaders are on their way and should arrive within the hour. We have anyone with local ties to the states doing reconnaissance now. Neither governor will return our calls. We'll try to contact the senators and representatives next, but I doubt we'll have much luck with them answering either."

Jackson stands with one hand in his pocket and the other resting on the mantle above the fireplace. His head bows in contemplation. The slump of his shoulders speaks volumes to Haddie. He closes his eyes and takes a deep, purging breath. "I'll call Governor Marchio. Maybe he'll have some insight."

"We can't be sure he knew and didn't warn us."
Madison treads carefully out of respect for the man, but her
first priority is Jackson. "If he knew, he could be complicit in
hiding it from you."

"I know." Jackson runs his hand through his greying
hair. "What's the saying, prepare for the worst, hope for the
best? Let's keep hope."

Rich stands, "I need to brief my team and make sure
no one from the press is lurking around my office. I don't
trust the new interns yet. Let me know if you hear anything."

Madison asks Mrs. Pennington to call the governor's
mansion in West Virginia.

Haddie tells Jackson she's going up to the residence,
but he grabs her hand. "I need you to stay. Just for a little
while." The three of them wait in silence. The stress on his
face worries her. She prays for wisdom and peace in the
silent moments as they wait for the call to be answered. Mrs.
Pennington's voice has them all sitting at attention.

"The governor is not accepting calls at this time."
Jackson's head falls into his hands. Surprise and betrayal
crease his face.

Haddie's phone vibrates inside the pocket of her skirt.
She pulls it out to silence it when she sees an unknown
number with a West Virginia area code. Haddie quickly
realizes this text isn't for her. She shows the screen to
Jackson then to Madison. The three of them quietly walk
into the private study off of the Oval Office. Jackson calls
the number from the text message on Haddie's phone,
"John, thanks for taking my call. I hope I didn't disturb
you."

"Jackson, it is always a pleasure to speak with you.
May I be so bold as to assume we are speaking privately?"

"I have Madison Lyn and Haddie in the room with
me. Madison is here to keep me straight. Haddie is here

because your ideology is rubbing off on her, putting her in the crosshairs of a reporter tonight."

"First Lady Cashe, I always knew I liked you." The chortle on the other end of the line puts them at ease, but only slightly. "While I am sorry you had an incident with a reporter, I would enjoy talking ideology with you any day, Haddie. However, I'm assuming your husband called me for a different reason tonight. Possibly two reasons, Colorado and New Mexico, perhaps?"

"John, did you know?" Jackson's question is short and to the point.

"I heard rumblings, but nothing concrete until this afternoon. Jackson, you have to understand my position. I support you and your passion for reunification, but I'm also a patriot bound by duty to my country. You, my friend, are not the only one under suspicion of collusion. You know I can't officially take your call or even tell you everything I know."

Jackson sighs heavily, "I understand. A little warning would have been nice."

John ignores the dig. "From what I know the negotiations have been very secretive. I presume they wanted a surprise attack, so the government couldn't block them."

Madison weighs in, "They got the surprise factor right. We're scrambling now for information."

"I imagine our president will call you with a declaration when the votes are official, but I don't know more. If it helps, New Mexico is voting on independence and secession, so we may only gain one state."

"It doesn't. Do you know why they're favoring secession?"

"Jackson, you already know. The United States wanted more government control. Now, the entire country runs like the DMV. No one from any party, likes the DMV.

Regulations and taxes have decimated small business and industry. You have more government programs and departments than ants in an ant farm. You're top-heavy. It is crushing the states you govern."

"John, there has to be some way to stop this. What if I call the governors and invite them to the next summit in exchange for temporarily pausing the secession votes? Can you get word to them? Surely we can get a summit together quickly."

Haddie and Madison exchange glances as they sit around Haddie's cell phone. Jackson paces and brainstorms. John patiently listens, like a good mentor, but everyone knows that Jackson is grasping at straws.

"They didn't have the decency to negotiate with us. This is a cheap shot from the Allied States."

"Jackson, the US blew up all the checks and balances by eradicating the electoral college, adding to the number of justices, and ending the filibuster. Then you had the judicial system completely dismantle state rights and governance. Instead of all men being created equal with unalienable rights, the US began stripping one freedom at a time. Government control by the masses is the antithesis of the individual freedoms fought for by the Founding Fathers. This has nothing to do with political parties or agendas. What if, before the Separation, Republicans controlled the masses? Would you have been amenable to Republican control? I wouldn't, and I'm a die-hard Republican. The Allied States are not perfect, but we balance individual liberty with government control. Allowing the majority to set the rules destroys the freedom of the individual. You are losing states because you are stripping away their freedoms and silencing their voices. At some point, you have to acknowledge the problem."

Jackson stares at the phone. He looks as if John has just slapped him in the face.

"John, this is Madison. We appreciate your candor, but what we need to know is if we have a chance. Is the vote a formality, or are there still some state leaders on the fence?"

"I'm sorry, but I don't know. Jackson, I truly am sorry the reunification has another setback. I admire your tenacity and passion. I know you have a lot to do on your end. You're probably waiting for the four horsemen to come and devise a plan. This is my wife's cell phone. If you need to talk to a friend, you can reach me on this line."

"Thank you, John." Haddie pushes the red button to end the call.

Jackson falls back into the leather sofa and drops an arm over his face.

Frankie

Sunshine illuminates her bedroom. Beams of light dance across the floorboards and along the walls. Her curtains sway with the gentle morning air. Frankie left the window open a crack last night so she could hear the cacophony of night creatures on the farm. She regretted the decision at six this morning when Mr. Bubbles started his reveille, but she managed to fall back asleep.

She had a fitful night's sleep, but the nightmares didn't loom over her. Baring her soul to Nunnie and then to Tony lifted the weight, but the rawness left behind is exhausting. She rolls to her side and looks out the window just as a strong wind blows through and flips the pages of the book Nunnie gave her last night. A handwritten note falls out and onto the floor. Frankie picks it up and reads the quote written on it. "God never uses a person greatly until He has wounded him deeply. The privilege He offers you is greater than the price you have to pay. -Helen Roseveare"

Frankie holds the yellowed paper in her fingers. The fragility of the note itself moves her. It has obviously been touched and handled many times. Frankie picks up the book and flips to the front cover. Aunt Connie's initials are in the top right corner. She closes the book and places it back on her nightstand. She rereads the quote as another breeze caresses her bare arms. A shiver runs through her body.

God, I'm deeply wounded. I have no clue how you can use me. I don't know what to do with all of this anger. I'm mad. I'm scared. I'm confused. I don't understand how someone could do this to another person. I'm angry at myself for letting it happen. I'm mad at you for letting it happen, but more than that, I'm sad it happened. I feel broken and useless. I don't know how you can use this or me, but I can't hold it anymore. I'm giving it to you. I don't want to feel like this anymore. I know prayer isn't a magic wand, but I could use some of the healing

Nunnie talks about all the time. I don't want this to rule me anymore. I want to live again. So, here it is, it's Yours, not mine.

Frankie sits on the edge of her bed with the note tightly in her grip. A softer breeze blows open the curtains and swishes her wispy hair. She takes a deep, cleansing breath before standing and heading to the bathroom. Her morning routine is shortened because she needs to get ready for the festival today. Tony will be picking her up soon.

Frankie quickly dresses and ties back her hair. The routine is comforting. She pulls on her skinny jeans and a maroon Rafaluzza Vineyard t-shirt. Slipping into her favorite tennis shoes, Frankie heads downstairs. The delicious aroma of bacon hits her before she makes it to the kitchen. Nunnie has her travel coffee mug and a breakfast plate waiting.

"Good morning, Nunnie. Everything smells yummy." Frankie kisses her grandmother's cheek.

"How are you feeling this morning, Sugar?" Nunnie pours coffee into the mug and hands Frankie the creamer.

"Thanks." Frankie finishes chewing a bite of toast. "I feel much better today."

"Make sure you drink lots of water. It will be a long day."

Frankie grins, "I know. I'll be careful. I'm sure Tony and my dad will be watching me like hawks."

"Look at that, he must have known we were talking about him." Nunnie looks out the window and spies Tony's truck coming up the road.

Frankie stuffs a few bites in and grabs her coffee. She hugs Nunnie tightly. "Thank you. I love you very much."

Nunnie pats her back. "Francesca, God must have some really big plans for you. You could be a real firecracker for Christ."

Frankie laughs, "I don't know about that, but I'm ready to listen."

Tony honks the horn.

"We must be late if he's honking," Frankie laughs. "Wish us luck!"

"I don't 'wish' for anything, I pray," Nunnie shouts after her.

Frankie skips down the backstairs and climbs up into the cab of the truck to see Tony looking for something on the floor bed. He's mumbling in Italian.

"What did you lose?"

"My phone." He lifts the console and looks inside before closing it and grumbling more.

"That one?" Frankie points to the dashboard.

Tony sighs, "That would be the one. Thanks." He winks at her then places the phone in the cup holder, where it usually sits. He reverses the truck and heads back down the drive, reaching over to take her hand in his. "How are you feeling?"

"I'm fine. I told you that last night before you left, and again when you texted when you got home, and again when you texted this morning, twice. Truly I'm fine. I don't know how to explain it, but I feel at peace for the first time in a long time. Nunnie says it's because I'm letting others bear my burdens, but it's something bigger. I can't explain it."

He rubs her hand with his thumb. "Well, I do have something to tell you. It's kind of a surprise I guess."

"Ooh, that sounds interesting." Frankie turns in her seat to stare at him.

"I had a meeting for a bid yesterday. The guy wants to build a warehouse near the interstate. Turns out, he's considering renting his building in town, but he'd rather sell it outright. It's on Main Street. The bottom floor could easily be flipped into a bakery and the second floor is currently his office space. It could be used as an office, a studio, extra dining space, or even an apartment."

Butterflies fill her stomach, and tingles go up her arms. "Seriously?"

"Seriously. If you're interested, he said we could look at it."

Her face lifts into a broad, cheek busting grin. "Let's do it."

"All right. I'll text him." Tony is relieved. He has faith in her, but for a while, she didn't have it in herself.

"I'm so excited. I can't believe it." Frankie stares out the windshield, looking beyond the road to something else, something better.

Tony's voice cracks a little, which causes Frankie to be concerned. "You know, if you go with the option of an apartment upstairs, it would be a big area. You might want a roommate."

Frankie laughs. "You think Sam Marchio will let you shack up with his daughter? He doesn't like you that much."

"Who said anything about shacking up? I'm talking about something bigger." He looks like a little boy as he stares at her, like he just sent her a note asking her to check yes or no for the dance. "I'm not asking anything, just testing the waters."

"I just started liking you, now you want to get married?" She nervously laughs.

"You can't say we don't know each well enough. Technically, it's been over a twenty-year courtship. How much more time do you want? I'll wait, but I wanted you to know I'm ready. Whenever you are, I'm ready. That's all I'm saying."

"Well, that's saying a lot. I need time to think about it, but I'm not saying no."

Tony smiles and fiddles with the radio. By the time they make it to the fairgrounds, Sammy and Beau have already set up tables and chairs. Sam is helping Maryssa organize the tent. Frankie offers hugs to everyone, with Tony trailing behind her. She jumps right into work mode. Tony looks down at Sam's bandaged arm, "Frankie?" Sam nods with a shoulder shrug. Tony shakes his head and smirks. An unspoken comradery passes between them. The team from Rafaluzza Vineyard works well together. The melodious sounds of jazz musicians serenade them throughout the day. The sweet fall air mixes with hay bales and food trucks. Maryssa and Frankie pump out food orders with the help of Sam and Malik. The father-daughter duos are unstoppable and entertaining. Hannah helps Sammy, Tony, and Beau fill tasting glasses as Jo sells bottles and cases to customers. Victoria, Esther, and Wes are enjoying the festival before their shift begins this afternoon.

In between pulling out another container of cookies and refilling the baskets of business cards, Frankie notices that Tony has taken a break. She is too busy to keep track of everyone else, but she feels his absence. Maryssa nudges her when their relief workers finally show up to give them a break. She pulls out water bottles from the cooler and hands one to Maryssa. Just as she tries to find a seat in the shade, Frankie hears her father call over to her and Maryssa. They sigh before exiting the tent into the sunlight.

As the women approach, Frankie recognizes Ben Stanley and his nephew, Chase.

"This should be interesting," Maryssa whispers.

The whole family thinks Ben Stanley and his daughter Angelica are crazy. Angelica keyed Beau's truck, and Ben terminated their distribution partnership with the vineyard and Poppy's after unsuccessfully hitting on Maryssa. The Stanleys are hotheads when they don't get what they want, and two years ago, they wanted Maryssa and Beau, literally. Frankie hesitantly joins the group, wiping a bead of sweat from her forehead.

"Frankie, you remember the Stanleys?" Frankie has always admired her father's gracious demeanor. The man can forgive anyone. She nods and greets the men, "Hello, Mr. Stanley. Chase."

"It's good to see you again, Frankie. It's been a while. You are still as beautiful as you were in college." Chase reaches over and shakes her hand with both of his. He was always a politician, even at school. She offers a half-smile out of courtesy.

Ben Stanley shakes Maryssa's hand longer than socially acceptable. "I wanted to offer congratulations on the string of awards you've been accumulating. Rafaluzza and Poppy's seem to be the talk of the fairs and festivals circuit this year." Even Mr. Stanley's accolades sound sleazy.

"Thank you, Ben. We've worked really hard over the past two years to combine efforts and market all three brands as one." Maryssa isn't suffering fools today, as Nunnie would say. She offers nothing more. Mr. Stanley is oblivious to her line in the sand, which probably explains his unsuccessful businesses as of late.

"I noticed that you haven't found a distributor for the Poppy's brand. We may have been premature in our parting of ways. I wonder if we could meet next week to discuss some possibilities." Ben Stanley attempts to mend the fences he obliterated two years ago.

"We don't have a distributor because we haven't signed any contracts yet, but we are entertaining many offers. We currently have a list of national distributors sending us packages. I would be happy to add your name to the list when we begin taking meetings." If Mr. Stanley missed her meaning the first time, he sees it now. His arrogant sneer is chilling, causing Frankie to shiver. He and Chase have similar features.

"I understand. Well, I wish all the best to you, Maryssa." Mr. Stanley turns toward Sam. "Now, how about that new line you've been bragging about with the hops? I'd love a taste."

Sam pats Ben Stanley on the shoulder and directs him to the back of the tent, "Sure, you'll love it." *Gracious and kindhearted.*

Maryssa walks away, rolling her eyes. Frankie assumes Chase will follow his uncle. He doesn't. She warily smiles at him as he stares at her with the same creepy smile as his uncle. "So, Chase, are you out politicking today?"

Even his laugh is condescending. "Indeed, I am. Getting out into the public is the key. I need to meet with the people so they can put a face with the name."

Frankie nods, wondering how long this conversation will last. She wants to find Tony and eat lunch. "I'm sure all the socializing is exhausting."

"I love it. I feed off of the energy people give."

Awkward. "Good for you, Chase. Well, good luck. It was nice seeing you again." Frankie's attempt to find a way out of this annoying conversation is thwarted by Chase continuing it.

"Yes, it has been a while. In fact, the last time I saw you was my senior year. If I recall, you were pretty out of it that night."

His voice causes a sickness to creep up from the pit of her stomach. She instinctively wants to vomit. She takes a big swig of her water bottle, remembering Nunnie's warning to stay hydrated. The last thing she needs right now is to remember that night.

"We shared a bottle of champagne, then you wanted to leave with your friends. I was hoping to get to know you better, but you ran off with your roommate."

A cool breeze wafts his cologne past her and ruffles her hair. The smell burns her nose. She will never forget that smell. "If I ran off with my roommate, how would you have known that I was 'out of it' later that night?" Her voice shakes as much as her insides. Her feet instinctively shift to balance her stance, shoulder-width apart. Her spine straightens, and her breathing regulates. Deena's training kicks into gear. Vomit still wants to rise, but she is not running. She processes. Flickers of scenes flash through her mind like an old movie. Bits and pieces from nightmares and new memories fall into place.

"I ran into you at a bar downtown. Don't you remember?" His thumb wipes at the corner of his smug mouth. He sniggers again. "You were all over me. You don't remember that either? That's a shame. We had a great time." Chase's eyes pierce hers before breaking away to wave at someone passing by.

Frankie's eyes focus, but she is looking beyond him to that night. The smell of his cologne, the sickening sweetness of his voice. Vomit is building in her stomach. It burns from the inside.

"But you were so drunk, I had to do the gentlemanly thing and say goodnight to you and your friends. What a shame. You should have stayed with me at the party. There are a lot of bad guys out there, anything could have happened to you." His face gives nothing away, but his arrogant smile is icy.

Frankie breathes and centers herself. She cannot allow herself to pass out now. "It was you. It's all coming back to me. You popped the cork. You gave me the drink. I trusted you because I knew your family. You're the one." Clarity fills her mind as resolve abounds.

He menacingly stares at her and speaks in a placatingly obnoxious voice. "I have no idea what you are talking about,

Frankie. I told you, you were all over me. I said goodnight and left you at the bar. Maybe you dreamt of me."

"You could be right, and I may live to regret this, but I highly doubt it." Frankie's right shoulder drops before she draws her fist around in an arc. She connects and draws blood, which is exactly her intent. The restraint that follows is nothing short of Divine. Her bloodied hand lifts straight into the air, where no one can touch it.

The moments that follow are a blur, but her one job is to keep her hand away from everyone. Frankie hears her dad, Mr. Stanley, and Maryssa yelling. Hannah is grabbing a bag of ice for Chase. Sammy laughs hysterically. She hears Tony's voice in the distance and pulls herself back to the moment. She needs to think quickly.

Her voice is forceful, her directions concise. She was helpless alone, but she is not alone. She was never alone. She just didn't realize it at the time. "Maryssa, Beau needs to do everything in his power to keep Tony away. Daddy, call over the police and medics. I think I broke my hand, and hopefully his jaw." Frankie stands like a statue as she waits for justice.

She feels arms scoop her up from behind before she can protest. Tony is careful not to touch her bloody fist.

"What are you doing?" She asks breathlessly.

"You were shaking. I didn't want you to fall."

"I didn't want you here, around him."

"I don't want to be around him either, but I need to be here for us." Tony's voice is resolved.

"You know who he is, don't you?"

Tony nods. "I'm trying not to think about right now."

"Where were you?" She remembers his absence earlier.

"I went to find you a lemon square. I heard someone say they were the best they've ever tasted."

They both laugh sadly as her head collapses onto his shoulder.

Tony

The smell of coffee replaces the staleness of the apartment. Tony and Sammy aren't messy, but they certainly aren't living in a swanky bachelor pad either. Two grown men, both running their own businesses. They don't have time to make it homey. Tony kicks a tennis ball out of the way as he heads down the hallway, following the scent of coffee.

"I'm shocked you're up before me. I'm even more surprised you remembered how to make coffee." Tony sleepily swipes his hand through his thick curly hair and yawns.

"I didn't. But you may want to put some clothes on, moron." Sammy snarls at his roommate.

Tony concentrates on his surroundings as soon as he hears Frankie's giggle. He freezes in the doorway of the kitchen before smelling the wrinkled undershirt he wore to sleep, grateful that he slipped shorts on over his boxers before leaving his room. Deciding he doesn't smell that bad, Tony crosses the room and kisses the top of Frankie's head as he heads to the counter to pour a cup of coffee. "I just texted you."

"I saw. I'm awake and I'm fine." Her quiet laughter lifts some of the weight from his shoulders.

After spending yesterday at the hospital and then the police station, he knew she had to be exhausted. The police escorted her to the ER, worried that her hand was broken. Tony was amazed at the way she calmly explained to the police her story. The ER doctor swabbed the blood from her knuckles after Frankie claimed to be a serial battery suspect who wanted to turn herself in. Within two hours, they had the rapid DNA results, and the DA was at the hospital interviewing Frankie. The police felt terrible taking her to the station for booking, but Chase filed assault and battery charges on her. As they waited, the entire precinct made an effort to talk to the girl boxer who cracked the worst cold case in the county. Tony was by her side the entire time.

"How's my hardened criminal?" Tony chuckles as he sips the hot coffee.

"Fine, same as I was the last three times you texted me."

"Did you know?" Tony has never seen Sammy's face like this. Darkened eyes, squinting down, with a menacing scowl.

"I told him the night before yesterday," Frankie tries to intervene.

"You didn't tell me?" He scowls at Tony. A seething Sammy is very out of character.

"I asked him not to. I wasn't ready for the family to know."

"Why don't you let your *boyfriend* talk for himself? He knew and didn't tell me."

Tony sets his mug on the counter and stiffens, straight like the two by fours in his truck. Frankie holds out her hand, stopping the testosterone challenge.

"Okay boys, let's settle down." She turns to her brother, making sure he understands. The last thing Frankie wants is to harm their friendship. "Don't be mad at Tony. This isn't about him, and you know it. Why do you think I didn't tell you?"

"Probably because you know I would have killed the guy, which I'm still considering." Sammy spits out the words.

"Exactly, and what would that have accomplished? Nothing. That's why I didn't tell anyone."

"That guy is scum. He walked away yesterday so smug, vowing to press charges because you broke his precious jaw. I wish I knew then. I would have ended him right there."

Frankie's hand reaches out to cover her brother's. Her cast rests under the table where he can't be reminded of it. "Nunnie has always preached to us that we reap what we sow and that things work out exactly how God needs them to. Chase Stanley, Mr. Narcissist himself, will have to face all of his victims in court. His dreams of a political career are shattered. That's better than having him in the ground and you in prison in his place. You look terrible in orange."

"When did you tell Dad?"

"Last night. He was at the farmhouse with Mom when Tony brought me home."

"I'm surprised he didn't go after the Stanleys last night."

"He tried to call Mr. Stanley, but I stopped him. The DA is building her case and doesn't want it leaking that Chase is a suspect. I need the two of you to let this run its course. Promise?" Frankie's eyes plead with her big brother, her forever protector.

He nods. That's the best he can do. "I need to get ready for the festival. You're staying with her today, right?" Sammy stares at Tony. It wasn't a question. They both knew it. Tony nods.

"I'm going to the festival. I'm not letting Chase Stanley take away any more of my life." Frankie's defiant streak has always amused Tony.

He takes another sip while pulling out his phone from his pocket and swiping through his news feed. He hands it to Frankie with a video of her being swarmed by police, her bloody hand raised in the air. "You're not going anywhere today. I have a feeling Lisa will be calling you shortly."

Her head falls to the table.

Sammy actually laughs. "Well, that was entertaining."

"Beau texted this morning. The media is camped out on the main road. I'm surprised you didn't see them when you left. The sheriff runs them off, but they keep coming back. Maryssa and Jo have already changed the shifts to cover for us today. Your whole family will be working in the tents, so you are stuck with me." Tony drinks more coffee, smiling.

"Can we at least go see the building in town today? I can't sit around all day hiding from the press." She panics and runs to the front window.

"They have no idea where you are now. We can probably sneak you into the building. I'll call my guy then take a shower."

"I need to head out for the festival." Sammy hugs his sister tighter than he ever has before. "Call me if you need anything at all, okay?" She nods and closes her eyes. "I love you, Frankie."

"I know. I love you too." Frankie kisses her brother on the cheek and hugs him one more time.

Her phone begins ringing. "Lisa," Frankie groans. "Talk to Lisa. I'll jump in the shower."

Tony walks down the hallway as Frankie slides the green button, "I can explain everything."

Thirty minutes later, Frankie and Tony climb into his truck and head into town. "How is Deena?"

"She's relieved to have a face for her punching bag. The DA called last night right after I got off the phone with her. She's going in for an interview today."

"Chase might pee his pants in public when he finds out the Fighting Finnegans are after him. That would scare the snot out of me. Didn't her dad kill a man in the ring?"

Frankie relaxes for the first time since yesterday, "That's a myth."

"What about Lisa?"

"Once I explained the whole story, she felt better. She wants me to lay low until they figure out a way to approach

277

the subject. She wants me to meet with her and her bosses to work out a plan that makes me feel comfortable. It might be as early as tomorrow morning. She's going to text me later."

"Do you have to go to Georgia?" Tony grips the wheel tighter.

"I'm sure they'd rather me go in person, but I'll probably just attend by laptop in my pajamas." Frankie stares out the windows as they drive into town and reach Main Street.

"Look over there, that's the storefront. We're going around to the back." Tony points over to the two-story brick building.

"That one? That's so cute. I never noticed it before. I'm always looking across the street."

"I know. I think we should paint it a bright color and add some curb appeal. We could really make it pop."

She smiles brightly at him.

"What? Why are you looking at me like that?" Tony questions her.

"You keep saying 'we,' it's cute."

Tony blushes as he parks in the back lot.

Frankie's phone vibrates as she climbs out of the truck. She groans then tucks it into her back pocket. "Lisa wants to know if I can fly to Atlanta for a face-to-face tomorrow or Tuesday. I can't even fathom that right now."

Just as Tony is about to ask her plans, the door swings open for them. They meet the owner and tour the entire space. Frankie visualizes display cases and a coffee bar. A seating area by the front window and outside on the sidewalk. Color ideas splash through her mind as she runs her hand along the walls. Tony talks to the owner about the plumbing and electrical upgrades. She asks about taxes and the local business association fees. Frankie recognizes they make a great team.

By the time they make it upstairs, Frankie is sold. The owner's sister and nephew lived in the upstairs apartment. It's been vacant since they moved out last winter. He didn't want to find a new tenant until he decided what he would do with the building. They discuss utility bills and upgrades he has made over the years.

The owner goes outside to take a phone call as they walk through the rooms. "The space is much bigger than I anticipated from the outside. This is the best location I've seen so far. I think I should make an offer. Do you think he would sell or rent? I'd rather own the building outright."

"I think if you made the right offer, he'd sell. It's move-in ready. You could live here during the construction if you wanted. The bones are great downstairs too. It would only take a few weeks to build your kitchen and storefront." Tony turns on the kitchen faucet to check how it runs.

"Now, I just need to find a contractor. I'll have to get a few recommendations. It's hard to find a good builder these days." Her sarcastic smile has him crossing the room and pulling her into his arms.

"I actually know a guy. He might give you a discount." Tony breathes her in as he laughs.

"I don't know, I heard your schedule is booked for the next two weeks." Frankie feigns innocence.

"Do you know something I don't know?" His confused look eases her nerves a little bit.

"You are driving to Georgia with me today. We're going to make the face-to-face meeting with Lisa and her bosses. Then we will head to Jekyll Island, where we will get married. We'll spend the next two weeks exploring the Georgia coast and looking for the perfect lemon square together." Frankie holds her breath, waiting for the answer to her proposal.

A slow smile inches across his face. "Well, well, well. Francesca Josephine Marchio, did you just ask me to marry you? I mean, I'm not surprised, you've never been conventional. I am irresistible, and you have always had a crush on me."

She swats his arm with her cast but hurts herself instead. "Ouch! I didn't hear an answer. I will rescind the offer if you're not interested."

"Now, wait a minute. I didn't say no." He searches her eyes for understanding. He has loved this woman since he hit puberty. In all of his thoughts about her, a proposal never went down like this. Then again, nothing with Frankie has ever been boring.

"Are you sure this isn't the adrenaline talking? You've had some life-changing things happen this weekend. Maybe we should think about it. Not to mention, getting married without your family could be harmful to my health and well-being. I'd hate to start our marriage in a full-body cast."

"I'll protect you." Frankie smiles.

"Are you serious about this?"

"Dead serious."

"We just started dating, don't you want to make sure you like me first?"

"Unless you have some secret life that you have managed to keep hidden from me for over twenty years, I think I know all I need to know."

Tony studies her face. "Don't you want a big wedding? You know, the dress, the flowers, the cake?"

"Nope. I've never been one of those girls who dreamt about my wedding day. I don't need the bells and whistles, just the groom. If it's a game-changer for you, I can bake you a cake and buy you flowers."

He laughs as he tucks a stray curl behind her hair. "One condition."

"What, you need to call my Dad first?"

"No, I already did that, but we do need to make a call."

He waits for her shocked expression, then smiles when she gives it. "You what?"

"After they stitched up your hand from the glass squeezing event. You fell asleep waiting on the discharge nurse. Your dad came to check on you. I told him that my intentions were to marry you if you ever gave me a chance. He told me that we would make a formidable pair and that I better spend every day making myself worthy of the honor."

"Aww, that's so sweet. Wait, if it's not my dad, then who do we need to call?"

"*We* don't have to call anyone. *You* have to call Rosie Devono."

"Your mom loves me!" Nervousness starts to creep over her. "Oh no, will she be upset if we don't have a wedding?"

"No, but she does have my grandmother's ring. We can swing by on our way out of town. There is one flaw to your plan though."

"What? Didn't we cover everything? I'm starting to rethink my offer. You're kind of a diva, Anthony."

"It's just a point of clarification." He holds her tighter. "We'll never find the perfect lemon square, because you haven't made it yet."

Her smile melts his heart. Frankie stands on her tiptoes and kisses his nose. "I want to buy this place, but let's ask the guy if we can rent it now until the sale is final. We'll need a place to live when we return. I don't want to live with my brother, and the farmhouse is pretty crowded with busybodies."

"We're really doing this?" Tony studies her face.

"That's up to you. You still haven't said yes, yet."

"Yes, I will marry you, Francesca Josephine." Tony lifts her feet off of the ground and swings her around the room.

Epilogue

Fall in West Virginia is breathtaking. The green grass is lush and thick. Orange, red, purple, and yellow leaves paint the mountainsides as warm days transition into cool evenings. The aroma of moss and dried leaves mix into a fragrant potpourri. Tonight is perfect wedding weather.

Wildflowers and votives decorate the long rectangle table that is set against the backdrop of the vineyard. Off to the side, a two-tiered, Italian buttercream wedding cake is decorated with flowers of red, orange, and yellow. The large family oak tree is draped in white twinkle lights. Rows of chairs face the bride and groom.

Tony holds Frankie tight in his arms. "Are you still glad we ran off, or do you wish you had this?"

"This is beautiful, but I'm glad that our wedding was just ours." She sinks into his embrace and turns to kiss him.

The family cheers as Wes Anderson finally kisses Esther as his bride. "Did you know that Wes was Daddy's best friend in high school? Apparently, the Marchio girls have a thing for baseball players who befriend their brothers."

"I'm glad I didn't have to wait forty years to marry you like Wes did. Of course, I was starting to wonder. You weren't easy to convince."

"Convince? I asked you!" Frankie protests.

Tony plants a kiss on his new bride's soft lips. "And I will say yes again, every day for the rest of my life."

"Vomit. Please keep your PDAs to yourselves. I can't stomach it." Sammy gets up from his chair. "I'm going to get food and get away from you two."

Tony stands and pulls Frankie to her feet. "That sounds good. I want a piece of wedding cake. I hear the baker has her own television show."

They curl into each other's arms as they walk up toward the rest of the family. Maryssa is passing out glasses of champagne with Uncle Malik and Victoria. Nunnie and Aunt Jo are uncovering the platters of food. Uncle Dom is lighting the candles that line the table. Frankie watches as her dad and brother bicker over the sound system. Soft music finally begins playing in the background.

Aunt E and Wes are taking pictures with Haddie and Wes's daughter. Frankie points over at them under the tree, "Do you think the Secret Service will photobomb the pictures?"

"They're dressed for it. I don't know how they do it. I could never wear a suit and tie every day."

"I agree. You look very handsome in your jeans and plaid shirts, but you do look awfully handsome and spiffed up tonight." Frankie squeezes him tighter.

"You two are truly over the top. I totally understand Sammy's side of this. Seriously, it's out of control." Beau walks up behind them as they make their way to the table and find their seats.

"Leave them alone. Love is a beautiful thing."

"Thank you, Nunnie." Frankie leans over and kisses Nunnie's cheek.

The family gathers around the table. This family has gathered for weddings, births, birthdays, funerals, and any other time they can be together. The saying, "A family who prays together stays together" is accurate for the Marchio family. They break bread together every chance they get. Strength comes in numbers, and they are strong.

Every seat is filled. Food is served and passed up and down the table. Soft music provides ambiance with the soothing sounds of stringed instrumentals. Laughter and conversation fill the early evening air. Lights twinkle all around them.

Aunt E and Wes cut their cake to cheers and sparklers. They gently feed one another cake, sizing up the other. Aunt E swipes his nose with icing from her fingers. Wes quickly gives her a peck, sharing the icing with her cheek. Laughter abounds before the newlyweds head toward a makeshift dance floor.

Frankie, Maryssa, and Haddie stay at the dessert table to serve pieces of heavenly cake. Frankie cuts, Maryssa holds out the plates, Haddie adds a fork and passes the plates to Aunt Jo's kids, who are delivering them to guests. All three girls simultaneously recite Nunnie's favorite words, "Many hands make light the work."

As their giggling subsides, the questions Frankie has been dreading begin. "How are you feeling since the arrest yesterday?"

"I don't know. Okay, I guess. I'm relieved Chase is in custody, but I'm dreading the trial. I'm praying that he will make a plea, but I'm not holding my breath. The evidence is solid from what I'm told. Fifteen unsolved rape cases, all directly linking his DNA to the crime. I keep looking over my shoulder for the press. As of now my name is shielded, but based on the media coverage from the punching incident at the Wine and Jazz Festival, the court of speculation has already unmasked me."

"Jackson and Madison both read the grand jury inditement. They said they would be shocked if he doesn't want to plea for all ten victims. There is too much evidence stacked against him," Haddie licks icing from her thumb.

"Lisa said you two worked out a PR plan with the execs for if, or when, your name is released." Maryssa hands Frankie another plate to fill.

"We did. At some point, I may just release the statement regardless. We talked about a sexual assault special on the network where I do a series of fundraisers or dessert competitions and donate all the money to victim non-profits. I just don't want people to suffer in silence like I did." It is getting easier for Frankie to talk about it now that the burden is shared.

"Why did you suffer in silence? What? Someone had to ask her." Maryssa defensively ignores Haddie's glare. "She worked with me every day and never said a word. We were all here for her."

Frankie smiles at Haddie, warmed by her protectiveness. "It's okay. I honestly don't know. My dad asked the same question. At first, I was in shock and denial. I tried to pretend it never happened, push it out of my mind. Part of me was ashamed that it happened. The other part didn't want anyone's pity. I coped by learning to fight and protect myself, then I went overboard."

"You can say that again. Your anger management issues were epic at times, and your poor hands." Maryssa gives Frankie a shake of the head.

Frankie closes her eyes and inhales. "Don't remind me. I still cringe every time I think about punching Tony." She drops her head.

"At least you weren't mean and snotty to him on a national television dating show like Haddie." Maryssa cracks herself up with that one.

"Talk about cringe. I'm glad I wasn't fawning all over Jackson like the other contestants, but I could have at least been civil. I don't know how on earth he fell in love with me." Haddie covers her face with her hand.

"Well, you are drop-dead gorgeous and have a brilliant mind and an enormous heart. I think the question is, how did you fall in love with me?" Jackson approaches from behind and wraps his arms around Haddie's waste.

"You wore me down with your sheer determination." Haddie smirks as Jackson leans around and kisses her cheek.

"My determination had to be greater than your stubbornness." Haddie gently elbows his ribs for that comment. "Did you tell them yet?"

Haddie blushes, "I was just going to." Frankie and Maryssa stare at Haddie in anticipation. It seems these two always have some big announcements. Usually, it involves public policy. "I'm pregnant!" Haddie quietly squeals, leading the other two to follow suit. Jackson is nudged out of the way to make room for a three-way hug.

"No way! How far along are you? I can't believe you didn't tell me!" Maryssa is crying and smiling.

"I'm ten weeks. I finally verified it two weeks ago. I refuse to have special treatment just because I'm the First Lady, so I tried to make an appointment with the National Health Care doctor. The DMV would have been faster. I realized I couldn't get an appointment without telling the entire NHC system that I was pregnant. It would have been leaked faster than the assassination attempt. Finally, I just called Priscilla. Remember her from *Future FLOTUS?* She is a certified nurse-midwife. She came for a visit and gave me an exam. I didn't call because Jackson thinks someone might be tapping our phone lines. I was afraid to say anything until I saw you in person and I didn't want to take attention from Mom's big day."

"There is a lot to unwrap there, but let's focus on you. How are you feeling?" Frankie watches how Maryssa instinctively touches her own belly while talking.

"I'm completely exhausted. I could take three naps a day. My morning sickness is mild, but all day. I don't want to complain, but I'm definitely nervous. My stress level was crazy before, now I have a whole new layer."

"I'm making sure she's resting and taking it easy. The wedding was a perfect excuse for Ashleigh to lighten

Haddie's schedule without raising any suspicion." Jackson quickly jumps back into the conversation.

"What about when you return to Washington? Won't they expect your schedule to go back to normal?" Frankie states the obvious.

"Well, that's a whole other bombshell. The mandatory family breakfast Nunnie called for tomorrow is actually for us. We have a pretty massive announcement. You'll have to wait until then to find out the rest." Haddie and Jackson share a conspiratorial glance before he spins her out of his arms and takes her hand.

"Mrs. Cashe, may I have this dance?" She smiles over her shoulder and waves to them, effectively ending the conversation.

"Well, that was odd and intriguing." Frankie turns to Maryssa.

"Tell me about it!" Maryssa indignantly stands with hands on her hips. "She never keeps secrets from me, and that's two in one night. I'm losing my touch."

Frankie pats her on the shoulder. "Haddie has always been able to keep secrets better than you."

Maryssa's harrumph has Frankie walking away quickly. "I'm going to find my husband." *Husband? How my life has changed in four months.*

Frankie finds Tony on the edge of the party with Sammy, Beau, and Dominick. They found a deck of cards and are playing Briscola, a card game from the old country.

"You four are like a bunch of old ladies." She laughs before resting her arms on Tony's shoulders.

"You just called your husband an old lady. I think I need to change your mind later." Tony reaches up and squeezes her arms.

Sammy puts his cake plate on the table. "And I've lost my appetite. You two are killing me."

"Come dance with me." Frankie holds out her hand for Tony's.

They glide over the grassy area near the tree with sparkled lights. Tony pulls Frankie into him. Her head rests on his shoulder as his arms tighten around her waist. They sway to the sweet music as the October breeze kisses their skin.

Frankie looks up at him. His brown eyes, like chocolate, glistening back at her. "Thank you."

"For what?" Tony's grin is so pure.

"For fighting for me, even when I was fighting against you."

"You, Francesca Josephine Marchio Devono, are worth fighting for."

Frankie reaches up and places her hand on his cheek. "I have loved you my whole life."

"That tells me two things." He beams down at her.

She giggles, "What?"

"You are way more stubborn than I am, and I loved you first." Tony swiftly kisses her lips before she can argue with him…..for now.

The End

Discussion Questions

1. Frankie and Tony were on a quest to find the perfect lemon dessert. Is there a popular dessert, and, like Frankie and Tony, you just don't understand the hype? What is your favorite dessert?

2. The Marchio girls keep finding themselves on television. If you could star in your own reality TV show, what would it be called?

3. Frankie used boxing and baking as her coping mechanisms during the trials of life. Do you have a go-to hobby or source of comfort when you need to let off some steam?

4. What do you think Jackson and Haddie's big announcement is for the family?

5. Who is your favorite Marchio and why?

6. Do you have a favorite quote or piece of advice from Nunnie Mary?

Ethel's Menasha

Ingredients:
Potatoes
Green Beans
Minced Garlic
Olive Oil
Garlic Salt
Onion Salt
Salt & Pepper
Bacon pieces
Optional: (Anything from your kitchen you want to throw into the pot.) Ham, beans, spinach, Italian sausage, etc..

Instructions:
1. Heat olive oil, bacon pieces, and minced garlic in a pot.
2. Toss in potatoes and let them sizzle in the hot oil for a few minutes.
3. Add green beans and any other vegetables. If you are adding meat (sausage, bacon, ham), make sure you cook it first in another pan or cook it in the pan before adding the garlic and bacon.
4. Season to taste.
5. Cover and let simmer for an hour or two.
6. Serve with fresh bread to sop up the liquid.

As I'm sure you've picked up on already, Menasha is an everything-but-the-kitchen-sink recipe. My Nunnie made hers with green beans and potatoes, but I have seen countless versions growing up in many Italian kitchens. I've also heard it called, "Greens Soup." There are no set ingredients or amounts, just toss in what looks good, and season to taste. My dad adds banana ring peppers to his (yuck) and my cousin eats it on bread. If you're familiar with the children's book *Stone Soup*, this is the Italian version. This is my favorite comfort food. Every time I eat it, I am transported back to my Nunnie's kitchen. I hope you enjoy your own version of Menasha!

Thank you for reading!

If you enjoyed *Frankie's Confections*, please take a minute and write a review. As a new author, your recommendation means the most to me!

Check out www.amydensonbooks.com for other books and updates!

I am an Indy author. I am human. My beta readers and editors are human. If you catch a typo, please shoot me an email and let me know (amydensonbooks@gmail.com).
Thanks, friend!

Acknowledgments

"Sugar and spice and everything nice. That's what little girls are made of."

Coffee, tears, laughter, sleepless nights, and lots of chocolate-covered almonds are what books are made of. Every project is a labor of love, but *Frankie's Confections* left her mark on me. I could not have written this book without the encouragement and support of my fantastical team. You weighed in on book covers, plot twists, and dessert discussions.

Thank you to my crack team of beta readers. Your insights make me a better writer.

To Courtney, thank you for your strict deadlines. I hope you enjoy your cruise!

To Ashleigh, you are a gifted editor. You are strong and brave like Frankie, wise beyond your years, and full of grace. I cannot wait to see what God has planned for you.

To my parents, sister, niece, forever friends, and prayer warriors, thank you. When I wanted to quit, you fed me and encouraged me to take naps. I love you bunches and bunches.

My children have sometimes eaten dinner late, cold, or leftover. You are my greatest cheerleaders and a fierce marketing team. You have embraced characters as members of our family. You allowed me to write "just one more paragraph" many times without complaint. You are my precious gifts from God.

To my long-suffering husband. Thank you for dodging apples and praying over me when I wanted to throw my formatting software at the wall. I love you more than words (and we both know I have a lot of words).

While writing *Frankie's Confections,* I learned many valuable lessons. I have grown both as an author and a publisher. I have learned when to let go, when to hold on, and when to ask for help. As an independent author, my support team is invaluable. **You, dear reader, are part of that team. I do not take lightly the precious time you share with me. Thank you, from the bottom of my heart!**

I loved watching Frankie's story unfold in front of my eyes. Her story is one of endurance, forgiveness, and redemption. No one is perfect, and every life is marred from the daily act of living in a world filled with broken people. I am humbled and honored to tell Frankie's story. She is a fighter. I pray that each one of you knows how to be a fighter, but more importantly, I hope you know the God who fights for you.

"This is what the LORD says: Do not be afraid or discouraged because of this vast number, for the battle is not yours, but God's." 2 Chronicles 20: 15

About the Author

Amy Denson grew up in a big Italian family from West Virginia. She loves hearing and telling stories about her family history. Her Nunnie and mother taught her to love Jesus with all her heart. She loves cooking, reading, writing, and learning. In her spare time (obvious sarcasm), Amy is the mother of four kids, one scrappy dog, and another dog who thinks she's a cat. She is married to her college sweetheart. Together, they ride the unpredictable rollercoaster of life, hanging on by the seats of their pants. Amy loves spending time with her friends and family, usually around a table breaking bread and laughing a lot.

Made in the USA
Monee, IL
30 April 2022

95675778R00177